BEWILDERMENT

BEWILDERMENT

a novel

RICHARD POWERS

W. W. NORTON & COMPANY
Independent Publishers Since 1923

Bewilderment is printed on 100 percent recycled paper. By using recycled paper in place of paper made with 100 percent virgin fiber, the first printing has saved:

1,796 trees

134,266 gallons of water

257,494 pounds of CO_2

Totals quantified using the Eco Calculator at https://rollandinc.com/.

For information about permission to reproduce selections from this book, write to Permissions, W. W. Norton & Company, Inc., 500 Fifth Avenue, New York, NY 10110

For information about special discounts for bulk purchases, please contact W. W. Norton Special Sales at specialsales@wwnorton.com or 800-233-4830

Manufacturing by Lake Book Manufacturing
Production manager: Beth Steidle

Library of Congress Cataloging-in-Publication Data

Names: Powers, Richard, 1957– author.
Title: Bewilderment : a novel / Richard Powers.
Description: First Edition. | New York, NY : W. W. Norton & Company, [2021]
Identifiers: LCCN 2021008991 | ISBN 9780393881141 (hardcover) |
ISBN 9780393881158 (epub)
Classification: LCC PS3566.O92 B49 2021 | DDC 813/.54—dc23
LC record available at https://lccn.loc.gov/2021008991

W. W. Norton & Company, Inc., 500 Fifth Avenue, New York, N.Y. 10110
www.wwnorton.com

W. W. Norton & Company Ltd., 15 Carlisle Street, London W1D 3BS

1 2 3 4 5 6 7 8 9 0

Those who contemplate the beauty of the earth find reserves
of strength that will endure as long as life lasts.
—RACHEL CARSON

Therefore, for a similar reason, we must admit that the Earth,
the sun, the moon, the ocean and all other things are not
unique, but number in numbers beyond number.
—LUCRETIUS, *DE RERUM NATURA*

BEWILDERMENT

BUT WE MIGHT NEVER FIND THEM? We'd set up the scope on the deck, on a clear autumn night, on the edge of one of the last patches of darkness in the eastern U.S. Darkness this good was hard to come by, and so much darkness in one place lit up the sky. We pointed the tube through a gap in the trees above our rented cabin. Robin pulled his eye from the eyepiece—my sad, singular, newly turning nine-year-old, in trouble with this world.

"Exactly right," I said. "We might never find them."

I always tried to tell him the truth, if I knew it and it wasn't lethal. He knew when I lied, anyway.

But they're all over, right? You guys have proved it.

"Well, not exactly proved."

Maybe they're too far away. Too much empty space or something.

His arms pinwheeled as they did when words defeated him. We were closing in on bedtime, which didn't help. I put my hand on his wild auburn mop. Her color—Aly's.

"And what if we never heard a peep from out there? What would that say?"

He held up one hand. Alyssa used to say that when he concentrated, you could hear him whirring. His eyes narrowed, staring down into the dark ravine of trees below. His other hand sawed the cleft of his chin—a habit he resorted to when thinking hard. He sawed with such vigor I had to stop him.

"Robbie. Hey! Time to land."

His palm pushed out to reassure me. He was fine. He simply wanted to run with the question for another minute, into the darkness, while still possible.

If we never heard anything, like ever?

I nodded encouragement to my scientist—*easy does it*. Stargazing was finished for tonight. We'd had the clearest evening, in a place known for rain. A full Hunter's Moon hung fat and red on the horizon. Through the circle of trees, so sharp it seemed within easy reach, the Milky Way spilled out—countless speckled placers in a black streambed. If you held still, you could almost see the stars wheel.

Nothing definitive. That's what.

I laughed. He made me laugh once a day or more, in good stretches. Such defiance. Such radical skepticism. He was so me. He was so her.

"No," I agreed. "Nothing definitive."

Now, if we did *hear a peep. That would say tons!*

"Indeed." There would be time enough another night to say exactly what. For now, it was bedtime. He put his eye up to the barrel of the telescope for a last look at the shining core of the Andromeda Galaxy.

Can we sleep outside tonight, Dad?

I'd pulled him from school for a week and brought him to the woods. There had been more trouble with his classmates, and we needed a time-out. I couldn't very well bring him all the way down to the Smokies only to deny him a night of sleeping outside.

We went back in to outfit our expedition. The downstairs was one great paneled room smelling of pine spritzed with bacon. The kitchen reeked of damp towels and plaster—the scents of a temperate rain forest. Sticky notes clung to the cabinets: *Coffee filters above fridge. Use other dishes, please!* A green spiral folder of instructions spread on the battered oak table: plumbing quirks, fuse box location, emergency numbers. Every switch in the house was labeled: *Overhead, Stairs, Hallway, Kitchen.*

Ceiling-high windows opened onto what, tomorrow morning, would be a rolling expanse of mountains beyond mountains. A pair of pilled rustic sofas flanked the flagstone fireplace, emblazoned with parades of elk, canoes, and bears. We raided the cushions, brought them outside, and laid them on the deck.

Can we have snacks?

"Bad idea, buddy. *Ursus americanus*. Two of them per square mile, and they can smell peanuts from here to North Carolina."

No way! He held up a finger. *But that reminds me!*

He ran inside again and returned with a compact paperback: *Mammals of the Smokies*.

"Really, Robbie? It's pitch-black out here."

He held up an emergency flashlight, the kind you charge by cranking. It fascinated him when we arrived that morning, and he'd demanded an explanation of how the magic worked. Now he couldn't get enough of making his own electrons.

We settled into our makeshift base camp. He seemed happy, which had been the whole point of this special trip. Lying down on beds spread out on the slats of the sagging deck, we said his mother's old secular prayer out loud together and fell asleep under our galaxy's four hundred billion stars.

I NEVER BELIEVED THE DIAGNOSES the doctors settled on my son. When a condition gets three different names over as many decades, when it requires two subcategories to account for completely contradictory symptoms, when it goes from nonexistent to the country's most commonly diagnosed childhood disorder in the course of one generation, when two different physicians want to prescribe three different medications, there's something wrong.

My Robin didn't always sleep well. He wet the bed a few times a season, and it hunched him over with shame. Noises unsettled him; he liked to turn the sound way down on the television, too low for me to hear. He hated when the cloth monkey wasn't on its perch in the laundry room above the washing machine. He poured every dollar of allowance into a trading card game—*Collect them all!*—but he kept the untouched cards in numeric order in plastic sleeves in a special binder.

He could smell a fart from across a crowded movie theater. He'd focus for hours on Minerals of Nevada or the Kings and Queens of England—anything in tables. He sketched constantly and well, laboring over fine details lost on me. Intricate buildings and machines for a year. Then animals and plants.

His pronouncements were off-the-wall mysteries to everyone except me. He could quote whole scenes from movies, even after a single viewing. He rehearsed memories endlessly, and every repetition of the details made him happier. When he finished a book he liked, he'd start it again immediately, from page one. He melted down and exploded over nothing. But he could just as easily be overcome by joy.

On rough nights when Robin retreated to my bed, he wanted to be on the side farthest from the endless terrors outside the window. (His mother had always wanted the safe side, too.) He daydreamed, had trouble with deadlines, and yes, he refused to focus on things that didn't interest him. But he never fidgeted or dashed around or talked without stopping. And he could hold still for hours with things he loved. Tell me what deficit matched up with all that? What disorder explained him?

The suggestions were plentiful, including syndromes linked to the billion pounds of toxins sprayed on the country's food supply each year. His second pediatrician was keen to put Robin "on the spectrum." I wanted to tell the man that everyone alive on this fluke little planet was on the spectrum. That's what a spectrum *is*. I wanted to tell the man that life itself is a spectrum disorder, where each of us vibrated at some unique frequency in the continuous rainbow. Then I wanted to punch him. I suppose there's a name for that, too.

Oddly enough, there's no name in the *DSM* for the compulsion to diagnose people.

When his school suspended Robin for two days and put their own doctors on the case, I felt like the last reactionary throwback. What was there to explain? Synthetic clothing gave him hideous eczema. His classmates harassed him for not understanding their vicious gossip. His mother was crushed to death when he was seven. His beloved dog died of confusion a few months later. What more reason for disturbed behavior did any doctor need?

Watching medicine fail my child, I developed a crackpot theory: Life is something we need to stop correcting. My boy was a pocket universe I could never hope to fathom. Every one of us is an experiment, and we don't even know what the experiment is testing.

My wife would have known how to talk to the doctors. *Nobody's perfect*, she liked to say. *But, man, we all fall short so beautifully.*

HE WAS A BOY, so naturally he wanted to see Hillbilly Vegas. Three towns jammed together with two hundred places to order pancakes: What's not to love?

We drove from the cabin, down seventeen winding miles along a stunning river. It took us almost an hour. Robin watched the water, scanning the rapids from the back seat. Wildlife bingo. His new favorite game.

Tall bird! He called out.

"What kind?"

He flipped through his field guide. I was afraid he might get carsick. *Heron?* He turned back to the river. Half a dozen more curves and he shouted again.

Fox! Fox! I saw him, Dad!

"Gray or red?"

Gray. Oh, man!

"The gray fox climbs persimmon trees to eat the fruit."

No way. He looked it up in his *Mammals of the Smokies*. The book confirmed me. He groaned and slugged my arm. *How do you know all this stuff, anyway?*

Skimming his books before he woke up helped me keep one step ahead of him. "Hey. I am a biologist, aren't I?"

Ass . . . trobiologist.

His grin tested whether he'd just crossed a terrible line. I gaped, equal parts stunned and amused. His problem was anger, but it almost never turned mean. Honestly, a little meanness might have protected him.

"Whoa, mister. You just missed getting a time-out for the rest of your eighth year on Earth."

His grin firmed, and he returned to scouting the river. But a mile down that winding mountain road, he put his hand on my shoulder. *I was just joking, Dad.*

I watched the road and told him, "Me, too."

We stood in line for the Ripley's Odditorium. The place unnerved him. Kids his age ran all over, forming bands of improvised mayhem. Their screaming made Robbie wince. Thirty minutes of the horror show and he begged me to leave. He did better with the aquarium, even if the stingray he wanted to sketch wouldn't hold still for its portrait.

After a lunch of french fries and onion rings, we took the lift to the sky platform. He almost vomited all over the glass floor. White-knuckled, jaw clenched, he declared it fantastic. Back in the car, he seemed relieved to have gotten Gatlinburg out of the way.

He was thoughtful on the drive back to the cabin. *That would not have been Mom's favorite place on the face of the planet.*

"No. Probably not even in her top three."

He laughed. I could get him to laugh, if I chose my moments.

That night was too cloudy for stargazing, but we slept outside again, on our rustic cushions with their parades of elk and bear. Two minutes after Robin snapped off his flashlight I whispered, "Your birthday tomorrow." But he was asleep already. I recited his mother's prayer softly for the both of us, so I could reassure him if he woke up horrified at forgetting.

HE WOKE ME IN THE NIGHT. *How many stars did you say there are?*

I couldn't be angry. Even yanked from sleep, I was glad he was still stargazing.

"Multiply every grain of sand on Earth by the number of trees. One hundred octillion."

I made him say twenty-nine zeros. Fifteen zeros in, his laughter turned to groans.

"If you were an ancient astronomer, using Roman numerals, you couldn't have written the number down. Not even in your whole lifetime."

How many have planets?

That number was changing fast. "Most probably have at least one. Many have several. The Milky Way alone might have nine billion Earth-like planets in their stars' habitable zones. Add the dozens of other galaxies in the Local Group . . ."

Then, Dad . . . ?

He was a boy attuned to loss. Of course the Great Silence hurt him. The outrageous size of emptiness made him ask the same question Enrico Fermi did over that famous lunch in Los Alamos, three quarters of a century ago. If the universe were larger and older than anyone could imagine, we had an obvious problem.

Dad? With all those places to live? How come nobody's anywhere?

IN THE MORNING I PRETENDED I'd forgotten what day it was. My new nine-year-old saw through me. While I made super-deluxe oatmeal with half a dozen mix-ins, Robin bobbed in place, pushing off the counter and pogo-sticking with excitement. We set a land speed record eating.

Let's open the presents.

"The what? You're making a pretty big assumption, aren't you?"

Not assumption. Hypothesis.

He knew what he was getting. He'd been bargaining with me for months: a digital microscope that attached to my tablet and let him display magnified images on the screen. He spent all morning trying out pond scum, cells from inside his cheek, and the underside of a maple leaf. He would have been happy looking at samples and sketching notes into his notebook for the remainder of our vacation.

Afraid of pushing him over the top, I wheeled out the cake I'd bought on the sly at the little 1950s grocery store at the bottom of the mountain. His face shone before he caught himself.

Cake, Dad?

He made a beeline for the box, which I'd failed to hide. He studied the ingredients, shaking his head.

Not vegan, Dad.

"Robbie. It's your birthday. That only happens, what . . . ? Barely once a year?"

He refused to smile. *Butter. Dairy products. Egg. Mom would not have gone for it.*

"Oh, I watched your mother eat cake, on more than one occasion!"

I regretted the words as soon as they left my mouth. He looked like a timid squirrel, not sure whether to take the outstretched goodness that he craved or to flee back into the woods.

When?

"She made exceptions now and then."

Robin stared at the cake, a carroty, sinless thing whose virtue would have disgusted any other child. His brief little birthday Eden had just been overrun with snakes.

"It's okay, champ. We can feed it to the birds."

Well. We could try a little, first?

We did. Every time the taste of cake made him happy, he caught himself and grew thoughtful again.

How tall was she?

He knew her height. But today he needed a number.

"Five-foot-two. You'll pass her, before long. She was a runner, remember?"

He nodded, more to himself than to me. *Small but mighty.*

She called herself that, when gearing up to go do battle at the Capitol. I liked to call her "compact, but planetary." Stolen from a Neruda sonnet I once recited to her on an autumn night that ended in a winter. I had to resort to some other man's words to ask her to marry me.

What did you call her?

It always rattled me when he read my mind. "Oh, all kinds of things. You remember."

But like what?

"Like Aly for Alyssa. And Ally, because she was my ally."

Miss Lissy.

"She never liked that one."

Mom. You called her Mom!

"Sometimes. Yes."

That is so flipping weird. I reached out to rough his hair. He jerked away but gave me a pass. *How did I get my name again?*

He knew how he got his name. He'd heard the story more often than was healthy. But he hadn't asked for months, and I didn't mind repeating it.

"On our first date, your mother and I went birding."

Before Madison. Before everything.

"Before everything. Your mother was brilliant! She kept spotting them left and right. Warblers and thrushes and flycatchers—every one of those birds was an old friend. She didn't even have to see them. She knew them by ear. Meanwhile, there I was, poking around, stumbling over these confusing little brown jobs that I couldn't tell apart . . ."

Wishing you'd asked her to the movies?

"Ah. So you *have* heard this one before."

Maybe.

"At last I saw an amazing patch of bright orange-red. I was saved. I started shouting, *Ooh, ooh, ooh!*"

And Mom said, "What do you see? What do you see?"

"She was very excited for me."

Then you swore.

"I may have sworn, yes. I was so humiliated. 'Gee. Sorry. It's only a robin.' I figured I'd never see this woman again."

He waited for the punch line that, for some reason, he needed to hear out loud once more.

"But your mother was looking through her binoculars like my find was the single most exotic life-form she'd ever seen. Without taking her eyes off it, she said, 'The robin is my favorite bird.' "

That's when you fell in love with her.

"That's when I knew I wanted to spend as much time around her as I could. I told her so, later, when I knew her better. We started saying it all the time. Whenever we were doing anything together—reading the paper or brushing our teeth or doing the taxes or taking out the trash. Whatever blah or boring thing we were taking for granted. We'd trade a look, read each other's minds, and one of us would blurt out, 'The robin is my favorite bird!' "

He stood and stacked his dish onto mine, brought them to the sink, and turned on the faucet.

"Hey! It's your birthday. My turn to wash dishes."

He sat back down across from me with his *Look me in the eye* look.

Can I ask you something? No lies. Honesty is important to me, Dad. Was the robin actually her favorite bird?

I didn't know how to be a parent. Most of what I did, I remembered from what she used to do. I made enough mistakes on any one day to scar him for life. My only hope was that all the errors somehow canceled each other out.

"Actually? Your mother's favorite bird was the one in front of her."

The answer agitated him. Our curious boy, as strange as anyone. Weighed down by the world's history, before he even learned to talk. *Six going on sixty,* Aly said, a few months before she died.

"But the robin was the national bird, for her and me. It kept things special. We just had to say the word, and life got better. We never thought of naming you anything else."

He bared his teeth. *Did you have any idea what being a Robin is like?*

"What do you mean?"

I mean, at school? At the park? Everywhere? I have to deal with it, every day.

"Robbie? Listen to me. Are kids bullying you again?"

He closed one eye and pulled away. *Does the entire third grade being a total jerk-face count?*

I held out my hands, asking forgiveness. Alyssa used to say, *The world is going to take this child apart.*

"It's a dignified name. For men and women. You could do good things with it."

On some other planet, maybe. A thousand years ago. Thanks again, guys.

He gazed into his microscope's eyepiece, avoiding me. The note-taking grew diligent. Someone looking in from outside might have thought his research was real. In a confidential report, his second-grade teacher had called him *slow but not always accurate*. She was right about the slow, wrong about the accurate. Given time, he'd converge on more accuracy than his teacher could imagine.

I went out on the deck to breathe in the trees. A tract of forest ran in all directions. Five minutes later—it must have felt an eternity to him—Robin came out and slipped underneath my arm.

Sorry, Dad. It's a good name. And I'm okay with being . . . you know. Confusing.

"Everyone's confusing. And everyone's confused."

He put a sheet of paper into my hand. *Check it out. What do you think?*

From the upper left, a colored-pencil bird, in profile, looked toward the center of the page. He'd drawn it well, down to the streaked throat and white splotches around the eye.

"Well, look at that. Your mother's favorite bird."

How about this one?

A second bird in profile looked back from the top right. This one, too, was unmistakable: a raven with its wings tucked in, like a tuxedoed man pacing with his hands behind his back. My family name derived from *Bran*—raven in Irish. "Nice. From the Mind of Robin Byrne?"

He took the sheet back and appraised it, already planning slight corrections. *Can we print up some stationery from this when we get back? I really, really need some stationery.*

"This could happen, Birthday Boy."

I TOOK HIM TO THE PLANET DVAU, about the size and warmth of ours. It had mountains and plains and surface water, a thick atmosphere with clouds, wind, and rain. Rivers wore the rocks into great channels that ran the sediment down to rolling seas.

My son jittered, taking it in. *It looks like here, Dad? It looks like Earth?*

"A little."

What's different?

The answer wasn't obvious, on the reddish rocky coast where we stood. We turned and looked. Across the entire landscape, nothing grew.

It's dead?

"Not dead. Try your microscope."

He knelt and scooped some film from a tidal pool onto a slide. Creatures everywhere: spirals and rods, footballs and filaments, ribbed, pored, or lined with flagella. He could have taken forever, just sketching all the kinds.

You mean, it's just young? It's only getting started?

"It's three times older than the Earth."

He looked around the blighted landscape. *Then what's wrong?* For my boy, large creatures wandering everywhere were a God-given right.

I told him Dvau was almost perfect—the right place in the right kind of galaxy, with the right metallicity and low risk of annihilation from radiation or other fatal disturbances. It revolved at the right distance around the right kind of star. Like Earth, it had floating plates and volcanoes and a strong magnetic field, which made for stable carbon cycles and steady temperatures. Like Earth, it was showered with water from comets.

Holy crow. How many things did Earth need?

"More than a planet deserves."

He snapped his fingers, but they were too rubbery and small to make a sound. *Got it. Meteors!*

But Dvau, like Earth, had large planets in a farther orbit shielding it from extreme bombardment.

Then what's wrong? He seemed about to cry.

"No large moon. Nothing nearby to stabilize its spin."

We lifted into near orbit and the world wobbled. We watched as the days changed chaotically and April blinked into December, then August, then May.

We watched for millions of years. Microbes bumped up against their limits, like a float thumping a dock. Every time life tried to break loose, the planet twirled, beating it back down to extremophiles.

Forever?

"Until a solar flare burns away its atmosphere."

His face made me kick myself for telling him this one too soon. *It's cool*, he said, faking bravery. *Kind of.*

Dvau ran barren all the way to the horizon. He shook his head, trying to decide whether the place was a tragedy or a triumph. He looked at me. When he spoke, it was the first question of life, everywhere in the universe.

What else, Dad? Where else? Show me another one.

THE NEXT DAY, WE TOOK to the woods. Robin was wired. *Nine, Dad. I get to ride in front!* The law finally freed him from his safety seat in back. He'd waited for the front-seat view his whole life. *Geez. Tons nicer, up here.*

Fog clotted in the mountain folds. We drove through the little town that spread two buildings deep along both sides of the parkway: hardware store, grocery, three barbeque pits, inner tube rentals, outfitters. Then we entered half a million acres of recovering forest.

Before us, the remnant of a range once much higher than the Himalayas endured as rounded foothills. Lemon, amber, and cinnamon—the whole run of deciduous colors—flowed down the watersheds. Sourwoods and sweet gums covered the ridge in crimson. We rounded the bend into the park. Robin breathed out a long, astonished vowel.

We left the car at the trailhead. I carried a frame pack with our tent, sleeping bags, and stove. Slender Robin humped a day pack full of bread, bean soup, utensils, and marshmallows. He hunched forward under its weight. We headed over a ridge and back down toward a backcountry campsite that would be all ours tonight, a spot by the side of a stream that had once been all the planet I needed.

Fall's extravagance ran through the Southern Appalachians. Rhododendrons plunged down ravines and crowded up rises in thickets that made Robin claustrophobic. Above that manic shrub layer rose a canopy of hickories, hemlocks, and tulip poplars just as lush.

Robin stopped every hundred yards to sketch a patch of moss or swarming ant nest. That was fine by me. He found an eastern box turtle feeding on a mass of ocher-colored pulp. It stood defiant, neck stretched, as we bent near. Fleeing wasn't an option. Only when Robin dropped to his knees alongside it did the creature retract.

Robin traced the Martian cuneiform letters spelling out unreadable messages on the dome of the creature's shell.

We climbed up into the cove hardwood along a CCC path laid by unemployed boys not much older than Robin, back in the days before communal enterprise became the enemy. I crushed the star-shaped leaf of a sweet gum, half August jade, half October brick, and told him to sniff. He shouted in surprise. The scratched husk of a hickory nut shocked him even more. I let him chew the tip of a burgundy leaf and taste how sourwood got its name.

Humus tainted the air. For more than a mile, the trail ascended as steeply as a set of stairs. Spectral shadows followed us as we passed through the shedding broadleaves. We rounded an outcrop of mossy boulders, and the world changed from damp cove hardwood into drier pine and oak. It was a mast year. Acorns piled up across the trail. With each step, we scattered them.

Rising from the leaf duff in a bowl-shaped opening off the path was the most elaborate mushroom I'd ever seen. It mounded up in a cream-colored hemisphere bigger than my two hands. A fluted ribbon of fungus rippled through itself to form a surface as convoluted as an Elizabethan ruff.

Whoa! Whaaat . . . ?

I had no answer.

Farther down the trail he almost stepped on a black and yellow millipede. The animal writhed into a ball in my hand. I fanned the air above it toward Robin's nose.

Holy crow!

"What does it smell like?"

Like Mom!

I laughed. "Well, yes. Almond extract. Which Mom sometimes smelled like when she was baking."

He pressed my palm to his nose, traveling. *That is so wild.*

"That's the word for it."

He wanted more, but I laid the creature back in a patch of sedge and we carried on down the trail. I didn't tell my son that the delicious smell was a cyanide, toxic in large doses. I should have. Honesty was very important to him.

A MILE OF DESCENDING TRAIL DROPPED US into a clearing by a rocky stream. Patches of white cascade gave way to deeper, open pools. Mountain laurel and stands of mottled sycamore flanked both banks. The site was more beautiful than I remembered.

Our tent was an engineering marvel, lighter than a liter of water and not much larger than a roll of paper towels. Robin pitched it himself. He fitted the thin poles, bent them into the tent's eyelets, snapped the fabric clips onto the tensed-up exoskeleton, and hey presto: our home for the night.

Do we need the fly?

"How lucky do you feel?"

He felt pretty lucky. I did, too. Six different kinds of forest all around us. Seventeen hundred flowering plants. More tree species than in all of Europe. Thirty kinds of salamander, for God's sake. Sol 3, that little blue dot, had a lot going for it, when you could get away from the dominant species long enough to clear your head.

Above us, a raven the size of an Oz winged monkey flew up into a white pine. "He's here for the opening of Camp Byrne."

We cheered, and the bird flew away. Then the two of us, after a stiff climb with packs on a day that had broken yet another all-time heat record by five degrees, opted for a swim.

A footbridge cut from a girthy tulip poplar crossed a chute in the cascades. Rocks on both sides were splattered with an action painting of lichen, moss, and algae. The creek was clear down to its stony bottom. We bushwhacked upstream and found a flat boulder. I steeled myself and eased into the rush. My doubtful son watched, wanting to believe.

The water shocked my chest and shoved me toward a tumble of rocks. What looked level from the shore was a whole rolling range of submerged micro-mountains. I plunged into the turbulence. My foot slid on a slick stone worn smooth by centuries of falling water.

Then I remembered how to do this. I sat down in the torrent and let the chill river crash over me.

At his first touch of frigid current, Robin screamed. But the pain lasted only half a minute and his shrieks turned to laughter. "Keep low," I called. "Crawl. Channel your inner amphibian." Robbie surrendered to the ecstatic churn.

I'd never let him do anything so dangerous. He fought the current on all fours. Once he found his cascade legs, we worked our way to a spot in the middle of the surge. There we wedged ourselves into a rocky bowl and braced in the pummeling Jacuzzi. It felt like surfing in reverse: leaning back, balancing by constant adjustment of a hundred muscles. The film of water over the stones, the light that etched its rippled surface, and the weird fixed flow of the standing waves roaring over us where we lay in the frothy rapids mesmerized Robin.

The stream felt almost tepid now, warmed by the force of the current and our own adrenaline. But the water coiled like something wild. Downstream, the rapids dropped under orange trees that arched in from both banks. From behind us, upstream, the future flowed over our backs into the sun-spattered past.

Robin gazed at his submerged arms and legs. He fought against the warping, twisting water. *It's like a planet where the gravity keeps changing.*

Black-striped fish the length of my pinkie swam up to kiss our limbs. It took me a moment to see they were feeding on the flakes of our sloughed skin. Robin couldn't get enough. He was the main exhibit of his own aquarium.

We crab-walked upstream, legs splayed, arms patting for underwater handholds. Robin scuttled sideways from one cascade to another, playing at being a crustacean. Wedged into a new scoop of rocks, I inhaled the percolating foam—all the negative ions broken by the churn of air and water. The play of sensations elated me: the frothed-up air, the biting current, the free-falling water, a last swim together at the end of the year. And like some surge in the rocky stream, I lifted for a moment before crashing.

A hundred yards upstream, Alyssa tumbled feetfirst down this channel in a wet suit that fit her like skin. I anchored downstream to catch her, but she still yelped as the flow tossed her down the chutes. Her body bobbed toward me, small but mighty, swelling as it swept downstream, and just as my muscles reached to catch her, she passed right through me.

Robbie let go of his hold and scudded down the rapids. I stuck out an arm and he snagged it. He grappled to me and brought his eyes up to mine. *Hey. What's up?*

I held his gaze. "You're up. I'm down. Only a little, though."

Dad! He jabbed with his free hand, waving it at the evidence all around us. *How can you be down? Look where we are! Who gets this?*

Nobody. Nobody in the world.

He sat down in the cascade, still hanging on to me, working it out. It took him no longer than half a minute. *Wait. Were you here with Mom? Your honeymoon?*

His superpower, really. I shook my head in wonderment. "How do you do that, Sherlock?"

He frowned and raised himself out of the water. Tottering in place, he surveyed the whole watershed with new eyes. *That explains everything.*

BACK AT CAMP, I FELT A CRAVING for current events. Urgent things were happening across the world that I knew nothing about. Notes from colleagues were piling up in my offline in-box. Astrobiologists on five continents huddled in a scrum over the latest publications. Ice shelfs were breaking off Antarctica. Heads of state were testing the outermost limits of public gullibility. Little wars were flaring everywhere.

I pushed back against the informational DTs, while Robin and I shaved pine twigs for a fire. We'd strung our packs up on a wire between two sycamores where not even the fattening bears could reach them. With the fire blazing, our only responsibility in the whole world was to cook our beans and toast our marshmallows.

Robin stared into the flames. In a robotic monotone that would have alarmed his pediatrician, he droned, *The good life*. A minute later: *I feel like I belong here*.

We did nothing but watch the sparks, and we did that well. One last purple rib of sun lined the ridges to the west. The forested mountainsides, having inhaled all day long, now began to breathe back out again. Shadows flickered around the fire. Robin swung his head at every noise. His wide eyes blurred the line between thrill and fear.

Too dark to draw, he whispered.

"Yes," I said, although he probably could have managed, even in the dark.

Gatlinburg used to look like this?

The question startled me. "Bigger trees. Much older. Most of these are younger than a hundred."

A forest can do a lot in a hundred years.

"Yes."

He squinted, sending all kinds of places—Gatlinburg, Pigeon Forge, Chicago, Madison—back to wilderness. I'd done the same thing, on my own worst nights after Alyssa died. But in the mind of this child, the one who'd kept me going, the wish seemed unhealthy. Every decent parent in the world would have argued him out of it.

Robin saved me the effort. His voice was still low, still robotic. But I saw his eyes spark as he studied the fire. *Mom used to read poetry at night, to Chester?*

Who knows how he leapt from one thought to another? I'd stopped trying to trace him a long time ago.

"She did." It had been Alyssa's favorite ritual, long before I showed up on the scene. Two glasses of red wine, and she'd submit the homeliest beagle–border collie rescue that ever walked the Earth to her favorite stanzas.

Poetry. To Chester!

"I'd listen, too."

I know, he said. But clearly, I didn't count.

The embers spat, then settled again into reddish gray ingots. For a moment I worried that he'd ask me to name her favorite poems. Instead, he said, *We should get another Chester.*

Chester's death had almost killed him. All the grief over Alyssa that he'd suppressed in order to protect me tore out of him when the crippled old beast gave up. The rages took over, and I let the doctors medicate him for a while. All he could think about was getting another dog. For a long time, I'd fought him off. Somehow, the idea traumatized me.

"I don't know, Robbie." I poked the cinders with a stick. "I don't think there is another Chester."

There are good dogs, Dad. Everywhere.

"It's a lot of responsibility. Feeding, walking, cleaning up after it. Reading it poetry every night. Most dogs don't even like poetry, you know."

I'm very responsible, Dad. More responsible than I ever am.

"Let's sleep on it, okay?"

He doused the fire in several gallons of water, to show how

responsible he could be. We crawled into the two-man tent and lay faceup, side by side, no fly, just the lightest netting between us and the universe. The tops of trees waved in the Hunter's Moon. A thought formed on his face as he studied their moving tips.

What if we hung a huge Ouija board upside down, above them? Then they could send us messages, and we could read them!

A bird started up in the woods behind our heads, another cryptic message no human would ever decode. *Whip-poor-will. Whip-poor-will.* I started to name it, but there was no need. The bird would not quit. *Whip-poor-will. Whip-poor-will. Whip-poor-will. Whip-poor-will.*

Robin grabbed my arm. *It's going nuts!*

The bird looped its name into the cooling dark. We started to count together, under our breaths, but gave up when we reached one hundred and the bird showed no sign of flagging. That bird was still perseverating when Robin's eyes started to close. I nudged him.

"Hey, mister! We forgot. 'May all sentient beings . . .' "

". . . be free from needless suffering." Where does that come from, anyway? I mean, before Mom.

I told him. It came from Buddhism, the Four Immeasurables. "There are four good things worth practicing. Being kind toward everything alive. Staying level and steady. Feeling happy for any creature anywhere that is happy. And remembering that any suffering is also yours."

Was Mom a Buddhist?

I laughed, and he slugged my arm through two sleeping bags. "Your mother was her own religion. When she said something, it was worth saying. When she spoke, everybody listened. Even me."

Half a vowel trickled out of him, and he hugged himself. Some large forager snapped twigs on the slope above our tent. Smaller creatures rooted through the leaf layer. Bats mapped the canopy in frequencies beyond our ears. But nothing troubled my son. When Robin was happy, he had all the Four Immeasurables covered.

"She once told me that no matter how much bad stuff she had to deal with during the day, if she said those words before bed, she'd be ready for anything the next morning."

ONE MORE QUESTION, he said. *What exactly do you do, again?*

"Oh, Robbie. It's late."

I'm serious. When somebody at school asks me, what am I supposed to say?

It had been the cause of his suspension, a month before. The son of some banker had asked Robin what I did. Robin had answered, *He looks for life in outer space.* That made the son of a brand executive ask, *How is Redbreast's Dad like a piece of toilet paper? He circles Uranus, looking for Klingons.* Robin went nuts, apparently threatening to kill both boys. These days, that was grounds for expulsion and immediate psychiatric treatment. We got off easy.

"It's complicated."

He waved toward the woods above us. *We're not going anywhere.*

"I write programs that try to take everything we know about all the systems of any kind of planet—the rocks and volcanoes and oceans, all the physics and chemistry—and put them together to predict what kind of gases might be present in their atmospheres."

Why?

"Because atmospheres are parts of living processes. The mixes of gases can tell us if the planet is alive."

Like here?

"Exactly. My programs have even predicted the Earth's atmosphere at different times in history."

You can't predict the past, Dad.

"You can if you don't know it yet."

So how do you tell what kind of gases a planet has from a hundred light-years away when you can't even see it?

I exhaled, changing the atmosphere inside our tent. It had been a long day, and the thing he wanted to know would take ten years of coursework to grasp. But a child's question was the start of all things. "Okay. Remember atoms?"

Yep. Very small.

"And electrons?"

Very, very small.

"Electrons in an atom can only be in certain energy states. Like they're on the steps of a staircase. When they change stairs, they absorb or give off energy at specific frequencies. Those frequencies depend on what kind of atom they're in."

Crazy stuff. He grinned at the trees above the tent.

"You think *that's* crazy? Listen to this. When you look at the spectrum of light from a star, you can see little black lines, at the frequency of those stairsteps. It's called spectroscopy, and it tells you what atoms are in the star."

Little black lines. From electrons, a gazillion miles away. Who figured that out?

"We're a very clever species, we humans."

He didn't reply. I figured he'd drifted asleep again—a good end to a fine day. Even the whippoorwill agreed and called it a night. The hush in its wake filled with the bandsaw buzz of insects and the river's surge.

I must have dropped off, too, because Chester was sitting with his muzzle on my leg, whimpering as Alyssa read to us about the soul recovering radical innocence.

Dad. Dad! I figured it out.

I slipped upward from the net of sleep. "Figured out what, honey?"

In his excitement, he let the endearment slide. *Why we can't hear them.*

Half asleep, I had no clue.

What's the name for rock-eaters, again?

He was still trying to solve the Fermi paradox—how, given all the universe's time and space, there seemed to be no one out there. He'd held on to the question since our first night in the cabin, looking through our telescope at the Milky Way: Where was everybody?

"Lithotrophs."

He smacked his forehead. *Lithotrophs! Duh. So, say there's a rocky planet full of lithotrophs, living in solid rock. You see the problem?*

"Not yet."

Dad, come on! Or maybe they live in liquid methane or whatever. They're super-slow, almost frozen solid. Their days are like our centuries. What if their messages take too long for us to even know that they're messages? Like maybe it takes fifty of our years for them to send two syllables.

Our whippoorwill started up again, far away. In my head, Chester, infinitely long-suffering, was still struggling with Yeats.

"It's a great idea, Robbie."

And maybe there's a water world, where these super-smart, super-fast bird-fish are zooming around, trying to get our attention.

"But they're sending too fast for us to understand."

Exactly! We should try listening at different speeds.

"Your mother loves you, Robbie. You know that?" It was our little code, and he abided it. But it did nothing to calm his excitement.

At least tell the SETI listeners, okay?

"I will."

His next words woke me again. A minute, three seconds, half an hour later: Who knew how long?

Remember how she used to say: "How rich are you, little boy?"

"I remember."

He held up his hands to the moonlit mountain evidence. The wind-bent trees. The roar of the nearby river. The electrons tumbling down the staircase of their atoms in this singular atmosphere. His face, in the dark, struggled for accuracy. *This rich. That's how rich.*

WHEN HE FINALLY LET ME SLEEP, I couldn't. The two of us were doing fine, camping in the woods with a few cooked beans and a sketchbook. But the minute we returned to civilization, I'd be neck-deep in work and Robin would be back in a school he hated, surrounded by kids he couldn't help spooking. Eden would be clear-cut again, back in Madison.

Everything about parenting terrified me, long before the day Alyssa burst into my office in Sterling Hall and shouted, "Ready or not, Professor—company's coming!" I hugged her, to an ovation from my amused colleagues. But that was the last time I executed my paternal responsibilities with unambiguous success.

I could no more raise a child than I could speak Swahili. The prospect terrified Alyssa, too, in her own ecstatic way. But somehow the collective wisdom of family, friends, doctors, nurses, and Internet advice sites sufficiently emboldened us to ignore everyone and muddle through on our own best guesses. Tens of thousands of generations of clueless humans had managed to work out the kinks in child rearing well enough to keep the game in play. We wouldn't be the worst, I figured. As it turned out, Alyssa and I never had time to keep our parenting score. Life became a fire drill from the moment Robin came out of the incubator.

But it turns out children have a tolerance for mistakes that I never imagined. Who'd have believed a four-year-old could pull a grill full of hot charcoal down onto himself and walk away with no lasting harm beyond a brand like a shiny pink oyster on his lower back?

On the other hand, the ways of going wrong never failed to stun me. I once read my six-year-old *The Velveteen Rabbit* and only learned from my eight-year-old about the months of nightmares it had given him. Two years of night terrors he'd been too ashamed to tell me about: that was Robin. God only knew what the eleven-year-old might confess to me about the things I was right now doing wrong. But he'd survived his mother's death. I figured he'd survive my best intentions.

I lay in our tent that night, thinking how Robbie had spent two days worrying over the silence of a galaxy that ought to be crawling with civilizations. How could anyone protect a boy like that from his own imagination, let alone from a few carnivorous third-graders flinging shit at him? Alyssa would've propelled the three of us forward on her own bottomless forgiveness and bulldozer will. Without her, I was flailing.

I twitched in my sleeping bag, trying not to wake Robin. A chorus of invertebrates swelled and ebbed. Two barred owls traded their call-and-response: *Who cooks for you? Who cooks for you-all?* Who would ever cook for this boy, aside from me? I couldn't imagine Robin toughening up enough to survive this Ponzi scheme of a planet. Maybe I didn't want him to. I liked him otherworldly. I liked having a son so ingenuous that it rattled his smug classmates. I enjoyed being the father of a kid whose favorite animal for three straight years had been the nudibranch. Nudibranchs are deeply underappreciated.

Late-night anxieties of an astrobiologist. I smelled the trees respiring and heard the river where Alyssa and I first swam together, polishing its boulders even in darkness. A noise came from the bag next to me. Robin was pleading in his sleep. *Stop! Please stop! Please!*

ONE OF THE SOLUTIONS TO THE FERMI PAR-
ADOX was so strange I never dared tell Robin. He would have
had bad dreams for months. One quadrillion neural connections
lay on the inflatable camping pillow next to me: one synapse for
every star in two thousand five hundred Milky Ways. Lots of ways
to overheat.

But here's the solution I never told him: Say life is easy to kick-
start from out of nothing. Say it'd been springing up in every
crack of the cosmic sidewalk for billions of years before the Earth
appeared. After all, it sprang up here the moment this planet stabi-
lized, from the same stuff that exists everywhere in the universe.

And say that over the eons, countless millions of civilizations
arose, many of them lasting long enough to venture into space.
Spacefaring creatures found each other, linked up, and shared
knowledge, their technologies accelerating with each new contact.
They built great energy-harvesting spheres that enclosed entire
suns and drove computers the size of whole solar systems. They harnessed the energy from quasars and gamma ray bursts. They filled
galaxies the way we once spread across continents. They learned to
weave the fabric of reality itself.

And when this consortium mastered all the laws of time and
space, they fell into the sadness of completion. Absolute Intelligence
surrendered to nostalgia for the camping and woodcraft of its own
lost origins. They created consoling playthings—countless sealed-
off planets where life could evolve again in its pristine state.

And say that life in one of those terrariums evolves into creatures with two thousand five hundred times as many synapses as
there were stars in a galaxy. Even with such brains, it would take
those creatures millennia to discover that they were trapped forever
in a simulated wilderness, looking out onto a virtual firmament,
trapped in childhood, alone.

The catalog of solutions to the Fermi paradox calls this the Zoo

Hypothesis. Zoos made Robin queasy. He couldn't stand to see sentient beings confined.

My own parents raised me a Lutheran, but I lost all religion at the age of sixteen. All life long I've believed that when a person dies, all the beauty and insight and hope—but also all pain and terror—everything stored in her one thousand trillion synapses disperses into noise. But that night in the Smokies, in our two-person tent, I couldn't help petitioning the person who knew Robin best in all the world. "Alyssa." My wife of eleven and a half years. "Aly. Tell me what to do. We're fine together, in the woods. But I'm afraid to take him home."

AT THREE A.M., IT POURED. I scrambled into the rain to put the fly on. The bedlam terrified Robin at first. But, running around in the downpour, he began cackling like a crow. He was still laughing when we got back in the tent, soaked to the bone in a puddle of our foolish optimism.

"I guess I should have insisted on the fly."

Worth it, Dad. I'd leave it off again!

"You would, would you? You and your inner amphibian."

We cooked oatmeal over the portable stove and broke camp late that morning. The trail looked different from the other direction. We headed back up and over the ridge. It surprised Robin, how much was still growing, so late into the season. I showed him witch hazel, waiting to flower in January. I told him about the snow scorpionfly, which would skate on ice and feed on moss all winter.

Too soon, we were back at the trailhead. The sight of the road through the trees crushed me. The cars, the asphalt, the sign listing all the regulations: after a night in the woods, the trailhead parking lot felt like death. I did my best not to show Robin. He was probably protecting me, too.

We hit traffic on the road back to our rented cabin. I pulled up behind a Subaru Outback loaded down with high-performance mountain bikes. The queue stretched in front of us, out of sight: half a mile of backed-up SUVs, all starved for the last little scraps of eastern wilderness.

I looked over at my passenger. "You know what this is? Bear jam!" I'd told him we might see one, here in the densest population of black bears on the continent. "Hop out. Walk down a ways and see. But stay close to the road."

He studied me. *Serious?*

"Of course! I'm not going to leave you here. I'll stop and pick you up when I reach you." He didn't move. "Go on, Robbie. There's all kinds of people up there. The bears won't hurt you."

His look withered me: he wasn't worried about the quadrupeds. But he let himself out of the car and stumbled ahead, alongside the stopped cars. The small victory should have cheered me.

Traffic crept along. People started honking. Cars tried to U-turn on the narrow mountain road. Cars pulled off onto the shoulder, haphazard, their passengers milling out into traffic. People grilled each other. Bear. Where? A mother and three little ones. There. No, there. A ranger tried to get the cars to move on through. The queue ignored her.

Minutes later, I reached the throng. People pointed into the woods while others lifted binoculars to their eyes. People aimed tripod-mounted cameras with howitzer lenses. A line of people warded off nature with their cell phones. It looked like a crowd outside an office building watching a person on the tenth-floor ledge.

Then I noticed the family of four, drifting diffidently back into the undergrowth. The sow cast a look over her shoulder at the assembled humans. I saw Robin in the crowd, gazing down, in the wrong direction. He turned and saw me and trotted toward the car. The traffic was still stopped dead. I rolled down the window. "Stay and look, Robbie."

He jogged to the car, got in, and slammed the door behind him. "Did you see them?"

I saw them. They were fantastic. His voice was belligerent. He stared straight ahead, at the Outback still in front of us. I felt an incident coming on.

"Robbie. What's wrong? What happened?"

His head turned away and he shouted, *Didn't you see them?*

He stared at his hands in his lap. I knew enough not to push things. The spectacle over, traffic started to move at last. Half a mile down the road, Robbie spoke again.

They must really hate us. How would you like to star in a freak show?

He stared through the side window at the snaking river. Minutes later, he said, *Heron.* The word was nothing but flat fact.

I waited for two more miles. "They're very smart, you know. *Ursus americanus.* Some scientists say they're almost as smart as hominids."

Smarter.

"How do you figure?"

We'd popped out of the park and were driving back through the gauntlet of recreational economy. Robin held his hands out toward the evidence. *They don't do this!*

We passed the fudge shop and the hamburger stand, the tube rentals, dollar store, and bumper cars. We made a left past the visitor center, back uphill to our cabin. "They're just lonely, Robbie."

He looked at me as if I'd renounced my citizenship in the clan of sentient beings. *What are you talking about? They weren't lonely. They were disgusted.*

"Don't shout, okay? I'm not talking about the bears."

The puzzle slowed him down, at least.

People are lonely because we're jerk-faces. We stole everything from them, Dad.

Warnings were everywhere, from his rigid fingers and twitching lips to the purple flush rising around his neck. Another few minutes would undo all the gentleness of the last few days. I didn't have the stamina for two hours of wounded screaming fit. Years of experience had taught me that my best course now was distraction.

"Robbie, listen. Suppose the Allen Telescope Array had a press conference tomorrow where they announced indisputable evidence of intelligent aliens."

Dad.

"It would be the most exciting day on Earth. One announcement would change everything."

He stopped twitching, still disgusted. But curiosity beat disgust in Robin, nine times out of ten. *So?*

"So . . . say they held a press conference and said alien intelligence was discovered all over the Smokies and—"

Gee, God . . . ! He jabbed his hands in the air. But I'd successfully derailed him. I could see his eyes toy with the idea. His mouth twitched in resentful amusement. That line of people along the side of the road holding out their cell phones were turning back into kin. He saw it now: We humans were dying for company. Our species had grown so desperate for alien contact that traffic could back up for miles at the fleeting glimpse of anything smart and wild.

"No one wants to be alone, Robbie."

Compassion struggled with righteousness and lost. *They used to be everywhere, Dad. Before we got to them. We took over everything! We deserve to be alone.*

THAT NIGHT WE WENT TO FALASHA, a planet so dark we were lucky to find it. It wandered in empty space, an orphan without a sun. It had its own star once, but got ejected during its home system's troubled youth. "When I was in school, no one even mentioned them," I told him. "Now we think rogue planets might even outnumber stars."

We watched Falasha drift through interstellar emptiness, in timeless night and temperatures a few degrees above absolute zero.

Why did we come here, Dad? It's the deadest place in the universe.

"That's what science thought, too, when I was your age."

Every belief will be outgrown, in time. The first lesson of the universe is to never reason from only a single instance. Unless you only have one instance. In which case: find another.

I pointed out the thick greenhouse atmosphere and the hot, radiating core. I showed him how the tidal friction from a large moon bent and pinched the planet, further warming it. We touched down on Falasha's surface. *Nice!* my excited son said.

"Above the melting point of water."

In the middle of empty space! But no sun. No plants. No photosynthesis. No nothing.

"Life can eat all kinds of things," I reminded him. "And only one of those is light."

We went to the bottom of Falasha's oceans, into their volcanic seams. We aimed our headlamps into the deepest trenches, and he gasped. Creatures everywhere: white crabs and clams, purple tube worms and living draperies. Everything fed on the heat and chemistry oozing from hydrothermal vents.

He couldn't get enough. He watched as microbes and worms and crustaceans learned new tricks, fed on themselves, and spread their nutrients across seafloors into the surrounding waters. Whole periods went by, eras, even eons. The oceans of Falasha filled with forms, all kinds of outrageous designs, swimming and evading and outmaneuvering.

"We should call it a day," I said.

But he wanted to keep watching. The vents spewed and cooled. The currents of the waters shifted. Small upheavals and local catastrophes favored the cagey. Sessile barnacles turned into free swimmers, and swimmers developed the power to predict. Pilgrim adventurers colonized new places.

My son was hypnotized. *What will happen in a billion more years?*

"We'll have to come back and see."

We rose from the pitch-black planet. It shrank beneath us, and in no time it was invisible again.

How on Earth did we ever discover this place?

And that's where the story turned surreal. A lineage of slow, weak, naked, awkward creatures on a far luckier planet had lasted through several near-extinctions and held on long enough to discover that gravity bent light, everywhere in the universe. For no good reason and at insane expense, we'd built an instrument able to see the tiniest bend in starlight made by this small body, from scores of light-years away.

Get out, my son said. *You're making that up.*

And we were, we Earthlings. Making it up as we went along, then proving it for all the universe to see.

WE HIT THE ROAD BY DAWN. Robbie was at his best as the sun came up. He got that from his mother, who could solve dozens of not-for-profit crises before breakfast. That morning, he was willing to treat even banishment as an adventure.

The country had been so volatile when we left, and days of spotty reception left me anxious about what was waiting for us back out here. I waited until we got out of Tennessee to tune in the news. Two headlines in, I regretted it. Hurricane Trent's hundred-mile-an-hour winds returned a good stretch of the South Fork of Long Island to the sea. U.S. and Chinese fleets were playing nuclear cat-and-mouse off Hainan Island. An eighteen-deck cruise ship named *Beauty of the Seas* exploded off St. John's, Antigua, killing scores of passengers and wounding hundreds more. Several groups claimed responsibility. In Philadelphia, stoked by social media flame wars, True America militias attacked a HUE demonstration and three people were dead.

I tried to change the station, but Robbie wouldn't let me. *We have to know, Dad. It's good citizenship.*

Maybe it was. Maybe it was even good parenting. Or maybe it was a colossal error in judgment, to let him go on listening.

Following the fires that had taken out three thousand homes across the San Fernando Valley, the President was blaming the trees. His executive order called for two hundred thousand acres of national forest to be cut down. The acres weren't even all in California.

Holy crap, my son shouted. I didn't bother with a language check. *Can he do that?*

The news announcer answered for me. In the name of national security, the President could do pretty much anything.

The President is a dung beetle.

"Don't say that, bud."

He is.

"Robin, listen to me. You can't talk like that."

Why not?

"Because they can put you in jail, now. Remember when we talked about it, last month?"

He fell back in his seat, having second thoughts about good citizenship.

Well, he is. A you-know-what. He's wrecking everything.

"I know. But we can't say so out loud. Besides. You're being totally unfair."

He looked at me, baffled. Two beats later, he broke into a spectacular grin. *You're right! Dung beetles are pretty amazing.*

"Did you know that they navigate by mental maps of the Milky Way?"

He looked at me, mouth agape. The fact seemed too weird to be invented. He pulled out his pocket notebook and made a note to fact-check me when we got home.

UP THROUGH THE DIMINISHING HILLS of Kentucky, past the Creation Museum and Ark Encounter, through counties that had little use for science of any kind, we listened to *Flowers for Algernon*. I'd read it at age eleven. It was one of the first books in my two-thousand-volume library of science fiction. I bought it in a used bookstore—a mass market paperback bearing a creepy image of a face halfway between mouse and man. Paying for it with my own money felt like cracking the code of adulthood. Holding it open in my hands, I wormholed into a different Earth. Small, light, portable parallel universes turned out to be the only thing in this life I'd ever collect.

Algernon didn't quite start me down the path of science. That was the "sea monkeys," a kind of brine shrimp shipped to me in an astonishing state of cryptobiosis. By Robbie's age, I'd already tabulated my first data sets on their hatching rates. But Algernon lit up my proto-scientific imagination and made me want to experiment on something the size of my own life. I hadn't read the story in decades, and a twelve-hour drive seemed the perfect excuse to revisit with Robin in tow.

The story gripped him. He kept making me pause for questions. *He's changing, Dad. You hear his words getting bigger?* A little later, he asked: *Is this for real? I mean: Could it ever be for real, someday?*

I told him everything could be for real, somewhere, someday. That may have been a mistake.

By the time we reached southern Indiana's long stretch of factory farms, he was swept up, limiting his commentary to cheers and jeers. We went for miles at a shot, Robin leaning forward, a hand on the dash, forgetting even to look out the window. He was spawning synapses as fast as Charlie Gordon, whose IQ rose to precarious heights. Robbie winced through Charlie's rejection at the hands of his coworkers. The moral ambiguity of the experimenting scientists Nemur and Strauss hurt him so much I had to remind him to breathe.

When Algernon died, he made me stop the recording. *Really?* He couldn't wrap his head around the fact. *The mouse is dead?* His face flirted with quitting the story altogether. But *Algernon* had already ended much of the innocence Robin still possessed. The mind's eye had two bafflements: coming out of the light and going into it.

"You know what that means? You see what's coming?" But Robin couldn't see the consequences for Charlie. Nor did he much care. I resumed the story. A minute later, he made me pause again.

But the mouse, Dad. The muh-hu-hu-mouse! His voice mock-mourned, like a smaller, younger kid. But not far down, the play was real.

We stopped for the night at a motel near Champaign-Urbana, Illinois. He wouldn't sleep until the story ended. He lay on his bed, suffering through Charlie's final decline with sphinxlike stoicism. At the end, he nodded, and motioned for lights-out. I asked him what he thought, but he simply shrugged. Only in the dark did it come out of him.

Did Mom ever read this story?

The question blindsided me. "I don't know. I think so. Probably. It's kind of a classic. Why do you ask?"

Why do you think? he said, sharper than perhaps intended. When he spoke again, he was contrite. He was going into the light, or coming out of it. I couldn't tell which. *You know. The mouse, Dad. The mouse.*

WE GOT TO MADISON A LITTLE AFTER NOON
on the day I'd promised to get Robin back to school. I got the automated text saying he was absent without excuse and asking if I knew
that (*Please reply Y or N*). I should have brought him straight to
class. But there were only a few hours left of school, and I was feeling how I always felt whenever I had to hand him over to people
who didn't get him. I wanted him to myself a little longer.

I brought him to campus with me. I dreaded going in after so
long away. We got my mail, and I checked in with my grad assistant, Jinjing, who'd taught my undergrad classes in my absence.
Jinjing fussed over Robin like he was her own little brother back in
Shenzhen. She took him to see the display case of meteorites and the
photos from *Cassini*. I took the opportunity to get chewed out by
Carl Stryker, my colleague and coauthor on a paper about detect-
ing biosignature gases from lensing-revealed exoplanets that I was
holding up.

"MIT is going to scoop us," Stryker said. Of course it was.
MIT or Princeton or the EANA was always scooping us. It wasn't
enough for anyone simply to do science. Everything was a race for
priority, for professional advancement, for a share of the shrinking
grants pool and a raffle ticket to Stockholm. The truth was, Stryker
and I were never going to win the Swedish Sweepstakes. But con-
tinued funding was nice. And I was jeopardizing that by failing to
refine my model data for the article.

"Is it the boy, again?" Stryker asked.

I wanted to say: *He has a name, jerk-face*. But yes, I said, it was
the boy, silently begging my collaborator to cut me a little slack.
Stryker didn't have much slack to give. Fifteen years ago, the exoplanet bonanza had turned the grants agencies as generous toward
astrobiology as the Renaissance courts had been to any adventurer
with a caravel. But Earth was shakier now, and the funding winds
had changed.

"We need the edits by Monday, Theo. I'm serious."

I told him I could manage by Monday. I left Stryker's office wondering what my career in this infant field might have been like, had I never married. A little luckier, maybe. But nothing in existence could ever be luckier than Alyssa and Robin.

MY LIFE WENT THROUGH ITS OWN LITTLE HADEAN EON, back in my Muncie childhood. Hell everywhere. The details are blissfully fuzzy now. I grew up fast. By rough count, my mother harbored six different personalities inside herself, and half of them were capable of doing me and my two older sisters real harm. By the time my father commenced his slow suicide by painkillers, I'd already traded in boy soprano for the more demanding hobby of sitting in my room and panicking.

When I was thirteen, Dad made us kids scrub up and sit behind him in court as he was sentenced for embezzling. The ploy must have worked because he got only eight months. But we lost the house, and my father never again earned more than minimum wage. I wouldn't have made it through those years without brains in a vat, Dyson spheres, arcologies, spooky action at a distance, Afrofuturism, Retro-pulp, and psi machines. From Alpha-beams to the Omega Point, I lived in a parallel place that spawned scenarios of such infinite variety that they made a laughingstock of the little parochial rock in the galactic sticks where I lived. Nothing could hurt me so long as consensual reality was just a tiny atoll in an ocean without shores.

By twelfth grade, I was fast-track apprenticing for my own career as a drunk. My two best friends and netherworld partners called me Mad Dog. Remarkably, I made it through to graduation without going to jail. But absent the scholarship from the electronic-organ company where a couple of my mother's personalities worked as a secretary, I would never have gone to college. As it was, I went only because it beat the summer job I had, cleaning out septic tanks for a company whose slogan was, "A Straight Flush Beats a Full House."

I headed downstate, to the flagship public school. There I took a biology survey picked at random out of the course catalog to meet a general education requirement. It was taught by a bacteriologist name Katja McMillian. She was cylindrical and stork-like, a superannuated Big Ethel Muggs. But Mondays, Wednesdays, and Fridays, she stood in a bowl of four hundred undergraduates, on fire. Week after week she worked to show us how none of us had a clue what life could do.

There were creatures that retooled themselves into something unrecognizable halfway through their life. There were creatures that saw infrared and sensed magnetic fields. There were creatures that changed sex based upon straw polls of the neighborhood, and single cells that acted en masse by sensing quorums. Lecture by lecture, it dawned on me: *Astounding Stories* had nothing on Dr. McMillian.

In week twelve, almost through the semester, she arrived at the creatures she loved. A revolution was under way, and Dr. McMillian was on the barricades. Researchers were finding life where science knew it could not live. Life was eking out a living above the boiling point and below freezing. It staked out places Dr. McMillian's own professors once insisted were too salty, too acidic, and too radioactive for any creature to survive. Life made a home high up on the edge of space. Life lived deep in solid rock.

I sat in the back of the auditorium thinking: *My people. At last.*

Dr. McMillian hired me to assist on a summer field expedition to study alien life-forms in a sinkhole under Lake Huron that someone had discovered by accident. They were among the most bizarrely creative creatures on this planet—switching like Jekyll and Hyde from anoxic to oxygenic photosynthesis when the tasty sulfur ran out. The crazy biochemistry behind Dr. McMillian's bipolar extremophiles suggested how life took hold and shaped a hostile planet into something more conducive for life. Working for her was a waking dream, for a guy who loved to stay out in any weather.

Professor McMillian's inflated letter of recommendation—*largely accurate,* she told me, *if still mostly predictive*—got me a graduate assistantship at U Dub. Seattle was the best place I could have landed, given my skill set, which consisted of holding still and looking at things, the stranger the better. The microbiology program was strong, and the extremophile people adopted me as close enough for kin.

I joined a multidisciplinary team modeling how oxygenated meltwater between glaciers and the seas kept organisms alive when Earth was frozen up like a giant snowball. According to our models, that sliver of life, over agonizingly long stretches of time, helped turn the snowball planet back into a runaway garden.

While I studied, crazy things were happening far away. Data flowed back from instruments flying all over the Solar System. The planets were wilder than anyone suspected. Moons of Jupiter and Saturn turned out to be hiding liquid oceans beneath their suspiciously smooth crusts. All the Earthly chauvinisms began to fall. We'd been reasoning from a sample of one. Life might not need surface water. It might not need water at all. It might not even need a surface.

I was living through one of the great revolutions in human thought. A few years before, most astronomers thought they'd never live to see the discovery of even a single planet outside the solar system. By the time I was halfway through graduate school, the eight or nine planets known to exist turned into dozens, then hundreds. At first they were mostly gas giants. Then Kepler was launched, and Earth was flooded with worlds, some not much larger than ours.

The universe changed from one semester to the next. People were looking at infinitesimal changes in the light of immensely distant stars—reductions in brightness of a few parts per million—and calculating the invisible bodies that dimmed them in transiting. Minuscule wobbles in the motion of massive suns—changes of less than one meter per second in the velocity of a star—were betraying the size and mass of invisible planets tugging on them. The precision of these measurements defied belief. It was like trying to use a ruler to measure a distance a hundred times smaller than the amount the ruler would expand from the heat of your hand.

We did that. We Earthlings.

New habitats everywhere: no one could keep up. People were finding hot Jupiters and mini-Neptunes, diamond planets and nickel planets, gas dwarfs and ice giants. Super Earths in the habitable zones of K- and M-class stars seemed as suited for a spark of life as this place ever was. The whole idea of the Goldilocks zone got blown wide open. The life we'd found in Earth's harshest regions could easily thrive in many of the regions now springing up throughout space.

I woke one morning looking down on my body where I lay in bed. I saw myself the way my old mentor Dr. McMillian sized up a new species of archaea. I weighed where I'd come from, my cast of mind, the sum of my failings and capabilities, and I knew what I wanted to do before my small part of this giant experiment ended. I'd visit Enceladus and Europa and Proxima Centauri b, at least via spectroscopy. I'd learn how to read the histories and biographies of their atmospheres. And I'd comb through those distant oceans of air for the slightest signs of anything breathing.

ONE DAY NEAR THE END OF MY PH.D., back from a week of field sampling, I sat down in a campus computer lab next to a frantic but friendly woman who, by chance, was struggling with one of the few quirks in the university file system I knew how to solve. She leaned over to ask for help, a thing, it turned out, she never did. And the first words out of her earnest mouth—*Do you know how ttt-t . . . ?*—tripped on a stutter that caught even her by surprise.

She got the word out, and then the sentence. I worked my one little trick of digital wizardry. She thanked me for saving her from failing her course on animal law. By her third sentence, the stutter settled down. *If you ever need any advice about what constitutes legal cruelty, I'm your gal.*

Everything about her felt familiar, as if I'd been briefed on the local customs in advance. Her mouth puckered in permanent near-interruption, halfway between a- and be-mused. Her auburn frazzle was parted down the middle. The top of her head just reached my shoulder. She held her small frame like an athlete before the starting gun: challenges everywhere. She felt like a prediction, a thing on its way here. *Compact but planetary.* My favorite poet Neruda seemed to fall in love with her, too, the minute I did.

She had on Mil-Spec hiking boots and a green vest that made her look like something from the Shire. I lunged at my one entrée. "I'm just back from a week in the San Juans." She lit up. Even as I worked up the courage to ask if she'd like to see our field site, her lips formed her trademark look, half wince, half smirk. Laugh lines swamped her hazel eyes and she said, *I can go days without showering.* The stutter was nowhere.

It took some months to accept my luck. I'd met someone else who liked to hike more than most people like to sleep. It boggled me that a woman who looked like her would also be aroused by Latin nomenclature. Weirdest luck of all, she laughed at my jokes, even when I didn't know I was making one.

The fit between us was rough but useful. I gave her stamina and fed her curiosity. She taught me optimism and appetite, albeit plant-based. There it was: roll the dice and find your life catalyzed by another, one who, ten minutes later or three seats farther down at another computer screen, would have remained an undetected signal from deep space.

ALYSSA FINISHED HER JD as I wrapped up my doctorate. And still our streak kept rolling. We both landed decent jobs in the same unlikely city. Madtown, Cheeseland: from U Dub to U Double U. A place on neither of our radars soon made natives of us. We loved the city, and our only contention was east side or west. We found a place near Lake Monona, a healthy walk from campus. It was a good house, a little dowdy, a little old—pine-framed midwestern standard issue, renovated many times, with leaks around the flashing of the skylights. It was just right for two. It got snugger later, with three. Later still, with two again, it would feel cavernous.

Aly was a dynamo, cranking out fully researched action plans for one of the country's leading animal rights NGOs every other week while dashing off countless diplomatic emails and press releases in her spare minutes. In four years, she rose through the ranks from glorified fundraiser to Midwest coordinator. State legislators from Bismarck to Columbus both dreaded and adored her. She inched ahead on colorful profanity and sardonic cheer. The vilest factory farm brought out her steely will. Between occasional full-on collapses of confidence, her days remained as resolute as they were long. At night, there was red wine and poems for Chester.

Wisconsin gave me my first real home. I found a collaborator. Stryker handled the astrochemistry that was beyond me. I contributed the life science. Together, we studied how the absorption lines in the spectra of distant atmospheres might reveal biology. We refined our biosignature models by applying them to terrestrial satellite data, scaled down to what Earth would look like if spied on by a four-meter telescope from distant space. We learned to read its fluctuating images. In the shimmer of data points we detected the planet's makeup, calculated its cycling elements, watched the bright continents and swirling currents of ocean. The harsh Sahara and fertile Amazon, mirror-like ice sheets and changing temperate forests: all appeared in the fluctuations of a few pixels. It thrilled me to peer through that narrow keyhole on the breathing Earth and see it the way alien astrobiologists would from a trillion miles away.

We had lucky days, lots of them. Then the climate in Washington changed and funding fell off. The great telescopes we needed—the ones that would give us *real* data to run through our models— slipped and missed their development deadlines. But there I was, still getting paid to prepare how to discover whether we were alone or surrounded by crazy neighbors.

Aly and I had more projects than we had hours. Then our lives changed, thanks to the one-point-five percent failure rate of our favored birth control. The unlikely roll stunned us both. It seemed a break in our long streak, the worst possible timing for an event we might never have chosen for ourselves. Our careers already stretched us to the limits. Neither of us had the knowledge or where-withal to raise a child.

A decade later, I see the truth, every morning I wake up. If Aly and I had been in charge, the luckiest thing in my life—the thing that kept me going when all the luck in the world went cold—would never have existed, not even in my wildest models.

THE FIRST NIGHT HOME was hard on Robin. Our mountain getaway had smashed all routines, and thermodynamics long ago proved that putting things back together is lots harder than taking them apart. He tore through the house, wired and erratic. After dinner, I felt him regressing: eight years old, seven, six . . . I braced myself for zero, and blastoff.

Can I check my farm?

"You can play for one hour."

Yesss! Gems?

"No gems. I'm still paying off that last little stunt of yours."

That was an accident, Dad. I didn't know your card was on the account. I thought I was getting gems for free.

He did look stricken. If his explanation wasn't the literal truth, regret had made it truer in the months since the disaster. He played for forty minutes, announcing his trophies as he earned them. I graded homework sets from the lecture course and worked on the edits for Stryker.

Following an especially manic harvesting clickfest, he turned to me. *Dad?* His shoulders hunched in supplication. Here it was at last—the thing that had nagged him since we got home. *Can we watch Mom?*

He'd been asking more often in recent weeks, in a way that had grown unhealthy. We'd watched some of her videos too many times, and seeing Aly in action didn't always have the best effect on Robin. But whatever the clips did to him, forbidding them would have done worse. He needed to study his mother, and he needed me to study her with him.

I let Robin search the video site. After two keystrokes, Alyssa's name rose to the top of previous searches. I have less than fifteen minutes of video of my own mother. Now the moving, talking dead are everywhere, available anytime, from any pocket. It's a rare week when we dead-to-be don't surrender a few more minutes of our souls to the overflowing archives. Not even the craziest SF story from my youth predicted it. Imagine a planet where the past never went away but kept happening again and again, forever. That's the planet my nine-year-old wanted to live on.

"Let's see. We need a good one." I took the mouse and scrolled, looking for a clip that would be gentle with us. Aly was up in my ear, whispering, *What in God's name are you thinking? Don't let him watch that!*

Pulling rank didn't work. Robin swung in the swivel chair and grabbed the mouse. *Not those ones, Dad! Madison. Here.*

For the magic to work, the ghost had to be nearby. He needed to see his mother lobbying at the state Capitol, an hour's walk from our two-bedroom bungalow. He remembered those days—afternoons with Alyssa practicing in the dining room, editing and re-editing her testimony, declaiming away her nerves, all those times he'd watched her don her owl pendant, wolf earrings, and one of three warrior dress suits—black, tan, or navy blazer with knee-length stretchy skirt and cream-colored blouse—then hop on her bike with her dress shoes in a shoulder bag to pedal off to the state assembly and do battle.

This one, Dad. He pointed to a clip of Alyssa testifying for a bill to outlaw killing contests.

"That one's for later, Robbie. Maybe when you're ten. How about one of these?" Aly lobbying against something called possum tosses. Aly fighting to protect pigs from abuse during the annual "Pioneer Days." Rough, too, but cakewalks compared to the one he wanted.

Dad! His force surprised us both. I sat still, certain he'd melt down and turn the evening into a screaming match. *I'm not a little kid anymore. We watched the farm one. I was fine with the farm one.*

He had not been fine with the farm one. The farm one had been a colossal mistake. Aly's description of chicks raised on tilted wire mesh, packed so closely they pecked each other to death, had given Robin nighttime screaming fits for weeks.

Our little two-man luge was poised to plunge off the mountainside. I took a breath. "Let's pick another one, buddy. They're all of Mom, right?"

Dad. Now he sounded old and sad. He pointed to the clip's date: two months before Alyssa's death. My son's equations came clear to me. The ghost had to be as close as possible, not just in space but in time.

I clicked on the link, and there she was. Aly, at full incandescence. The shock never weakened. My cell phone camera has this special effect: the object in the crosshairs stays saturated while everything around it fades to gray. That's how it was with the woman who let me marry her. She ionized any room, even a roomful of politicians.

All the nerves that plagued her in rehearsal vanished in the final performances. Behind the microphone, she came off consummately self-possessed, with flashes of wry bafflement in the face of our species. She turned her voice into this Platonic public radio announcer. She could blend stats and stories without hectoring. She empathized with all parties, compromising without betraying the truth. Everything she said came across as so damn reasonable. None of the ninety-nine assembly members would have believed she'd suffered from a massive childhood stutter and used to chew her lips until they bled.

As she gave her last recorded performance, her son watched from this side of the ground. Every detail had him so hypnotized that his questions never got past his gaping lips. He watched Aly talk about witnessing a celebrated event up north, near Lake Superior, one of twenty hunting contests held in the state that year. He sat up straight and smoothed his collar; I'd once told him how mature that made him look. For a kid with no self-control, he gave a masterful performance all his own.

Aly described the judging stand on the fourth and final day of the competition: an industrial-spec crane scale waiting for the contestants to deliver their hauls. Pickup trucks filled with carcasses pulled up and unloaded their mounds onto the scales. Awards went to those who had bagged the most poundage over four days. The prizes included guns, scopes, and lures that would make next year's contest even more one-sided.

She recited the facts: Number of participants. Weight of winning entry. Total animals killed in statewide contests every year. Effects of lost animals on ravaged ecosystems. Her sober eloquence would conclude later that night in a two-hour crying jag in bed, with me powerless to comfort her.

I kicked myself for imagining Robbie could handle this. But he'd wanted to see his mother, and truth be told, he was holding it together pretty well. Nine is the age of great turning. Maybe humanity was a nine-year-old, not yet grown up, not a little kid anymore. Seemingly in control, but always on the verge of rage.

Alyssa wrapped up. Her conclusion was masterful. She always nailed the landing. She said how this bill would restore tradition and dignity to hunting. She said how ninety-eight percent by weight of animals left on Earth were either *Homo sapiens* or their industrially harvested food. Only two percent were wild. Didn't the few wild things left need a little break?

Her closing words chilled me all over again. I remembered her working them out, in weeks of laboring over this testimony. *The creatures of this state do not belong to us. We hold them in our trust. The first people who lived here knew: all animals are our relatives. Our ancestors and our descendants are watching our stewardship. Let's make them proud.*

The clip ended. I canceled the one that queued up next. To my relief, Robin didn't argue. He held three fingers against his mouth. The gesture made him look like a four-foot-tall Atticus Finch.

Did that bill pass, Dad?

"Not yet, buddy. But something like it will, one of these years. And look at the number of views. People are still hearing her."

I mussed his hair. His locks were all over the place. He wouldn't let anyone cut them but me. That wasn't doing much for his social standing.

"Why don't you get ready for bed, and we'll burn the midnight oil." Our code for reading together for twenty minutes past his eight-thirty bedtime.

Can I have a juice, first?

"Juice might not be the best thing, right before bed." I didn't need a two a.m. disaster. I'd removed the plastic fitted sheet. It was too humiliating for him.

How do you know? Maybe it is. Maybe juice is exactly the perfect thing before bed. We should run a double-blind experiment.

I'd made the mistake of telling him about those. "Naw. We're gonna fake the data. Scoot!"

HE WAS THOUGHTFUL WHEN I CAME INTO HIS ROOM. He lay under the covers in his brown plaid canoe pajamas that he'd forbidden me from giving to Goodwill. The cuffs stopped two inches above his wrist and the waist pinched his boy's belly into a muffin-top. The pajamas had been a little too big when his mother had bought them. The way he was going, he'd still be wearing them on his honeymoon.

I had my book—*The Chemical Evolution of the Atmosphere and Oceans*—and he had his—*Maniac Magee*. I took my place beside him in the bed. But he was too thoughtful to read. He put his hand on my arm, as Aly always did.

What did she mean about our ancestors watching us?

"And our descendants. It was just an expression. Like saying that history is going to judge us."

Is it?

"Is what?"

Is *history going to judge us?*

I had to think about that. "That's what history *is*, I guess."

And are they?

"Are our ancestors watching us? It's a figure of speech, Robbie."

When she said that, I pictured them all together, on one of your exoplanets. TRAPPIST-whatever. And they had a huge telescope. And they were watching us and seeing whether we're doing okay.

"That's a pretty cool metaphor, all by itself."

But they're not.

"I . . . no. I don't think so."

He nodded, opened *Maniac,* and pretended to read. I did the same, with *Atmospheres and Oceans*. But I knew his next question was only waiting for a decent interval. As it happened, the interval was two minutes.

So . . . what about God, Dad?

My mouth pumped, like something in the Gatlinburg aquarium. "You know, when people say *God* . . . I don't, I'm not sure they always . . . I mean, God isn't something you can prove or disprove. But from what I can see, we don't need any bigger miracle than evolution."

I turned to face him. He shrugged. *I mean, duh. We're on a rock, in space, right? There are billions of planets as good as ours, filled with creatures we can't even imagine. And God is supposed to look like* us?

I gawked again. "Then why'd you ask?"

To make sure you weren't kidding yourself.

This, God help me, made me laugh out loud. There we were. Nothing. Everything. My son and me. I tickled him until he screamed for forgiveness, which took about three seconds.

We sobered up and read. The pages turned; we traveled easily, everywhere. Then, without taking his eyes off his book, Robin asked, *So what do you think happened to Mom?*

For one awful moment, I thought he meant the night of the accident. All kinds of lies presented themselves before I realized he was asking something much easier.

"I don't know, Robbie. She went back into the system. She became other creatures. All the good things in her came into us. Now we keep her alive, with whatever we can remember."

His head tipped, a little reticent. My son, growing away from me. *I think she's like a salamander or something.*

I rolled to face him. "Wait . . . *what?* Where'd you get *that?*" I knew: the thirty species the Smokies had.

Well, remember you said how Einstein proved nothing could be created or destroyed?

"That's right. But he was talking about matter and energy. How they keep changing from one form to another."

That's what I'm saying! The words tore out of him so wildly I had to shush him. *Mom was energy, right?*

My face got away from me. "Yes. If Mom was anything, she was energy."

And now she's changed into another form.

When I could, I asked him. "Why a salamander?"

Easy. Because she's fast, and she loves the water. And because how, like you always say, she's totally her own species.

Amphibious. Small but mighty. And she breathed through her skin.

There's a salamander that lives for fifty years. Did you know that? He sounded desperate. I tried to hug him, but he pushed away. *It's probably just a figure of speech. She's probably not anything.*

The words froze me. Some awful switch had been thrown in him, and I couldn't tell why.

Two percent, Dad? He snarled like a cornered badger. *Only two percent of all animals are wild? Everything else is factory cows and factory chickens and us?*

"Please don't shout at me, Robbie."

Is that for real? Is it?

I took our abandoned books and put them on the nightstand. "If your mother said it in a speech for the state legislature, it's for real."

His face bunched up like he'd been punched. His eyes curdled and his mouth opened in a silent scream. It took a moment for the soundless jag to turn into tears. I held out my arms, but he shook his head. Something in him hated me for letting that number be true. He backed into the corner of his bed, up against the wall. His head swung sideways in disbelief.

Just as suddenly, he deflated. He lay back down, his back to me, one ear to the mattress. He lay there listening to the hum of defeat. He felt around for my body in the space behind him. When he found it, he mumbled into the sheets, *New planet, Dad. Please.*

THE PLANET PELAGOS had many times more surface than Earth. It was covered in water—a single ocean that made the Pacific look like the Great Lakes. One sparse chain of tiny volcanic islands ran through that immensity, bits of punctuation sprinkled through an empty book hundreds of pages long.

The endless ocean was shallow in places, kilometers deep in others. Life spread through its latitudes from steamy to frozen. Hosts of creatures turned the ocean bottoms into underwater forests. Giant blimps migrated from pole to pole, never stopping, each half of their brains taking turns to sleep. Intelligent kelp hundreds of meters long spelled messages in colors that rippled up the length of their stalks. Annelids practiced agriculture and crustaceans built high-rise cities. Clades of fish evolved communal rituals indistinguishable from religion. But nothing could use fire or smelt ores or build any but the simplest tools. So Pelagos diversified and invented new forms, each stranger than the last.

Over the eons, the few scattered islands radiated life as if each were its own planet. None of them was large enough to incubate large predators. Each pinprick of land was a sealed terrarium sporting enough species for a small Earth.

Dozens of dispersed intelligent species spoke millions of languages. Even the pidgins numbered in the hundreds. No town was bigger than a hamlet. Every few miles we came across a speaking thing whose shape and color and form were wholly new. The most universally useful adaptation seemed to be humility.

The two of us swam along veins of shallow reef down into underwater forests. We scrambled up onto islands whose complex communities were threaded into immense trading networks with islands far away. Caravans took years, even generations, to complete a deal.

No telescopes, Dad. No rocket ships. No computers. No radios.

"Only amazement." It didn't seem like an outrageous trade.

How many planets are like this one?

"There might be none. They might be everywhere."

Well, we'll never hear from any of them.

I WAS STILL DREAMING UP NEW LAYERS to our creation when I realized I didn't need any more. I leaned in. Robin's breath came light and slow. The stream of his consciousness had broadened to a miles-wide delta. I slipped off the bed and reached the doorway without a sound. But the click of the light switch jolted his body upright in the sudden dark. He screamed. I flipped the light back on.

We forgot Mom's prayer. And they're all dying.

We said it together: May all sentient beings be free from needless suffering.

But the boy who took the next two hours getting safe enough to fall back asleep was no longer sure if that prayer was doing much of anything.

THEY SHARE A LOT, ASTRONOMY AND CHILD-HOOD. Both are voyages across huge distances. Both search for facts beyond their grasp. Both theorize wildly and let possibilities multiply without limits. Both are humbled every few weeks. Both operate out of ignorance. Both are mystified by time. Both are forever starting out.

For a dozen years, my job made me feel like a child. I sat behind the computer in my office looking at data sets from telescopes and toying with formulas that could describe them. I roamed the halls in search of minds who might want to come out and play. I lay in bed with a canary-yellow legal pad and a black fine liner, re-creating the journeys to Cygnus A or through the Large Magellanic Cloud or around the Tadpole Galaxy, trips I'd once made in pulp novels. This time around, none of the indigenous inhabitants spoke English or practiced telepathy or floated parasitically through the frozen vacuum or linked together in hive minds to enact their master plans. All they did was metabolize and respire. But in my infant discipline, that was magic enough.

I made worlds by the thousands. I simulated their surfaces and cores and living atmospheres. I surveyed the ratios of telltale gases that might accumulate, depending on a planet's evolving inhabitants. I tweaked each simulation to match plausible metabolic scenarios, then incubated the parameters for hours on a supercomputer. Out popped Gaian melodies, unfolding in time. The result was a catalog of ecosystems and the biosignatures that would reveal them. When the space-borne telescope that all my models waited for launched at last, we'd already have spectral fingerprints on file to match to any imaginable perpetrator of the crime of life.

Some of my colleagues thought I was wasting my time. What's the use of simulating so many worlds, many of which might not even exist? What's the use of preparing targets beyond the ability of current instruments to detect? To which I always answered: What's the use of childhood? I was sure that the Earthlike Planet Seeker that hundreds of colleagues and I lobbied for would come along before the end of the decade and seed my models with real data. And from those seeds, the wildest conclusions would grow.

Much of existence presents itself in one of three flavors: none, one, or infinite. One-offs were everywhere, at every step of the story. We knew of only one kind of life, arising once on one world, in one liquid medium, using one form of energy storage and one genetic code. But my worlds didn't need to be like Earth. Their versions of life didn't require surface water or Goldilocks zones or even carbon for their core element. I tried to free myself from bias and assume nothing, the way a child worked, as if our single instance proved the possibilities were endless.

I made hot planets with massive wet atmospheres where life lived in the plumes of aerosol geysers. I blanketed rogue planets under thick layers of greenhouse gases and filled them with creatures who survived by joining hydrogen and nitrogen into ammonia. I sank rock-dwelling endoliths in deep fissures and gave them carbon monoxide to metabolize. I made worlds of liquid methane where biofilms feasted on hydrogen sulfide that rained down in banquets from the toxic skies.

And all my simulated atmospheres waited for the day when the long-gestated, long-delayed space-borne telescopes would lift off and come online, blowing our little one-off Rare Earth wide open. That day would be for our species like the one when the eye doctor fitted my vain wife with her first pair of long-overdue glasses, ones that made her shout out loud with joy at being able to see her child from all the way across a room.

THE SHORT, HARD NIGHT made for a late morning. I didn't get Robin to school until ten: another demerit for us both. When I got him there at last, the hardware on my cargo pants set off the security scanner. We had to go to the office to sign the tardy sheet. By the time Robin rejoined his smirking class, he was humiliated.

I rushed from his grade school to the university, where I parked illegally to save time and wound up getting a stiff ticket. I had forty minutes to prep my lecture on abiogenesis—the origin of life—for the undergraduate astrobiology survey. I'd taught the same course only two years before, but dozens of new discoveries since then made me want to start over.

In the auditorium, I felt the pleasure of competence and the warmth that only comes from sharing ideas. It always baffles me when my colleagues complain about teaching. Teaching is like photosynthesis: making food from air and light. It tilts the prospects for life a little. For me, the best class sessions are right up there with lying in the sun, listening to bluegrass, or swimming in a mountain stream.

Over the run of eighty minutes, I tried to convey to a coven of twenty-one-year-olds with a wide spectrum of intellectual abilities just how absurd it was for everything to spring up out of nothing. The alignment of favorable circumstances for the emergence of self-assembling molecules seemed astronomically unlikely. But the appearance of protocells almost as soon as the molten Hadean Earth cooled suggested that life was the inevitable by-product of ordinary chemistry.

"So the universe is either pregnant everywhere, or barren. If I could tell you which, beyond all doubt, would it change your study habits?"

That got a polite, *Okay-Xer* chuckle out of the happy few who were paying attention. But the rest had signed off. I was starting to lose them. It takes a certain kind of strangeness to hear the cosmic symphony and to realize that it was both playing and listening to itself.

"Here on Earth, it was archaea and bacteria and nothing but archaea and bacteria for two billion years. Then came something as mysterious as the origin of life itself. One day two billion years ago, instead of one microbe eating the other, one took the other inside its membrane and they went into business together."

I looked down at my notes and came unstuck in time. My wife-to-be, twenty minutes after having me for the first time, was lying with her nose against my floating rib. *I love your smell,* she said.

I told her, "You don't love me. You love my microbiome."

When she laughed, I thought: I'll just stay here in these parts for a bit. Until I die, or so. I told her how a person had ten times more bacterial cells than human cells and how we needed a hundred times more bacterial than human DNA to keep the organism going.

Her eyes crinkled in love. *So we're the scaffolding, is that it? And they're the building?* Her scaffolding laughed again and climbed on top of mine.

"Without that bizarre collaboration, there'd be no complex cells, no multicellular creatures, nothing to get you out of bed in the morning. The friendly takeover took forever to happen. But here's the weird thing: *It took two billion years to happen. But it happened more than once.*"

That was as far as my lecture got. A buzz went off in my pocket— a text from one of the few numbers allowed past my afternoon block list. It was from Robin's school. My son, my own flesh and blood, had smashed a friend in the face and cracked the boy's cheekbone. The former friend was in the ER getting stitched up, and Robin was being held in the principal's office pending my arrival.

I let the class out, ten minutes early. My students would have to figure out the rest of the origin of life on their own.

THEY WOULDN'T LET ME SEE MY SON until I sat for my own punishment. Dr. Lipman's office walls were covered with accreditation. Her desk was not large, but she used it to tremendous effect. The previous two times she called me in, she'd tried empathy and posture-mirroring. This time she was considerably more Excel spreadsheet. She was younger than I was and dressed too well. Ed psych jargon enthralled her. In her own over-professionalized way, she cared about my son. She was a reformer, and she saved herself for the troubled ones. To her, I was a pigheaded scientist damaging a special child by not following established protocols.

She laid out the facts. Robin had been having lunch with Jayden Astley, his only real friend. They were seated across from each other at the long lunchroom table. The feral din of lunch hour gave way to Robin's shouts. All the witnesses agreed: he wouldn't quit screaming, *Tell me. Tell me, you freaking jerk-face.* Just as the lunch-room monitor got to their table to break things up, Robin snapped, scooped up his metal thermos and flung it hard in Jayden's face. Miraculously it only fractured the boy's cheek.

"But what happened? What made him go off?"

Jill Lipman stared at me as if I'd asked how life began. "Neither boy will say." It was clear where she placed the blame. "We need to talk about why this happened right after you took him out of school for a week."

"I took him out of school to give him a chance to calm down. I doubt my son smashed his only friend's face because of a week in the Smokies."

"He missed a week of class. That's five days in every academic subject. He needs continuity, focus, and social integration. He's not getting that, and that's stressful for him."

He'd missed class when Dr. Lipman suspended him, too. But I listened and kept still.

"Robin needs orientation and accountability. But since his unscheduled vacation, he has been late to school twice."

"I'm a single parent. When things beyond my control——"

"I'm not passing judgment on your parenting." Which, of course, she was. "Children deserve a safe, secure, and stable learning environment. Instead, we're all coping with a violent assault against another child."

A fractured cheekbone. A painkiller and an ice pack, and Jayden was fine. I fractured my own cheekbone, on the monkey bars, when I was seven, back when schools had monkey bars.

Anger makes me clam up. It's a deep-seated trait, one that has often saved me. Dr. Lipman's strange little lips moved, and stranger words came out. "You have a child with special needs. When all this happened the last time——"

"*This* didn't happen, the last time."

"When we had trouble before, you chose to ignore the recommendations of more than one doctor. You have another choice now. You can help your child by giving him the treatment that he needs, or we can get the state involved."

The principal of my son's school was threatening to investigate me if I didn't put my third-grader on psychoactive drugs.

"We'll need to see some progress by December."

When I spoke again, I sounded remarkably composed. "May I please talk to my son?"

Dr. Lipman led me out of her office through the administrative suite. The staff's eyes were on me throughout the perp walk: the man who kept his boy in misery rather than obey the doctors.

Robin was being held in the "Calm Room," a detention cubicle next to the vice principal's office. I saw him through the panel of shatterproof glass. He was hunched over on the too-large wooden chair, doing that thing with his hands he did whenever he was beaten down. He'd stick his thumbs between his index and second fingers and squeeze his fists until everything turned red.

The door opened and Robin looked up. He saw me and his pain doubled. The first words out of his mouth were something no boy at that school had ever said. *Dad, it's all my fault.*

I sat beside him and cuffed his slender shoulder. "What happened, Robbie?"

My anger was going nuts. I tried to let my good parts breathe, like you said to. But my hands got confused.

HE WOULDN'T TELL ME what Jayden Astley said to set him off. I called the boy's parents, half expecting them to sue me over the phone. Instead, they were weirdly sympathetic. Their boy had given them more information than mine had given me, but they weren't volunteering anything. Everyone involved was protecting me. I couldn't tell from what.

I surprised Robin by not forcing the issue, and he surprised me by not wetting the bed that night. The next day was Saturday. I still hadn't finished the edits for Stryker. Robin and I took a long walk down near Olbrich Gardens. For lunch, I scrambled tofu, using the exact ratio of black salt and nutritional yeast that he loved. We played his favorite board game about racing cars across Europe. I pretended to work while he played with his microscope and looked through his files of collectible cards. We read together in peace for half an hour, before he asked for another planet.

I had two thousand paperbacks scattered through our house and thirty years of reading to steal from. When was the golden age of science fiction? For me, it started at nine.

I gave him a planet where the dominant sentient species could merge into a compound creature with all the powers of its separate parts.

His slew of questions stopped the story. *Are you for real? How could that even be?*

"It's another planet. That's how."

But, I mean, are they still separate when they're together, or all one single brain?

"One single brain that can have their separate thoughts."

You mean, like telepathy?

"More than telepathy. A superorganism."

Can the big one, like, get inside the heads of the little ones? Does he need them all, to make it work? What if some of the little ones don't want to join? Or are they really just parts to begin with?

He worried the edge between friendly merger and hostile take-over. I tried to tilt his fascinated horror toward horrified fascination. "They do it voluntarily, when times are hard and they need something extra to survive. And later, when things get better, they split up again."

He leaned forward, suspicious. *Wait a minute! Like slime molds?*

I'd shown him, in the labs at the university: those independent single cells that merged into a community with its own aggregate behavior and rudimentary intelligence.

You stole that from Earth! He slugged my upper arm several times in slow motion. Then he lay back on the pillow. I risked smoothing his bangs out of his eyes, the way he liked me to do when he was little.

"Robbie? You're still upset. I can tell."

He jerked up. *How do you know?*

I pointed at his fists, holding his thumbs crimson captives again. He stared, amazed that his own parts had betrayed him. He shook his hands and liberated his thumbs. Then his head dropped back onto the pillow.

Dad? What happened to her? This time, he meant it. *That night, in the car.*

I looked down at my own hands, which were busy tagging me. "Robin? Did Jayden say something about Mom?"

Luckily, no heavy objects were within reach. But the force of his voice alone knocked me backward. *Just tell me. Tell me!* He slashed back and forth. *I'm nine years old. Just . . . TELL ME!*

I grabbed his wrist, and the pain startled him. "You will stop right now." I spoke with all the calm authority I could fake. "And get control of yourself. Then you will tell me what Jayden said."

He yanked his wrist free and nursed it. *Why did you do that?*

I waited out my pounding pulse. He rubbed his wrist, hating me. Then he burst into tears. When I could, I held him. He tried to work his red and worthless mouth. I signaled that he had all the time on Earth.

He bared his palm and caught his breath. *I was telling him about Mom's video. He said his parents said there was more to her crash than people knew. Jayden said they think that Mom was—*

I pressed his lips, as if I could push the thought back in. "It was an accident, Robbie. Nobody thinks anything else."

That's what I told him! But he kept on saying it. Like he knew the truth. That's why I went nuts.

"You know? I might have slugged him myself."

Half a syllable came up out of his throat, lost between sob and laugh. *Great.* He patted blindly at my upper arm. *Then we'd both be toast.*

"You're not toast, Robbie. Get a tissue and wipe."

His half-formed features smeared under his pressing hands. The squall had blown over, leaving him clear, small, but still winded.

So what did they mean, Jayden's parents?

What kind of people knew their son was torturing mine with something they themselves had said, and didn't alert me when I called them? Scared and scrambling, like everyone.

I'm nine, Dad. I can handle it.

I was forty-five, and couldn't. "Robbie? There were witnesses. Everyone agrees. Something ran in front of her car."

What do you mean? Like a person?

"An animal." He frowned, baffled, like some cartoon boy. "You remember it was dark and icy?"

He nodded at a tiny model he was making of that evening, a foot in front of his eyes. *January twelfth. Nine p.m.*

"It ran in front of her car. She must have jerked the wheel. The car skidded, and that's how she crossed the center line."

He kept his eyes on his tiny simulation. Then he asked a question I should have been ready for. Such an obvious thing. *What kind of animal?*

I panicked. "Nobody knows for sure."

Maybe a marten, or something really rare? Maybe it was a wolverine.

"I don't know, buddy. Nobody does."

Calculations ran through his head. The oncoming car. The nearby pedestrians. The two of us, waiting for her to come home. I lasted ten seconds. The shame of owning up couldn't be worse than the nausea I felt.

"Robbie? They think it might have been an opossum. It was an opossum."

But you said . . .

I needed him to say: The opossum is North America's only marsupial, Dad. Things Aly taught him: how hard winters were on opossums, how frostbite punished their hairless ears and tails. But he scowled in silence at the thought of the most despised large animal on Earth.

He swung his head toward me, stunned. *You lied to me, Dad. You said nobody knew what it was.*

"Robbie. It was only for a minute." But no: it was forever, really.

He tilted his head and shook, as if clearing his ears. His voice was flat and low. *Everybody lies.* I couldn't tell if he was forgiving me or condemning all humanity.

It was way past bedtime. But there we were, the two of us on his bed, the last of the crew of a generational spacecraft that had come to the end of its possibilities long before reaching its new home.

So she chose not to hit it, even though . . . ?

"She didn't choose anything. There wasn't time. It was a reflex."

He thought for a while. At last he seemed appeased, although some part of him was still mapping the changing coastline between reflex and choice.

So Jayden's parents are full of crap? Mom wasn't trying to hurt herself?

I felt no need to reprimand the language. "Sometimes, the less people know about something, the more they want to talk about it."

He got his notebook and scribbled in it, holding it away from me. He snapped it shut and squirreled it away in the nightstand drawer. Something brightened in him. Maybe he was happy that he might be friends with his friend again, tomorrow.

I stood and kissed him on the forehead. He let me, preoccupied with his hands, remembering how they'd deceived him.

How about this one, Dad? What does this mean?

He held one cupped hand upward on the stalk of his arm and twisted it back and forth. A tiny planet, spinning on its axis.

"Tell me."

It means the world is turning and I'm good with everything.

We traded the signal, and he nodded. I told him I was glad he was who he was. I twisted my own hand in the air again by way of saying good night. Then I turned out the light and left him to fall asleep in the comfort of my larger lie. I've always been especially good at lying by omission. And I lied wildly to him that night, by failing to tell him about the car's other passenger, his unborn little sister.

HE WOKE UP SUNDAY in high excitement. Before dawn, he was climbing all over me, shaking me awake. *Great idea, Dad. Listen to this.*

I was still half-asleep, and I cranked at him. "Robbie, for God's sake! It's six in the morning!"

He stormed off and barricaded himself in his lair. It took forty minutes and the promise of blueberry pancakes to coax him out.

I waited until he was sluggish with carbs. "So let's hear this great idea."

He weighed the quid pro quos of forgiving me. His chin jutted out. *I'm only telling you because I need your help.*

"Understood."

I'm going to paint every endangered species in America. Then I'll sell them at the farmers' market next spring. We can raise money and give it to one of Mom's groups.

I knew he'd never be able to paint more than a fraction of them. But I also knew a great idea when I heard one. We cleaned up breakfast and headed to the Pinney branch of the public library.

My son loved the library. He loved putting books on hold online and having them waiting, bundled up with his name, when he came for them. He loved the benevolence that the stacks held out, their map of the known world. He loved the all-you-can-eat buffet of borrowing. He loved the lending histories stamped into the front of each book, the record of strangers who checked them out before him. The library was the best dungeon crawl imaginable: free loot for the finding, combined with the joy of leveling up.

Usually he followed the same route through the trove: graphic novels, sword and sorcery, puzzles and brain teasers, fiction. That day, he wanted art lessons. The shelves were a total candy shop. *Wow. How come you never told me about these?* We found a book on how to draw plants and one on how to draw simple animals. From there we went to Nature, where we zeroed in on endangered species. Soon he was trying to choose from among a pile of books that came up almost to his waist.

I'm over my limit, Dad. He could make thrilled sound overwhelmed.

"You take your limit, and I'll take mine."

He sat on the floor of the aisle, narrowing down the choices. Opening one of the bigger volumes, he groaned.

"Tell me."

He read, robotic. *The United States Fish and Wildlife Service lists more than two thousand North American species as being either threatened or endangered.*

"That's okay, buddy. Small steps. One drawing at a time."

He toppled the tower of books and sank his head in his hands.

"Robbie. Hey." I almost said, *Grow up.* But that was the last thing I would have wished on him. "What would your mom do?"

That made him sit up again.

"Let's check these out and get some supplies."

The clerk at the Art Co-op fell in love with him. She was an art student herself, recently graduated. She took Robin around the shop. He was in heaven. They looked at pastels and colored pencils and little tubes of bright acrylic.

"What do you want to make?" Robin told her his plan. "That's so beautiful. You are so awesome." She didn't believe the project would outlast the day.

Robbie loved the watercolor brush pens. The clerk was impressed with what he could do with one, even on his first go.

"This one would make a nice starter set. Forty-eight colors. That's probably everything you'd need."

Why is that other one so much more expensive?

"That one's for pros."

He grabbed the starter set, hiding his eyes from me. I overruled and upgraded him. As investments went, it felt like a steal. We also got micro-pen fine liners, a pad of cheap drawing paper for practice, and some sheets of the good stuff for the finished works. The clerk wished him luck, and he hugged her on the way out. Robin did not hug strangers.

He painted all afternoon. My hot-tempered, ungovernable son knelt for hours on the slats of a wooden folding chair, copying examples from the art books with his face up close to the paper. Sometimes he snorted in frustration, like the cartoon bull from one of his favorite childhood picture books. He crumpled up botched efforts, but with more artistic flair than violence. Once he tossed a watercolor pencil against the wall, then shouted at himself for doing so.

I tempted him to take a break. Ping-pong or a walk around the block. He refused to be derailed.

Which creature should I start with, Dad?

Creature was his mother's favorite word. She used it for everything, even my extremophiles. I told Robin that no one ever lost an audience with charismatic megafauna.

No. I should do the most endangered one. The one that needs the most help.

"Pace yourself, Robbie. The first farmers' market is months away."

The amphibians are in trouble. I'm going to start with an amphibian.

After much agonizing, he settled on *Lithobates sevosus*, the dusky gopher frog. It was a strange, secretive animal that spread its webbed fingers in front of its face to shield its eyes from threats. It puffed up when frightened and oozed a bitter milk from the glands on its back. Wetlands development had reduced it to three small ponds in Mississippi.

He studied his drawing, doubtful. *Do you think people will like it?*

His creature was byzantine in both shape and pigment. Where my own eyes had seen only gray-black lumps in the frog's photo, Robin saw wild swirls that required half of his glorious rainbow tool chest. The difference between the drab original and his surreal copy didn't trouble Robin. Nor did it bother, in the least, the ghost of my wife.

When he was done, Robbie brought his painting to the picture window in the living room and held it up to the light for my inspection. The perspective was skewed, the surface texture clumsy, the outlining naïve, and the colors out of this world. But the thing was a masterpiece, warts and all—the portrait of a creature whose passing few humans would mourn.

Do you think anyone will buy it? It's for a good cause.

"It's great, Robbie."

Maybe there's a planet out there where amphibians are as good as it gets.

Then, after so much fierce looking, he was done with it. He stashed it in a portfolio where he kept his other drawings and went back to the art books. He hadn't been so happy since the night we camped out under the stars.

MONDAY MORNING, HE ROLLED OUT OF BED, got dressed, ate a bowl of hot cereal, and brushed his teeth, all as usual. But five minutes before his bus was due, he declared, *No school today, Dad.*

"What are you talking about? Of course there's school. Scoot!"

No school for me, *I mean.* He waved toward the dining room table. I'd let him leave out all his art studio materials from the day before. *Too much to do.*

"Don't be silly. You can work on it this afternoon and evening. You're going to miss the bus."

No bus today, Dad. Too much work.

Too quickly, I resorted to reason. "Robbie. Look. I'm in trouble at your school already. Dr. Lipman said I've had you out of class too many times already this year."

What about the days she kicked me out?

"I went over that with her. She threatened me with bad things if we didn't get our act together."

Like what?

"Hey. Hop on it. No kidding. We'll talk about it tonight."

I'm not going, Dad.

The one time since Aly's death that I'd threatened him with force, he bit my wrist and broke the skin. I checked my watch. The bus was no longer a viable target. I put my hand on his shoulder. He pushed it off.

"They have you on probation because of what happened with Jayden. We're on their list. If there's more trouble, Dr. Lipman . . . We can't give them anything to fuss about right now."

Dad. Listen to me. I'm begging you. Mom says everything's dying. Do you believe her?

"Robin. Come on. Let's go. I'll drive you." Even to myself, I sounded outmaneuvered.

Because if she's right, there's no point in school. Everything will be dead before I get to tenth grade.

I wondered whether this was a hill I wanted to die on.

Do you believe her or don't you? That's all I'm asking.

Did I believe her? Her facts were beyond doubt. Everything she claimed was common knowledge to scientists everywhere. But did I *believe* her? Had mass extinction ever once felt real?

"You're going to school. There's no choice."

You said everything's always a choice, Dad. For instance. You could homeschool me.

I rubbed my eyes until I saw stars. In my head, I was talking to a dead person again. And Aly was reminding me: *Listen. Sympathize. But we don't negotiate with terrorists!*

"I believe in you, Robbie. In what you're doing. But we can't change school in the middle of the year. If you still feel strongly about this in the spring, we'll find a solution."

That's why they'll all go extinct. Because everyone wants to solve it later.

I sat down at the table, his test sketches spread in front of me. He wasn't wrong. "Okay. Today, paint. All the creatures that are in trouble. As well as you can."

He must have felt my deflation, because the little victory made him darken. He looked at me, ready to beg me to change my mind. *Dad? What if it doesn't help at all?*

NO SITTER IN MY CONTACTS LIST could watch him all weekday on such short notice. Fortunately, I didn't teach that day and could work from home. At quarter to nine, while canceling and rescheduling appointments, I got the automated text. *Your child is absent without excuse. Are you aware of this (please reply Y or N)?* I pressed *Y*, then phoned the office and told a curt, skeptical staffer that Robin had a doctor's appointment I'd forgotten to call in.

I applied myself to email triage, then finished the delinquent edits for the article for Stryker: dimethyl sulfide and sulfur dioxide in our models of atmospheric disequilibrium. Sulfur-based life, in place of carbon: I thought about what lunch might look like in such a place, while cooking up Robin's favorite lentils with masses of melt-away onions and the barest hint of tomato. In the afternoon, Robin knocked on my office door with several small questions about his paintings for which any answer at all would do. He was lonely. By morning, I figured, he'd be ready to head back to school.

We knocked off again for dinner. Robin wanted Aly's signature eggplant casserole. He insisted on laying out the layers. Our finished result was not a success, but he ate with the appetite of some-one who'd put in a full day. After dinner, I asked for an exhibition. A few paintings remained from the many that he'd destroyed in anger. He mounted the day's work on a bare wall in the dining room using bits of reusable tape. I was forbidden to come in until he said to. There was an ivory-billed woodpecker and a red wolf and a Frank-lin's bumblebee and a giant anole and a clump of desert yellowhead. Some were more skillful than others. But they all vibrated, and the colors shouted, *Save us.*

That's a bird and a mammal and an insect and a reptile and a plant. To go with yesterday's amphibian.

I still don't see how a nine-year-old held still long enough to paint them. He was channeling some other maker. "Robin. They're incredible."

The woodpecker and the anole might already be extinct. How much should I ask for them? I want to send in as much as I can.

"You could ask people how much they might want to pay." Used-car trick, put to a good cause. He took the pictures down and stashed them in his portfolio. "Careful! Don't crumple them."

So many more to do, Dad.

The next morning, after breakfast, he announced he was staying home to work some more.

"No way. Get going, now. We had a deal."

When? What deal? You said you believed in me!

In one quick escalation, he went from nine to sixteen. Blocked from doing right, he stared me down with a fury bordering on hatred. His lips pursed and he spit near my feet. Then he wheeled, ran back down the hall to his bedroom, and slammed his door. Twenty seconds later, a skin-freezing scream turned into the thunder of toppling furniture. I pushed in his door against a mass of junk piled up behind it. He'd pulled down a five-foot-high bookshelf, and books, toys, model spacecraft, and arts-and-crafts trophies spilled across his bedroom floor. When I stepped into the room, he screamed again and swung Aly's old ukulele into the multi-paned window, breaking both the glass and the instrument.

He lunged at me, howling. We fought. He tried to claw my face. I took his arm and twisted way too hard. Robin screamed and dropped sobbing on the floor. I wanted to die. The back of his hand was half a crushed butterfly. Aly and I had had a pact, the only one she ever made me swear to. *Theo? Whatever happens, we must never hit that child.* I looked around the room, ready to throw myself at her mercy. But she was nowhere.

ON GEMINUS, WE WERE TRAPPED on opposite sides of a terrible meridian. The planet's sun was small, cool, and red. Geminus lay so close in that the star had captured its rotation. One side remained forever in scalding light. The other side stayed night, icy and perpetual.

Life germinated in the strip of twilight between permanent noon and midnight. In that band between burning and frozen, winds whipped the air and currents drove the water. Creatures evolved to exploit the loops of energy, moving bits of morning to warm the blackness and bits of night to cool the endless blaze.

Life pushed deeper into both halves of the wind-whipped landscape. Tendrils of habitability seeped down canyons and up watersheds, creeping from the temperate boundary toward the extremes. Life on Geminus split into two kingdoms, one of ice, one of fire, each adapting to half of the bipolar planet. For the boldest pilgrims, there was no turning back. Even the temperate boundary strip became fatal.

Intelligence arose twice. Each kind solved its own impossible climate. But the minds of day failed to find the night intelligible, while night's minds couldn't comprehend the day. They shared only one bit of common knowledge: life could never exist "over the edge."

We traveled to Geminus together, my son and I. But we each arrived alone. I found myself in a wind-fed channel on the side of constant day. I searched throughout the habitable strip but couldn't find him. The local inhabitants were no help. I'd imagined that people of endless day would be cheerful and upbeat. But their sky was filled with one single unchanging light, blocking out all signs of a universe. They lived as if there could be nothing but Here and Now and this. The thought stunted them. Their sciences and arts had stalled in infancy. They never even invented the telescope.

On Geminus, seasons were places. Walking a few miles toward the boundary belt took me from August to January. He had to be somewhere on the side of constant night. What people would he find there, shaped by lethal cold? Cunning and ingenious, diggers of heat mines and farmers of subterranean fungi. Brutal, barbaric, and depressed killers, competing for every priceless calorie.

He had been looking for me as well. Nearing the temperate boundary belt, I saw him a long way off, rushing from the other side. I broke into a run, but he held up his hands to stop me. I realized, there on the edge of darkness: he had seen the raw night sky. He'd looked at stars as no one on Earth ever would again. He'd seen change and time, cycles and variety. Math and stories, as countless, subtle, and various as the black-backed constellations.

He called to me, from over the standing edge of dark. *Dad. Dad! You have no idea.* But I was trapped in light and couldn't cross over.

LOTS OF PEOPLE LOVED MY WIFE. And Aly loved lots of people, as if that were the most natural thing in the world. She'd had partners before me and stayed on good terms with most of them, even with one woman who'd broken her heart. Flirting was a part of her job. I watched her work hallways full of legislators and ballrooms full of donors as if they were all her dear friends.

She was on the road a lot, directing her NGO across ten midwestern states. For the first two years of our marriage, it used to kill me. She'd call me from some budget interstate hotel to say, *We went to a great little Italian place downtown*, and when I croaked a casual, "We?" she'd say, *Oh, didn't I say? Michael Maxwell's in town. My ex from grad school?* And that would be another eight hours of night thoughts I didn't need.

Her ten-state area hosted an equal-opportunity harem of devoted women and men. Some of these friendships I knew about; others came as surprises, at her memorial service. The one time I asked whether she was ever tempted to stray, her jaw popped open in astonishment. *Oh my God. I am so not built that way! I'd split into little pieces if I ever tried that.*

I settled into a manageable mix of jealousy and thrill. Lots of good, kind people wanted my wife. My wife seemed to want me. Nature, as Aly often showed me, was quite ingenious in keeping people just happy enough.

So it didn't surprise me when she came home late from the farmers' market one Saturday, bubbly from a round of flattering attention. *I ran into Marty Currier at the Apple Lady's stand. We had a quick coffee. He wants us to be in an experiment!*

Martin Currier was one of Wisconsin's high-profile scientists: senior research professor in neuroscience, National Academy of Sciences fellow, Hughes Investigator—the kinds of recognitions I dreamed of winning once but never will. He was one of the few people in town Aly could bird with and learn something from. They'd go out together in all seasons, and it made me nuts.

"Does he, now? I'm sure he'd like to experiment on *you*."

She grinned and tucked into her pugilist stance, circling her fists in front of her face, bobbing and weaving. She always held her small fists way too close together when threatening to rabbit-punch me. I loved that.

Come on, buster. We should try it. He's doing wild things.

The Currier Lab was exploring something called Decoded Neurofeedback. It resembled old-fashioned biofeedback, but with neural imaging for real-time, AI-mediated feedback. A first group of subjects—the "targets"—entered emotional states in response to external prompts, while researchers scanned relevant regions of their brains using fMRI. The researchers then scanned the same brain regions of a second group of subjects—the "trainees"—in real time. AI monitored the neural activity and sent auditory and visual cues to steer the trainees toward the targets' prerecorded neural states. In this way, the trainees learned to approximate the patterns of excitation in the targets' brains, and, remarkably, began to report having similar emotions.

The technique dated back to 2011, and it claimed some impressive early results. Teams in Boston and Japan taught trainees to solve visual puzzles faster, simply by training them on the visual cortex patterns of targets who'd learned the puzzles by trial and error. Other experimenters recorded the visual fields of target subjects exposed to the color red. Trainees who learned, through feedback, to approximate that same neural activity reported seeing red in their mind's eye.

Since those days, the field had shifted from visual learning to emotional conditioning. The big grant money was going to desensitizing people with PTSD. DecNef and Connectivity Feedback were being touted as treatments to all kinds of psychiatric disorders. Marty Currier worked on clinical applications. But he was also pursuing a more exotic side-hustle.

"Why not?" I told my wife. And so we volunteered in her friend's experiment.

IN THE RECEPTION AREA OF CURRIER'S LAB, Aly and I chuckled over the entrance questionnaire. We would be among the second wave of target subjects, but first we had to pass the screening. The questions disguised furtive motives. HOW OFTEN DO YOU THINK ABOUT THE PAST? WOULD YOU RATHER BE ON A CROWDED BEACH OR IN AN EMPTY MUSEUM? My wife shook her head at these crude inquiries and touched a hand to her smile. I read the expression as clearly as if we were wired up together: The investigators were welcome to anything they discovered inside her, so long as it didn't lead to jail time.

I'd given up on understanding my own hidden temperament a long time ago. Lots of monsters inhabited my sunless depths, but most of them were nonlethal. I did badly want to see my wife's answers, but a lab tech prevented us from comparing questionnaires.

DO YOU USE TOBACCO? Not for years. I didn't mention that all my pencils were covered with bite marks.

HOW MUCH ALCOHOL DO YOU DRINK A WEEK? Nothing for me, but my wife confessed to her nightly Happy Hour, while plying the dog with poetry.

DO YOU SUFFER FROM ANY ALLERGIES? Not unless you counted cocktail parties.

HAVE YOU EVER EXPERIENCED DEPRESSION? I didn't know how to answer that one.

DO YOU PLAY A MUSICAL INSTRUMENT? Science. I said I might be able to find middle C on a piano, if they needed it.

Two postdocs took us into the fMRI room. These people had way more cash to throw around than any astrobiology team any-where. Aly was having the same thoughts about her impoverished NGO. I hoped envy wouldn't cloud our brain scans.

I braved the scanner first. Aly sat with Martin Currier in the control booth behind a bank of monitors. That seemed suspect to me, but he was the one with all the research awards. The earpiece I wore inside the fMRI tube instructed me to relax, close my eyes, and listen to my breathing. They fed me some stimuli, for calibration. There was a bit of Moonlight Sonata and a snippet from something harsh and modern. They told me to open my eyes. A screen above my face showed, in turn, images of a bluebird on a branch, a happy baby, a magnificent holiday meal, and a close-up of a fractured forearm with bone coming through the skin. After that, I was told to close my eyes for another minute and mind my breathing again.

Then came the real experiment. Aly and I would each be given a random feeling from the eight core emotional states in Plutchik's typology: Terror, Amazement, Grief, Loathing, Rage, Vigilance, Ecstasy, or Admiration. We'd have four minutes to inhabit our given mental state. Software would make a three-dimensional map of part of our limbic system while we were absorbed in the task.

They gave me *Admiration*. I closed my eyes and settled into vague thoughts about Einstein, Dr. King, and Sydney Carton. But off in the booth, my wife was watching the ebb and flow of my feeling. The thought of her made me remember an evening we'd lived through together, in the depths of an upper midwestern winter four years before.

Aly had just been appointed midwestern coordinator, and the man replacing her as state supervisor was proving to be inept. In Maryland for the organization's three-day biannual national meeting, she'd spent hours on the phone nursing her successor through various crises. While there, she caught a nasty cold. Ice storms delayed her return flight by half a day. I picked her up at the airport at nine at night, little Robbie in tow. In her absence, he'd developed an ear infection. He howled until after midnight, when Aly let her sick and weary head touch the pillow at last.

The phone woke her at one-thirty in the morning: her hapless new state supervisor, calling in a tizzy. The police way upstate in Rhinelander had found a truck with a dozen caged dogs left for hours in subzero temperatures in a Walmart parking lot. They traced the truck to a sprawling puppy mill, which they shut down. Hundreds of dogs flooded into Oneida County's sole overwhelmed shelter. The locals reached out to Aly's NGO, although such a problem lay way outside her rights-oriented organization's bailiwick.

Her successor wanted to know who to dish the crisis off on. Aly told him, *What are you talking about? Go up and help them out.* The man said that was way below his pay grade. They talked for twenty minutes, with my zombied wife never once sounding anything less than rational. The man still refused. So at sunrise Alyssa packed a backpack and got in the car to drive three and a half hours on icy state roads by herself. I kept asking, "Are you *sure?*" Not exactly the support she deserved.

She returned forty-eight hours later, after shepherding two hundred dogs to shelters across upper Wisconsin. She got out of the car looking like a Central Casting nineteenth century French peasant dying of consumption. She went straight to wailing Robin and comforted him for an hour. Then she wrote a speech she had to deliver in Des Moines the next day. After midnight once again, she looked at me with comically crossed eyes, proclaimed herself *tuckered out*, and slept for five hours before getting up to drive to Iowa.

My wife was admirable the way I was tall. But *admiration* barely touched what I felt. The feeling flowing through me felt like a geometric proof. I *revered* my wife. She was who she should be in this world, without once worrying about what that meant. I could never hope to emulate her. I just hoped she could see, from the control booth, in front of those monitors, what flooded my brain.

The run ended and my trance broke. The techs recalibrated the software by showing me the earlier images and having me count backward from ten to one. Then they rolled the dice again and gave me a second target: *Grief.*

As soon as the word sounded in my earbuds, my pulse spiked.

Truth is, I'm profoundly superstitious—not in my head, which science has retrained, but in my limbs. I'm good at old feelings, and grief must be older than awareness itself. Way too easily, my body embraces my worst imaginings. The several minutes I'd just spent admiring my wife now turned inside out. I was back in that vivid night, now with disaster everywhere. My son's ear infection turned septic and fatal. Puppy mill killers captured my wife and tortured her. Sleep-deprived and overworked, she drove off the icy road and lay in a ditch for hours.

What's grief? The world stripped of something you admire. The things that swarmed me were utter, irrational nonsense. But I felt them as if, on some planet, they had really happened.

Aly jumped up and hugged me as I joined them in the booth. *Oh, my poor little guy!*

WE CHANGED PLACES. I sat with Currier, and Aly got into the fMRI tube. While two techs calibrated Aly with the images and music, I raised my doubts with Currier.

"Your methodology doesn't seem especially well controlled. Won't your results vary widely, depending . . . ?"

"Depending on how good a method actor the subject is?" His face was cheerful, but his voice turned condescending. I really struggled with the man, and not only because Aly liked him so much.

"Exactly. Not everyone can make themselves feel emotions on command."

"We don't need them to. We're looking at specific regions in the limbic system. Some of the targets' reactions will be truer than others. Some people will really feel the emotions while others will only think about them. But the AI can extract common patterns of activity from hundreds of runs and builds up a composite, 3-D map of shared salient features. We're testing whether averaged fingerprints of the eight core emotions are distinct enough to be recognized by trainees who are taught to match them."

"And? How's it looking?"

He tilted his head, like one of the birds he and my wife peeped at together. "Given pure chance and eight choices, a person would identify the target emotion correctly one in eight times. But after a few sessions of feedback, trainees can correctly name the target emotion a little more than half the time."

"Jesus. Emotional telepathy."

Currier raised his eyebrows. "You could say that."

I was still skeptical. But had I been on the grants committee, I'd have funded him. The idea deserved exploration, whatever its results. An empathy machine: it could have come from one of the two thousand SF novels in my collection.

Across the room, my wife seemed even smaller inside the scanner. They gave her *Vigilance*. I wouldn't even have called vigilance an emotion, let alone one of the eight core ones. But vigilance was to Alyssa what chant was to medieval nuns, so it didn't surprise me when, three minutes into her stint with it, Currier leaned in to the monitor. "Hoo. She's intense."

"You have no idea."

But maybe he did. We watched the activity swirl through Aly's brain like an animated finger painting. Maybe she was reliving the same night that I had. Yet scores of other nights could have served her as nicely. I watched the screen, learning something. Aly sang all of life's basic tunes in full voice, but *vigilance* was her national anthem. Her whole life was variations on one theme: whatever work your hands can do, do now, for there is no work for you in that place where you are going.

The patterns danced through Aly's brain. A tech told her to breathe deeply and relax. *Relax?* she called from inside the tube. *I'm just warming up!*

Then they gave her *Ecstasy*. "Wait," I told Currier. "I get Grief and she gets Ecstasy?"

The man grinned. His charm was undeniable. "I'll have a look at the random number generator."

Vigilance and Ecstasy lie right next to each other on Plutchik's wheel of emotions. Vigilance shades off into Anticipation and Interest, toward the wheel's rim. Ecstasy dials back into Joy and Serenity. In the wedge between Joy and Anticipation is Optimism. Day after day of hopeless triage used to knock Aly on her ass. I remember her weeping over clandestine video from an Iowa feedlot. She once damned humanity to hell while throwing a UN report about habitat destruction across the room. But my wife's cells pumped out optimism. Her soul aligned toward Ecstasy like iron filings mimic a magnetic field.

I watched Aly's brain-print of bliss on a screen in a booth alongside a man I was sure desired her. Currier stared at her unfolding pattern. "She's *perfect*!" I had no idea what he was looking at, but even I could see how different this flood was from her patterns a few minutes before.

I knew my wife as well as I've ever known anyone. But I had no clue what memories Aly used to generate this command performance. Was I somewhere in the mix? Was her son the center of her joy? Or did other things prompt her innermost bliss? I wanted so badly to know the source of the spreading colors that it filled me with a ninth primary emotion nowhere on Plutchik's wheel.

Currier studied her diencephalon on the monitor. He was part of a long, impressive exploration that would last for as long as society believed in science. But even if his kind did succeed at last in opening the locked room of another person's head, we'd still never know what it felt like to inhabit that place. Wherever we went, the view would always be from here.

The two techs helped Aly from the fMRI tube. She blushed with pleasure the way she did the day the nurses put her newborn in her hands. She joined us in the booth, a little wobbly. Currier whistled. "You sure know how to drive that thing."

My wife came and put her hands around my neck, as if my body alone might keep her small craft afloat in a large sea. We made it home still clutching at each other and paid off the babysitter. We fed our boy and tried to distract him with his favorite Star Wars Legos. Robin knew something was up and chose that moment to turn clingy. I reasoned with him.

"Your mother and I have a few things to take care of. You play quietly, and we'll go see the sailboats, later."

This worked long enough for Aly and me to barricade ourselves in the bedroom. She had me half undressed before I could whisper my first fierce words. "What were you thinking of, back there? I need to know!"

She ignored every sound from me but my pulse. Her ear was up to my chest and her hands everywhere below. *Oh, my poor little guy. You looked like you were about to cry, in that nasty machine!*

Then she towered above me, upright, alert, and huge. Lifting off, she cried out a little, like some nocturnal thing. I reached up to shush her, and the thrill doubled. It took only seconds for the knock on the door. *Is everybody okay in there?*

My wife, vigilant ecstatic, took all her will to keep from laughing. *So okay, honey! Everybody's so okay.*

ON A WEDNESDAY MORNING IN NOVEMBER, I walked across campus to Currier's building. It was a good long hike, but I didn't send a heads-up. I didn't want a paper trail. Martin seemed perplexed to see me. The closest emotion on Plutchik's wheel was probably Apprehension.

"Theo. Huh. How've you been?" He sounded almost like he wanted to know. That came from years of studying human emotions. "I felt miserable about missing Alyssa's service."

I lifted my shoulders and let them fall. Two years ago; ancient history. "Honestly? I couldn't tell you who was there and who wasn't. I don't remember much of it at all."

"How can I help you?"

"I need to ask something confidential."

He nodded and took me down the hall and out of the building. We sat in a cafeteria in the School of Medicine, each with a hot beverage that neither of us wanted.

"This is a bit embarrassing. I know you're not a clinician, but I have nowhere else to go. Robin's in trouble. His grade school is threatening me with the Department of Human Services if I don't dope him up."

He took an instant to place *Robin*. "Has he been diagnosed with something?"

"So far the votes are two Asperger's, one probable OCD, and one possible ADHD."

He smiled, bitter and sympathetic. "This is why I dropped out of clinical psych."

"Half the third-graders in this country could be squeezed into one of those categories."

"That's the problem." He looked around the cafeteria, scanning for colleagues who might overhear us. "What do they want to put him on?"

"I'm not sure his principal cares, so long as Big Pharma gets their cut."

"Most of the common meds are pretty normalized, you know."

"He's *nine years old*." I caught myself and calmed down. "His brain is still developing."

Martin raised his hands. "That's young, for psychoactive drugs. I wouldn't want to experiment on my nine-year-old."

He was a clever man. I could see why my wife liked him. He waited me out. At last I confessed, "He threw a thermos at a friend's face."

"Huh. I broke my friend's nose once. But he deserved it."

"Would Ritalin have helped?"

"My father's treatment of choice was the belt. And it turned me into the exemplary adult you see before you."

I laughed and felt better. Quite a trick on his part. "How do any of us make it to adulthood?"

My wife's friend squinted into the past, trying to remember her son. "How bad would you say his anger gets?"

"I don't know how to answer that."

"He did peg that boy."

"That wasn't entirely his fault." Nothing was ever entirely anyone's fault. *His hands got confused.*

"Are you afraid he might hurt someone? Has he ever come after you?"

"No. Never. Of course not."

He knew I was lying. "I'm not a doctor. And even doctors can't give you a reliable opinion without a formal consult. You know that."

"No doctor can diagnose my son better than I can. I just want some treatment short of drugs that will calm him down and get his principal off my back."

The man came to attention, as he once did while looking at my wife's brain scan. He leaned back in the plastic scoop of his chair.

"If you're looking for non-pharmacologic therapy, we could put him in one of our trials. We're testing DecNef's efficacy as a behavioral intervention. A subject your son's age would be a valuable data point. He'd even make a little pocket money."

And I could tell Dr. Lipman my son was enrolled in a behavioral modification program at U Double U. "There wouldn't be any human-subject concerns with someone that young?"

"It's a non-invasive process. We train him how to attend to and control his own feelings, the same way behavioral therapy does, only with an instant, visible scorecard. The Institutional Review Board has signed off on projects a lot dicier than ours."

We walked back to his office. The trees were bare and snow crystals wavered sideways in the air. It smelled like the year would end a little early, this year. But undergrads drifted past us still in shorts.

Currier explained how much had changed since Aly and I had volunteered to be target subjects. DecNef was maturing. Discovery and validation cohorts at universities here and throughout Asia were probing its clinical potential. DecNef was showing promise in pain management and the treatment of OCD. Connectivity Feedback was proving useful in managing depression, schizophrenia, and even autism.

"A high-performing trainee—someone who shows a knack with the feedback—can enjoy symptom amelioration for several weeks."

He described what was involved. The scanning AI would compare the patterns of connectivity inside Robin's brain—his *spontaneous brain activity*—to a prerecorded template. "Then we'll shape that spontaneous activity through visual and auditory cues. We'll start him on the composite patterns of people who have achieved high levels of composure through years of meditation. Then the AI will coax him with feedback—tell him when he's close and when he's farther away."

"How long does the training last?"

"We sometimes see significant improvement after only a few sessions."

"And the risks?"

"Lower than those of the school cafeteria, I'd say."

I bit down on my anger. But he saw it.

"Theo. Forgive me. I was being glib. Neural feedback is an assistive procedure. Anything happening to his brain is something he's learning to do himself, by reflection, concentration, and practice."

"Like reading. Or taking a class."

"That's right. Only faster and more effective. Probably more fun, too."

At the word *fun,* a look crossed his face, and the weirdest intuition told me he was remembering Alyssa. The two of them had sat still for hours, side by side in the middle of nowhere, just looking. *You don't always get them by the specific field marks,* Aly taught me, before boredom led me to abandon birding with her. *You know them by the shape, size, and impression. You* feel *them. We call that getting the jizz.*

"Marty, thank you. This is a lifesaver."

He waved me off. "Let's see what results we get."

I left him at the door of his office. When I stuck out my hand, he wrapped me in an awkward side-hug. On the wall behind him was a poster of a tree-lined beach with the words:

> The surface of the earth is soft and impressible by the feet of men; and so with the paths which the mind travels.

I was entrusting my traumatized son to a careerist neuroscientist-birder who still had a thing for my dead wife and decorated his office with cheesy posters quoting Thoreau.

YOU MEAN, LIKE A VIDEO GAME? My son loved games, but they also scared him. The fast-twitch shooters or the action scrollers where you had to jump at just the right moment made him nuts. He'd attack them with zeal, then retreat, routed, in a fury. They stood for the whole pecking order of competition that ruled the kingdom of his peers. When a certain racing game made him throw my tablet across the room and I banned him from playing it again, he seemed relieved. But he adored his farm. He could click on his fields to get wheat and click on the mill to grind flour and click on the oven to bake bread, all day long.

"Yes," I said. "A little like a game. You'll try to move a dot around on a screen or make a musical note sound softer or louder or higher or lower. It'll get easier with practice."

All with my brain? *That's insane, Dad.*

"Yep. Pretty crazy."

Wait. It's like something. It reminds me of something else. He paddled the air with one hand and sawed at his chin with the other—warning me to let him think. He snapped a finger. *Like one of your worlds.* "Imagine a planet where the people plug their brains into one another."

"This isn't quite like that."

Do you think that scanner could teach me to paint better?

It seemed like something Currier might try one day. "You paint perfectly. They could use your brain to train other people to paint better."

He beamed and ran to get his portfolio to show me his latest masterpiece, a birdwing pearlymussel. He had birds and fish and fungi now, and he was working on snails and bivalves.

We're going to need a big table at the market, Dad.

I held the painting with both hands, thinking: No therapy could be better than this. But then my boy looked down and smoothed the paper with his guilty hands, and I saw the marks of enraged crumpling. He traced his fingers on the painting with contrition. *I wish I could see one of these. For real, I mean.*

I GAVE CURRIER'S HANDOUTS to Dr. Lipman, along with three articles touting the therapeutic potential of the research. She seemed satisfied. Excited by the prospect of finger-painting with his brain, Robbie had two mercifully quiet weeks. For two weeks, I returned to my neglected duties and undid the damage to my in-box.

For Thanksgiving, we drove to Aly's parents on Chicago's West Side. The postwar, crowded suburban Tudor was the usual pressure cooker of glucose-fueled cousins, around-the-clock wall-sized sports no one was watching, and political shouting matches. Half of Aly's extended family backed one of the opposition candidates now gearing up for the primaries. The other half backed our defiant President in his return to the world of half a century ago. By noon on Thursday, the White House's new decree requiring everyone in the country to carry proof of citizenship or visas had Robin's blood relations sniping at each other across the trenches of a static front.

His grandmother spoke the Thanksgiving dinner prayer. The whole table said amen and began passing the food in four different directions. Robbie said, *Nobody's listening to that prayer, you know. We're on a rock, in space, and there are hundreds of billions of other rocks just like ours.*

Adele was horrified. She gaped at me. "Is that any way to raise a child? What would his mother say?"

I didn't tell her what her daughter would have said. Robin did that for me. *My mother's dead. And God didn't help her.*

The bickering table fell silent. Everyone looked to me to correct my son. Adele was on him before I could say a thing. "You need to apologize to me, young man." She turned to me. I turned to Robin.

I'm sorry, Grandma, he said. And the whole table went back to bickering. Only his favorite aunt and I, seated at each side of him, heard him mutter under his breath like Galileo, *but you're wrong.*

Throughout the meal, Robin pecked away at his beans, cranberries, and militantly gravy-free potatoes. His grandpa Cliff kept riding him, from across the table. "Have a little turkey, man. It's Thanksgiving!"

When Robin finally blew, it was geothermal. He started screaming, *I don't eat animals. I don't eat animals! Don't make me eat animals!*

I had to take him outside. We walked around the block three times. He kept saying, *Let's go home, Dad. Let's just go home. It's easier to be thankful there.*

We got back to Madison and finished the holiday alone together. He started the treatment the following Monday afternoon. He slid into the same fMRI tube his mother once disappeared into. The techs asked him to hold still, close his eyes, and say nothing. But when they played him the Moonlight Sonata, my son laughed and shouted, *I know that song!*

"WATCH THE DOT IN THE MIDDLE OF THE SCREEN." Robin lay tiny in the scanner, staring at the image on the monitor above him. Pads held his head swaddled in place. Martin Currier sat at the panel in the control room. I sat next to him. He coached Robin through the earbuds. "Now let the dot move to the right."

My son fidgeted. He wanted to click a mouse or reach up and swipe the screen. *How?*

"Remember, Robbie. No talking. Just relax and hold still. When you're in the right mood, the dot will know it and start to move. Just stay with it and let it travel. Try to keep it at a middle height. Don't let it go too far up or down."

Robin held still. We watched his results on a monitor in the booth. The dot jigged and jagged like a water strider on the surface of a pond.

Currier walked me through it again. "He's basically practicing mindfulness. Like doing meditation, but with instant, powerful cues steering him toward the desired emotional state. The more he learns how to get into that state, the easier that state is to get into. Get into it often enough, and we can take away the training wheels. He'll own it."

I watched my boy play a game of Blind Man's Bluff with his own thoughts: *Colder, colder, warmer . . .*

Currier pointed as the dot jerked toward the upper left quadrant. "See? He's frustrated. Now he's getting angry. Maybe mixed with a little sadness."

I pointed at the right-hand center, the place Robin was trying to reach. "What does this represent?"

Currier gave me that playful look that so annoyed me. "Step one of Enlightenment." Half a minute passed. Then another. The dot settled down and drifted back toward the screen's center. "He's getting the hang of this," Marty whispered. "He's going to be fine." Which made me anxious in whole new and creative ways.

I never knew what passed through my son's singular head at any given moment. Few days went by when he didn't surprise me. I know less about the planet he lived on than I know about Gliese 667 Cc. But I do know that when Robin settled into a groove, few things could deflect him. The dot swung in sullen, wary circles. It crept rightward under his nudging, even as it nudged him back. Massy and reluctant, the dot moved like a floater in your eye when you try to look at it. It crept, rocked back, and crept again, like a car getting pushed from a snowbank.

The prospect of victory excited Robin. Right at the finish line, he laughed, and the dot veered into the lower left quadrant. Inside the tube, Robin whispered, *Shit*, and the dot shot wildly around the screen. Contrition was instant. *Sorry to curse, Dad. I'll do the dishes for a week.*

Martin and I started laughing. So did the techs. It took a minute for everyone to sober up and continue the session. But Robin had found the trick of it, and after a few more false starts and faster recoveries, my son and his dot achieved their joint goal.

A tech named Ginny adjusted Robin's position in the scanner. "Wow," Ginny told him. "You're a natural at this."

Currier tweaked the software and started a new run. "This time make the dot as big as the background shadow. Then hold it there."

This new dot sat at the center of the screen. Behind it sat a paler disk, the target that Currier asked him to aim for. The dot shrank and grew in spasmodic concert with a different region inside Robin's head. "We're training intensity now," Currier said. The dot bobbed like an oscilloscope wave or the bouncing volume-level lights on an old stereo. Robbie fell into a trance. The fluctuating dot calmed down. Gradually it grew from dime-sized to a half-dollar.

He brought it into the target zone, then overshot. That upset him, and the dot fell away to nothing. He started again, lifting it on the wavering power of his mood alone.

Each time the dot aligned with the template size, it turned dusky rose. When the dot filled its background shadow long enough to glow, the scanner resounded with a short, victorious bell, and the dot reset.

"Now see if you can get it to turn green." New feedback for new parameters of affect. I thought Robin might revolt. He'd been in the scanner for almost an hour. Instead, he cackled with pleasure and tranced out again. Soon enough, he'd learned how to run the dot through a rainbow of colors. Currier smiled his wry, dry smile.

"Let's put this all together now. How about a green dot, the size of the background shadow, all the way on the center right? Hold it there for as long as you can."

Robbie nailed the day's final assignment fast enough to impress everyone. Ginny released him from the scanner, flush with success. He trotted into the control booth, swinging his palm above his head for me to high-five. His face had that look it got when I spun a planet into being for him at night: at home in the Milky Way.

That's the coolest thing in the world. You should try it, Dad.

"Tell me."

It's like you have to learn to read the dot's mind. You learn what it wants you to think.

We scheduled a follow-up for the next week. I waited until we'd left the building before grilling him. Currier could have his scans and data sets and AI analyses. I wanted words, straight from Robin's mouth. And I wanted them for myself.

"How did it *feel?*" I wanted to hand him a picture of Plutchik's wheel and have him point to the exact spot.

Still triumphant, he head-butted my ribs. *Weird. Good. Like I could learn to do anything.*

The words puckered my skin. "How did you get the dot to do all those things?"

He quit the billy-goat butting and turned serious. *I pretended I was drawing it. No. Wait. Like it was drawing me.*

THEY WANTED ROBIN ALONE for the second session. Currier thought I might distract him. As part of that painful feedback-training called parenthood, I surrendered Robin to the power of others.

I could tell things had gone well when I picked him up at the lab. Currier looked pleased, although he played his cards close to his chest. Robin was walking on air, but without the usual mania. A strange new awe possessed him.

They gave me music this time. Dad, it was totally crazy. I could raise and lower the notes, and make them go faster and slower, and change the clarinet to a violin, just by wanting it!

I cocked an eyebrow at Currier. His smile was so benign it made me queasy. "He did great with the musical feedback, right, Robin? We're learning to induce connectivity between the relevant regions of his brain. Neurons that fire together wire together."

Astonishingly, Robbie let another man tickle him on the most sensitive part of his ribs. Currier said, " 'For use almost can change the stamp of nature.' "

What's that supposed to be? Robin said. *Like poetry or something?*

"*You're* something," Currier said. Then he booked us for a third visit.

Robin and I walked from the neuroscience building to the lot where I was parked. He held my forearm, chattering. He hadn't grappled me so much in public since he was eight. Decoded Neurofeedback was changing him, as surely as Ritalin would have. But then, everything on Earth was changing him. Every aggressive word from a friend over lunch, every click on his virtual farm, every species he painted, each minute of every online clip, all the stories he read at night and all the ones I told him: there was no "Robin," no one pilgrim in this procession of selves for him ever to remain *the same as*. The whole kaleidoscopic pageant of them, parading through time and space, was itself a work in progress.

Robin tugged on my arm. *Who do you think that guy is?*

"What guy?"

The one whose brain I'm copying?

"It's not one guy. It's the average pattern of a few different people."

He slapped my hand from underneath, like he was patting a ball into the air. His chin lifted and he skipped a few yards, the way he used to when he was younger. Then he waited for me to catch up. My son looked happy, and it chilled me.

"Why do you ask, Robbie?"

I feel like they're coming over to my house to hang out or something. Like we're doing stuff together, in my head.

THE LAWS THAT GOVERN THE LIGHT FROM A FIREFLY in my backyard as I write these words tonight also govern the light emitted from an exploding star one billion light-years away. Place changes nothing. Nor does time. One set of fixed rules runs the game, in all times and places. That's as big a truth as we Earthlings have discovered, or ever will, in our brief run.

But the place is *big*, I tried to tell my son. "You can't imagine how big. Think of the most unlikely place . . ."

A planet made out of iron?

"For instance."

Pure diamond?

"They exist."

A planet where the oceans are hundreds of miles deep? A planet with four suns?

"Yes times two. And we'll find even stranger places, between here and the universe's edge."

Okay. I'm thinking of my perfect planet. My one-in-a-million place.

"At one in a million, there are roughly ten million of them in the Milky Way alone."

OUR DAYS SEEMED TO IMPROVE, and not just because I looked for evidence. His December school evaluations were his second-best ever. His teacher, Kayla Bishop, penned a message at the bottom of his report: *Robin's creativity is growing, along with his self-control.* He stepped off the bus in the afternoons humming. One Saturday he even went out sledding with a group of neighborhood kids he barely knew. I couldn't remember the last time he'd left the house to be with anyone other than me.

He came home the Friday before winter holidays with a length of jute twine taped to his rear belt loop. I slid it through my fingers. "What's this?"

He shrugged as he put his mug of ginger hazelnut milk into the microwave. *My tail.*

"Are you doing genetic engineering in science these days?"

His smile was as mild as the May-like December. *Some kids clipped it on to torture me. You know. Like: "Animal lover" or something. I just left it on.*

He took his hot milk to the table, where his art supplies had been spread out for weeks, and began poring over candidates for his next portrait.

"Oh, Robin. What jerk-faces. Did Kayla know?"

He shrugged again. *No biggie. Kids laughed. It was fun.* He lifted his head from his work and looked at some small revelation on the wall behind me. His eyes were clear and his face inquisitive, the way he used to look on his best days when his mother was still alive. *What do you suppose that's like? Having a tail?*

He smiled to himself. Painting, he made jungle sounds under his breath. In his mind, he was hanging upside down from a tree branch and waving his hands in the air.

I feel bad for them, Dad. I really do. They're trapped inside themselves, right? Same as everyone. He thought for a minute. *Except me. I've got my guys.*

It creeped me out, the way he said it. "What guys, Robbie?"

You know. He frowned. *My team. The guys inside my head.*

For Christmas we drove back down to Aly's parents' in Chicago. Cliff and Adele were a little stiff, welcoming us. They hadn't yet forgiven my little atheist's Thanksgiving assault on their core beliefs. But Robbie pressed his ear into each of their bellies, and they warmed to his embrace. He proceeded to hug every one of his cousins who put up with it. In a handful of minutes, he managed to freak out Aly's entire family.

Over the course of two days he sat through all the football and religion, took a ping-pong paddle to the temple, and watched his cousins react to his gifts—paintings of endangered species—with varying degrees of suppressed mockery. He did this all without melting down. When at last he showed signs of breaking, we were close enough to departure that I shoehorned him into the car and escaped before anything could mar our first incident-free holiday since Aly's death.

"How was that?" I asked him on the way back to Madison.

He shrugged. *Pretty good. But people are touchy, aren't they?*

THE PLANET STASIS looked so much like Earth. The flowing water and green mountains where we touched down, the woody trees and flowering plants, the snails and worms and flying beetles, even the bony creatures were cousins to those we knew.

How can that be? he asked.

I told him what some astronomers now thought: a billion or more planets at least as lucky as ours in the Milky Way alone. In a universe ninety-three billion light-years across, Rare Earths sprang up like weeds.

But a few days on Stasis showed the place to be as strange as any. The planet's axis had little tilt, which meant one monotone season at every latitude. A dense atmosphere smoothed out fluctuations in temperature. Larger tectonic plates recycled its continents with few catastrophes. Few meteors ever threaded the gauntlet of massive nearby planets. And so the climate on Stasis had stayed stable through most of its existence.

We walked to the equator, across the layers of planetary parfait. Species counts in every band were huge and filled with specialists. Each predator hunted one prey. Every flower kept a pollinator of its own. No creature migrated. Many plants ate animals. Plants and animals lived in every kind of symbiosis. Larger living entities weren't organisms at all; they were coalitions, associations, and parliaments.

We walked on to one of the poles. The boundaries between biomes ran like property lines. No flux of seasons blurred or softened them. From one step to the next, deciduous trees stopped and conifers began. Everything on Stasis was built to solve its own private spot. Everything knew one, infinitely deep thing: the sum of the world at their latitude. Nothing alive could thrive anywhere else. A move of even a few kilometers north or south tended to be fatal.

Is there intelligence? my son asked. *Is anything aware?*

I told him no. Nothing on Stasis needed to remember much or

predict much further out than now. In such steadiness, there was no great call to adjust or improvise or second-guess or model much of anything.

He thought about that. *Trouble is what creates intelligence?*

I said yes. Crisis and change and upheaval.

His voice turned sad and wondrous. *Then we'll never find anyone smarter than us.*

THE TECHS GOT A KICK OUT OF ROBIN. They liked to tease him, and, amazingly, he liked being teased. He enjoyed it almost as much as he liked conducting his own private feedback symphonies and directing his own private training animations. Ginny told him, "You're really something, Brain Boy."

"Definitely a high-performing decoder," Currier agreed. The two of us sat in his office surrounded by toys, puzzles, optical illusions, and life-affirming posters.

"Is that because he's so young? Like how kids learn a new language without trying?"

Marty Currier tipped his head to one side. "Plasticity has been documented at every stage of life. Habit impedes us as we age as much as any change in innate capacity. These days we like to say that 'mature' is just another name for 'lazy.'"

"What makes him so good at the training, then?"

"He's a distinctive boy, or he wouldn't be in the training in the first place." He picked up a Rubik's dodecahedron from his desk and toyed with it. His eyes turned absent and I knew who he was daydreaming about. He spoke, more to himself than to me. "Aly was the most incredible birder. I've never seen anyone so focused. She was pretty out there, herself."

My head snapped to attention in resentment and anger. Before I could tell him he was a creep who knew nothing at all about my wife, the door opened and Robin spilled in.

Best game ever.

"Brain Boy really racked up the points, today," Ginny said, squeezing his shoulders from behind like a coach massaging a prize boxer.

When everyone starts doing this stuff, it's going to be really cool.

"Exactly what we think." Martin Currier set down his puzzle and raised both hands in the air. Robin ponied up to his desk and gave him ten. I took my son home, feeling like the future's guardian.

I COULD SEE THE WEEKLY CHANGES. He was quicker to laugh now, slower to flare. More playful when frustrated. He sat still and listened to the birds at dusk. I wasn't sure which qualities were his and which came courtesy of *his team*. Each day's small changes blended into him and went native.

One night, I made a planet for him where the several species of intelligent life traded bits of temperament and memory and behavior and experiences as easily as Earthly bacteria trade snippets of genes. He grabbed my arm, smiling, before I could add the details. *I know where you stole that one from!*

"Do you, now? Who told you?"

He spread his fingers and attached them to my skull, making a sucking sound, as bits of our personality flew back and forth between us. *Wouldn't it be cool if everybody started to do the training?*

I put my fingers on his skull in exchange, sucking bits of his private emotions out through my fingertips and into me, accompanied by appropriate sound effects. We laughed. Then he clapped my shoulder, like he was calming me down before sending me to bed. The gesture was so preternaturally adult. It came from a place that hadn't been there the week before.

"So what do you think?" I tried for amused and offhand. "The mouse. He's changing?"

His eyes took hold of the puzzle. He remembered, and the solution blazed in his eyes. *Still the same mouse, Dad. I just have help now.*

"Tell me how that works, Robbie."

You know how when you talk to someone stupid and it makes you stupid, too?

"I do know that feeling. Very well."

But when you play a game against someone smart, you start making better moves?

I tried to remember if he'd spoken like this a month ago.

Well, it's like that. Like walking onto the playground. But three really smart, funny, and strong guys are walking with you.

"Do . . . they have names?"

Who?

"These three guys?"

He laughed like a much younger kid. *They're not really guys. They're just . . . my allies.*

"But . . . there are three of them?"

He shrugged, more defensive, more like my son. *Three. Or four. Who cares? That's not the point. Just: like, they're helping to row the boat or something. My crew.*

I told him he was my mouse of mouses. I told him his mother loved him. I said he should always feel free to tell me anything interesting that he was finding out about the boat ride.

Maybe I hugged him too hard on my way out of the room. He pulled away and shook me by the upper arms.

Dad! It's no big deal. Just . . . He stuck out a pair of fingers from each hand and crossed them against each other. *Hashtag life skills, right?*

GUSTS OF ROBIN'S OLD IMPATIENCE rocked him, waiting for the spring's first farmers' market. He hit on the idea of taking his paintings to school to find some buyers. He had a mailing tube under his arm and one foot out the door to catch the bus when he sprang that plan on me.

"Oh, Robbie. That's not a great idea."

Why? His voice wavered on the edge of raw. *You think they're too crappy?*

The respite had spoiled me. I thought we were in the clear. I thought his team had rowed us to safety.

"They're too good. Your classmates can't afford to pay you what they're worth."

He hunched over. *Anything would help. Thousands of creatures are going extinct every year. And so far I've raised ʒero dollars and ʒero cents to help them.*

He was right, on all counts. He lifted the tube in the air, challenging. My chin rose and fell half an inch, and he was out the door.

My morning passed in nervous distraction. By one-thirty I was so worked up I called the school and told them to tell Robin I'd pick him up when the day was over. I was waiting in the parking lot, practicing nonchalance and bracing for the worst, when he let himself into the car.

"How did it go?"

He held up the mailing tube, as if to show all the paintings still rolled up inside it. *Still ʒero dollars and ʒero cents.*

"Digame."

For a mile, he wouldn't. He beat the tube on the dash at a steady *andante*. I had to touch him on the shoulder to get him to quit. He breathed like he was on a ventilator.

They thought I was just being weird. They started in on me. "Dr. Strange." *Like that, okay? Then they started calling the paintings things.*

"What kind of things?"

Josette Vaccaro might have bought one, if nobody else had been there. I finally said I'd give whatever pictures they wanted, and they could pay whatever. Jayden said he'd give me a quarter for the Amur leopard. So I sold it to him.

"Oh, Robbie."

Ethan Weld thought that was funny, so he offered five cents for the eastern gorilla. He said he wanted it to remember me by when I went extinct. Other kids started giving me change, and I thought: Better than nothing, right? At least I can send something in. Then Kayla made me return all the money and take the pictures back.

I still wasn't used to students calling their teachers by first names. "She was trying to rescue you."

She gave me a demerit. She said it was against the rules to sell things on the school grounds, and I should have known that from the class hand-book. I asked her if she knew that half the large animal species on the planet would be gone by the time we reached her age. She said we were on social science, not biology, and don't talk back, or I'd get another demerit.

I drove. I doubted there was a useful thing to say. I was done with humans. We pulled into our driveway. He put his hand on my upper arm.

There's something wrong with us, Dad.

Right again. Something wrong with the two of us. Wrong with all seven and two-thirds billion. And it would take something faster, stronger, and more efficient than DecNef to save anyone.

IN EARLY MARCH THE PRESIDENT INVOKED
the National Emergencies Act of 1976 to arrest a journalist. She'd
been publishing accounts from a White House leaker and refused to
reveal her source. So the President ordered the Justice Department
to order the Treasury to release any Suspicious Activity Reports on
her. Based on those reports and on what the President called "cred-
ible tips from foreign powers," he took her into military custody.

The media cried bloody murder. At least, half the media did.
The top three opposition candidates for the next fall's election said
things the President condemned as "aiding and abetting America's
enemies." The minority Senate leader called the action the grav-
est constitutional crisis in our lifetime. But constitutional crises had
become commonplace.

Everyone waited for Congress to move. There was no movement.
Senators in the President's party—old men armed with polls—
insisted that no laws had been broken. They scoffed at the idea of First
Amendment violations. Violent clashes rolled through Seattle, Boston, and Oakland. But the general public, including me, once again
proved how good the human brain was at getting used to anything.

Everything had happened in broad daylight, and against shame-
lessness, outrage was impotent. The crisis gave way to another fla-
vor of craziness two days later. But for two days, I was strapped
to the news. I'd sit in the evenings, doom-scrolling, while Robbie
painted endangered species at the dining room table.

Sometimes I worried that Decoded Neurofeedback had left him
too calm. It didn't seem natural for any boy his age to be so single-
minded. But, addicted to the national emergency, I was no one to talk.

One night, the news channel I distrusted the least cut from the
fading constitutional crisis to an interview with the world's most
famous fourteen-year-old. The activist Inga Alder had launched
a new campaign, biking from her home near Zurich to Brussels.
Along the way, she was recruiting an army of teenage cyclists to

join her and shame the Council of the European Union into meeting the emissions reductions they had long ago promised.

The journalist asked her how many bicyclists had joined her caravan. Miss Alder frowned, looking for a precision she couldn't give. "The number changes each day. But today we are over ten thousand."

The journalist asked, "Aren't they enrolled in school? Don't they have classes?"

The oval-faced girl in tight pigtails blew a raspberry. She didn't look fourteen. She barely looked eleven. But she spoke English better than most of Robin's classmates. "My house is burning down. Do you want me to wait until the school bell rings before I rush home to put it out?"

The journalist plunged on. "Speaking of school, how do you answer the American President when he says you should study economics before telling world leaders what to do?"

"Does economics teach you to shit your nest and throw away all the eggs?"

My pale, odd son drifted from the dining room and stood at my side. *Who* is *that?* He sounded hypnotized.

The interviewer asked, "Do you think there's any chance this protest might succeed?"

She's like me, Dad.

My scalp burned. I recalled why Inga Alder sounded ever so slightly otherworldly. She'd once called her autism her special asset—"my microscope, telescope, and laser, put together." She'd suffered from deep depression and had even tried to take her own life. Then she found meaning in this living planet.

She cocked an eye at the bemused journalist. "I know our chance of failure if we do nothing."

That's what I'm saying! Exactly!

Robin twitched so hard I reached out to calm him. He pulled away. He had no use for calm. I don't know why it felt so painful and bottomless, to be sitting three feet away at the moment my son first fell in love.

HE ASKED FOR INGA ALDER as he once begged for videos of his mother. We watched the girl march and carry banners. We followed her posts. We sat through documentaries where she made honest commonplaces sound like urgent revelations. We saw her take over the little Tuscan hill town where the G7 met. We watched her tell the assembled UN how history would remember them, if there was a history.

Robin fell hard, as only a nine-year-old can fall for an older woman. But his was that rare love—pure gratitude untroubled by need or desire. In one go, Inga Alder opened my son's feedback-primed mind to a truth I myself never quite grasped: the world is an experiment in inventing validity, and conviction is its only proof.

Late April brought the first outdoor farmers' market of the year. We went down to the big square across from the Capitol. It felt like his mother was with us, just across the street. The stalls were few and the pickings slim. But there were lemony goat cheese and the last of last fall's apples and potatoes. There were carrots, kale, spinach, green garlic, and people glad that the land had come alive again. The Amish brought cakes and cookies of all colors and creeds. There were food trucks with cuisine from every continent. There were hand-built ceramics and scrap-metal jewelry and mandolin-saxophone duets, lathed bowls made from windfall oaks, marbleized shot glasses, and handsaws enameled with local landscapes. There were hanging ivy, flame flower, and spider plants. In the outer rim of that solar system were the fundraisers, community radio people, and public service folks. Alongside these was one fully fee-paid booth where customers could take their pick of one hundred and thirty-six wild pen-and-ink watercolors of creatures about to be relegated to memory.

Over the course of five hours, Robin became someone else. Maybe it was the trillion dollars of advertising that rained down each year, teaching children how to confuse themselves with stuff.

Every nine-year-old Earthling has long since learned how to pitch a sale. But I never imagined how cunning Robin could be at it, or how good. So good that for an entire Saturday, he passed for a native of this planet.

He reinvented every borderline-shyster trick in the traveling salesman's book. *What do you think would be a good price? I spent hours making that one! The golden-crowned sifaka matches your eyes. Nobody wants the thicklip pupfish; I don't know why.* He accosted gray-haired ladies from twenty yards away. *Help keep a beautiful creature alive, ma'am? Best few dollars you'll ever spend.*

People bought because he made them laugh. Several got a kick out of the salesman routine or wanted to reward a budding entrepreneur. Some took pity on him; others just wanted to assuage their guilt. Maybe someone among the hundred purchasers even liked the art well enough to hang it on her walls. But most people who stopped and bought were simply patronizing a child who'd spent months making things of little value on lots of misplaced hope.

In six hours, he made nine hundred and eighty-eight dollars. The guy who took our booth fee bought the black-chested spiny-tailed iguana—not Robin's most successful effort—for twelve bucks to make the grand total an even thousand. Robin was beside himself. Months of single-minded work had led to triumph. Any sum with that many zeroes in it was indistinguishable from a fortune. Who knew what such an amount might do?

Dad, Dad, Dad: Can we mail it tonight?

He'd worked for way too long for me to argue with this rush to the finish line. We took the money to the bank. I wrote a check to send off to the conservation organization he'd chosen after hours of agonizing. That night, after plant-based burgers and a couple of Inga videos, we lay reading on opposite ends of the sofa, our feet launching little border wars into the space between us. He closed his book and studied the beaded ceiling.

I feel great, Dad. Like I could die now and be pretty happy with how things went.

"Don't."

Uh, oh-kee, he said, in his clown voice.

Two weeks later, he got a letter from his not-for-profit saviors of choice. I put it on the front table for him to find when he came home from school. He opened it in high excitement, tearing the envelope. The letter thanked him for his contribution. It bragged about the fact that almost seventy cents on every dollar went directly or indirectly toward slowing the rate of habitat destruction in ten different countries. It suggested that if he wanted to donate another two thousand five hundred dollars, now was a good time, because matching funds and favorable exchange rates put them within reach of their quarterly fundraising goal.

Matching funds?

"That's when big donors give a dollar for every dollar someone else gives."

They have the money . . . but they won't give it unless . . .?

"It's incentive. Like your two-for-one deals, at the farmers' market."

That's different. Evil thoughts curdled his forehead. *They have the money, but they keep it back? And only seven hundred of my dollars goes to the animals? Species are dying, Dad. Thousands!*

He shouted at me, hands flailing. I suggested dinner, but he refused. He went to his room, slammed his door, and wouldn't come out, even to play his favorite board game. I listened for crashing, but the silence was scarier. I sneaked outside and peeked in his window. He was lying in bed, scribbling into a notebook. Plans everywhere.

Fourteen months earlier, he'd punched his bedroom door and fractured two bones in his hand because I'd accidentally thrown away a trading card of his. Now, faced with this crushing thank-you letter, he was concentrating himself, writing out some secret set of action points. For that remarkable metamorphosis, I had Martin Currier's neural feedback training to thank. Somehow, though, standing outside in the chilly spring wind while the maples showered me with red flowers, I wasn't sure *Thankful* was the emotion on Marty's ambiguous color wheel that best matched what I was feeling.

Right before bedtime, Robin came out of his room. He waved a handful of handwritten notes at me. *Can we apply for a protest permit?*

Little yellow warning triangles filled my head. "What are we protesting?"

He shot me a look so filled with disdain that I felt like his disappointing child. By way of answer, he held out a sheet of eleven-by-seventeen drawing paper, his sketch for a larger placard. In the middle of the rectangular landscape were the words:

HELP ME

I'M DYING

In a ring around these words ran a cartoon bestiary of soon-to-vanish plants and animals. My pride in his skill was offset by my dismay at the slogan.

"Is the protest going to be . . . just you?"

You're saying it's no good?

"No, I'm not saying that. It's just that protests usually work better when you join with other people."

Do you know any protests I can join? My head dipped. He touched my wrist. *I need to start somewhere, Dad. Maybe it'll inspire other people.*

"Where do you want to protest?"

His lips pinched and he shook his head. The man who'd watched all those Inga Alder videos with him—the man who'd married his mother—demeaned himself with such a question.

Duh. At the Capitol.

THE PEOPLE HAVE A RIGHT TO ASSEMBLE PEACEFULLY.

So my son informed me. Still, we read over the sections of the municipal code. We learned how the Constitution was one thing and the local powers of enforcement were another. That alone was enough civics lesson to show why legal public demonstration was never going to threaten the status quo.

Wow. They don't make it easy, do they? What if something really bad happens and a bunch of people want to protest, like, that same night?

"Good question, Robbie." One that was getting better with each passing month. I wanted to tell him that democracy had a way of working out, however ugly things got. But my son had this thing about honesty.

He spent three days on his poster. When he finished, it was a thing of beauty, halfway between an illuminated manuscript and a page from *The Adventures of Tintin*. His palette was simple, the lines clean, and the vibrant animals large enough to see from far away. Not bad, for a child who struggled with grasping the minds of others. He also prepared an illustrated handout of twenty-three species threatened or endangered in the state of Wisconsin, including the Canada lynx, gray wolf, piping plover, and Karner blue butterfly. *What else, Dad? What else?*

"Do you want to add a little message for the legislators?"

What do you mean?

"To say what actions you want them to take?"

His puzzled look turned to distress. If his own father was so blindly stupid, what hope was there for the world? *I just want to stop the killing.*

I knew it was asking for trouble, but I let his slogan ride. HELP ME. I'M DYING. Who knew what might move a stranger? After months of neural feedback, his empathy was surpassing mine. He and I would learn together how to enter the world that his mother had lived in like a native.

Dad? When will everyone be there?

"Who?"

The governor and the senators and the assembly people. Maybe those Supreme Court guys? I want as many of them as possible to see me.

"Weekday mornings, probably. But you can't miss any more school."

Inga doesn't even go *to school anymore. She says why bother to study how to live in a future that—*

"I'm familiar with Inga's ideas about education."

We made a deal with Dr. Lipman and his teacher, Kayla Bishop. Robin would keep up on his homework, and he'd do an oral report on his experiences at the Capitol when he got back to school the next day.

He dressed up. He wanted to wear the blazer he'd worn to his mother's funeral, but after two years, putting it on was like squeezing a butterfly back into the chrysalis. I made him wear layers; any kind of weather could blow in over the lake that time of year. He wore an oxford shirt, a clip-on tie, slacks with a crease, a sweater vest, a windbreaker, and boy's dress shoes that shone from long polishing.

How do I look?

He looked like a tiny god. "Commanding."

I want them to take me seriously.

I drove him downtown to the narrow isthmus between the lakes, where the Capitol sat like the center of a compass rose. Robin rode in the back seat, holding his poster on its foam-board handle across his lap. The act required his full attention. At the Capitol, a guard showed him where he could stand, off to the side of the south wing stairs leading to the senate. Relegation to the periphery of the steps upset him.

Can't I stand up by the doors so people see me on their way inside?

The guard's *No* left him grim but resolute. We headed to the area of confinement. Robin looked around, surprised at the sedate midmorning. Government employees drifted up the steps in dribs and drabs. A group of schoolchildren listened to their docent before touring the corridors of power. A block away on Main and Carroll, desperate pedestrians prowled the shops for caffeine and calories, picking their way through the many homeless people of all races. People who looked like elected officials but were probably lobbyists walked past, intent on the voices pressed to their ears.

The stillness confused Robin. *Nobody else is protesting anything? Everyone in the state is perfectly happy with everything just the way it is?*

He'd based his idea of this place on video clips of his mother. He wanted drama and showdown and righteous calls for justice from concerned citizens. Instead, he got America.

I took my place alongside him. He erupted. His free hand slashed the air. *Dad! What do you think you're doing?*

"Doubling the size of your protest group."

No. Freaking. Way. Go stand over there.

I walked thirty feet down the pavement. He waved me farther off.

Over there. Far enough that no one thinks you're with me.

He was right. The two of us standing together would look like an adult put-up job. But a nine-year-old standing alone with a sign reading HELP ME I'M DYING might be something you'd want to stop and talk over.

I relocated, as far off as I was comfortable going. We didn't need a well-meaning passerby calling Dane County Human Services. Satisfied, Robin picked up his painted sign and held it in the air. Then the two of us settled into the trenches of Earthly politics.

I'VE WAITED AT THE BASE OF THOSE STAIRS more times than I can remember. I'd meet Alyssa there, after she'd testified on bills that few people in the state would ever hear of. Often she was pleased with her day's work, sometimes elated, but never entirely satisfied. Coming down the steps, she'd wrap herself around me, dead with fatigue. She'd hold tight to my ribs and say, *It's a start.*

Eventually her turf expanded to include nine more Capitols. She traveled more and lobbied less, training others to do the testifying. But as I watched her son work the steps where Alyssa had so often battled against Things as They Are, I got turned around in time. The books in my sprawling science fiction library agreed: Time travel was not just possible. It was obligatory.

At our wedding, in a part of the vows I didn't know was coming, my wife-to-be gave me an oval loaf of ciabatta. *This is not a symbol. It's not a metaphor. It's just a loaf of bread. I made it. I baked it. It's food. We can eat it together tonight. From each according to her abilities, eh? Just stay with me, spring through winter. Stay with me when there's nothing left. I'll stay with you. There'll always be food enough.*

I lost it, idiot that I am. I don't even like bread. But I wasn't alone. After an equally unrehearsed pause, Aly sighed and said, *Okay. Maybe it* is *a metaphor.* And all the crying people laughed, even my mother. After, we had a great party.

She warned me, at the start, that she had nightmares. *I deal with some grim stuff, Theo. A lot of days. It gets into my dreams. You sure you want to sign on for sleeping next to someone with the screaming meemies?*

I told her if she ever needed company in the middle of the night to wake me up.

Oh, I'll wake you up, all right. That's the problem.

The first time, I thought she was screaming at someone coming into the room. I shot up, my heart seceding from my chest. My lunge woke her. Still in limbo, she broke out crying.

"Honey," I said. "It's okay. I'm here."

It's not *okay!*

Her rebuff was so violent I almost got up and went to sleep in the other room. Three in the morning, the woman I loved was weeping in the dark, and I wanted to tell her how badly she'd just hurt me. That's the ruling story on this planet. We live suspended between love and ego. Maybe it's different in other galaxies. But I doubt it.

"What was it, Aly? Tell me, and it'll go away." We like to say, *Tell me everything. Everything.* But always with the tacit proviso that there's nothing truly horrible to tell.

I can't *tell you. And it* won't *go away.*

Her sobbing subsided as she came awake. I tried again. "What can I do?"

She showed me: Shut up and hold her. It seemed too small a thing, something anyone at all might do. She fell asleep in my arms.

She woke early. By breakfast, it was as if nothing had happened in the night. Doing her mail, she basked in a pool of sun like some strong, green thing. I thought she might tell me now, describe the horror that had awakened her screaming. But she didn't volunteer.

"You were on the ropes last night. Bad dream?"

She shuddered. *Oh, sweetie. Don't ask.*

Her look begged me to let the whole thing drop. She didn't trust me; I wasn't a true believer. I hid that thought, but she read me like a primer.

My worst nightmare. She looked around the room for a way to placate me without getting into details.

"In my worst nightmare, you're lost in a foreign city when the sirens start going off. And I can't find you."

She took my hand, but her smile faltered. I was wasting my energy worrying about such a small thing when we were living in the middle of a vaster catastrophe.

They think we're neurotic, Theo. That we're a bunch of nutjobs.

I was not included in that disparaged *we*. She meant her kind, the ones who could feel their way across the species line.

Why is it so hard for people to see what's happening?

Her night screams grew so familiar they stopped waking me fully. Over time, she let me in on them. In her dreams, other kinds of life could talk, and she understood them. And they told her what was really happening on this planet, the systems of invisible suffering on unimaginable scales. Human appetite's final solution.

In sunlight, she worked flat-out. I'd drive her to the Capitol on days when she lobbied, and I'd pick her up at night, at the bottom of the southern stairs. The day's results mostly satisfied her. But in the evenings, after two glasses of red wine and a poetry session with her rescued mutt, she could turn panicky again.

What happens when they're gone? When it's just us? How is this going to end?

I had no answer. We'd fall asleep spooned against each other, making what comfort we could. And every few nights, she'd wake up screaming again.

But until the end, there would be battle. She was built for it. One afternoon, I watched her in front of the bathroom mirror, suiting up for war: blush, mascara, hair gel, lip gloss. She'd helped draft a call for nonhuman rights that she planned to promote throughout the Upper Midwest. That meant playing on the animal emotions of lawmakers of both sexes, in ten different states.

Take no prisoners. Right, man?

The barnstorm campaign was to start that evening, on home turf, in the southern wing of the Wisconsin Capitol. She hummed a song as she dolled up. *The cuckoo's a fine bird, she sings as she does fly. And when she cries cuckoo, then summer is nigh.* The bill she backed was decades ahead of its time. It had no chance in hell of passing, and she knew it. But Aly played the long game—a game as long as there was time left to play.

She came from the bathroom, glorious. She eyed me coyly. *Hey! You're the fella who once brought back my childhood stutter!* For this, she rewarded me with a teasing feel.

She needed the car, for a reception afterward. That justified the hassle of parking downtown. I walked with her out to the driveway. With one hand on the driver's-side door, she leaned forward and pointed campily in the air. *All right, then. Avengers, assemble!* She kissed me, nibbling my lip. Then she headed off to the Capitol. I would not see her again on this planet, except to identify the body.

THE FOOT TRAFFIC PICKED UP. People started to notice Robin. Several women approached near enough to make sure he was okay. Men walked by. One coiffed, gray-haired lady in a black skirt suit who looked like Aly's mother came up to him like she was ready to dial 911. I stood to intervene, but Robin talked her down. She dove into her purse and produced a handful of bills, which she tried to press on him. He glanced at me, begging, but he knew the rules. The protest permit strictly prohibited fundraising.

He managed to hand out some flyers, mostly to bemused people who didn't hang around to read them. The flyers rarely made it past the trash cans at the corners of the landscaped park. I figured his exploration of participatory democracy might last an hour, followed by a very short oral report at school the next day. But some combination of holy cause and many sessions of neural feedback turned my boy into a Zen bulldog. He dug in, developing a repertoire of playful patter with which he accosted people across the expanses of concrete and cut stone.

I sat on a backless bench with my laptop, tweaking a simulation of the atmospheres that might evolve on a Super Earth just discovered thirty light-years away. I got hungry before he did. I crossed to him, holding up the thermos of cold juice and the bag lunch he'd made for us the night before. He wolfed down half of a hummus-avocado sandwich, then ordered me back to my observation post, shaking his sign to make up for his few minutes away.

After lunch, time slowed down like some relativity thought experiment. I balanced my phone-tethered notebook computer on my lap and pretended to work while keeping one eye on my activist-in-training.

My in-box piled up with unaddressed urgencies. The department's Chinese graduate students had had their student visas revoked. Even Jinjing, my assistant and die-hard Packers fan, who knew more about this country than I did: more collateral victims in the President's two-front war against foreign powers and the scientific elites who supported them. Apparently God had made life on one planet only, and only one country of that planet's dominant species needed to manage it. The department called an emergency faculty meeting for late that afternoon.

When I looked up to check on Robin, he had buttonholed a white-haired black man in a crisp gray suit. My son was shaking his hand-painted sign, scattering facts and figures. The man listened, suspicious. He began grilling Robin.

I closed my computer and walked over. "Everything all right here?"

The man turned to size me up. "Is this your son?"

"I'm sorry. Do you have a problem with something he's doing?"

"I have a problem with you." His voice was stentorian and suffered no fools. "Did you put him up to this? Why isn't he in school? Is this your idea of manipulating strangers? What exactly are you trying to do?"

This is my protest, Robin said. *I told you already. He has nothing to do with it.*

"You left him out here unsupervised."

"I did nothing of the sort. I was sitting right over there."

The man turned to Robin. "Why didn't you tell me that?"

We did everything legally. I'm just trying to get people to believe the truth.

The man turned back to me. He pointed at the sign. "HELP ME, I'M DYING. You don't think there's something wrong with letting a young child stand in a public place, all by himself, holding—"

"Excuse me." I held my shaking hands behind my back. I couldn't remember the last time I'd interrupted anyone. "Who are you to tell me how to raise my child?"

"I'm the chief of staff of the assembly minority leader, and the father of four successful children. What are you teaching this boy, letting him stand out here by himself, holding *this*? You should be connecting him with existing groups. He could be helping to organize other kids. Write letters. Work on specific and useful projects." He looked me in the eye and shook his head. "I should report *you* for cruelty."

Then he turned and climbed the steps and vanished into government. I wanted to shout after him: *What do you mean, "successful children"?*

I looked at Robin. He was crumpling a corner of his poster. His first crushing legislative defeat, and his bill hadn't even been drafted.

I told you not to come over, he shouted. *I was handling it.*

"Robin. You've been here for a long time. Let's go home."

He didn't look up. He didn't even shake his head. *I'm staying. And I'm coming back tomorrow.*

"Robin. I need to get to a meeting. We have to leave now."

Hatred for his own kind rose in his eyes, as plain as the words on his placard. His brain was struggling to raise and lower its own pitches, to move the dots around, to grow and shrink them in the theater of his own head. His shoulders collapsed, and he turned away. He seemed ready to run or yell or smash his sign against the ground. When he spoke again, his voice was small and lost.

How did Mom do it? Every day. For years.

I COULDN'T FIND THE PLANET ISOLA. I looked across large swaths, for many years. My son came along to keep me company and witness my confusion.

"It should be right around here. All the data say so."

He no longer put much stock in data. My son was losing his faith in other planets.

The strange thing was, we could see it from far away. Transit photometry and radial velocity and gravitational microlensing all agreed on its exact location. We knew its mass and radius. We'd calculated its rotations and revolutions down to very small margins of error. But when my son and I came within a few thousand kilometers, it disappeared. The space where it should have been turned empty in every direction.

He took pity on my trouble with the obvious. *They're hiding, Dad. The creatures on Isola are going into our minds and cloaking themselves.*

"What? How?"

They've been around for a billion years. They've learned some things.

He was tired now, impatient with my failure to see. What were the odds of any contact ending well? All human history answered that one.

That's why the universe is silent, Dad. Everyone's hiding. All the smart ones, anyway.

"BUT WE'VE SEEN REAL PROGRESS," Martin Currier insisted. "You can't deny that. More than anyone expected."

We sat in a lunch booth in an abandoned dim sum shop almost shuttered by the Asian student visa crisis. The entire campus—all of American academia—was reeling. Those foreign students whose visas hadn't been curtailed were hiding out indoors. The crowded, cosmopolitan summer session had thinned out to a few safe white people.

Currier's chin nudged his point home. "No one promised you a cure."

I wanted to slap the bottom of his coffee cup as he lifted it to his face. "He won't get out of bed. I have to go to war just to get him up and dressed. He doesn't want to go outside. He's ready to go to sleep again as soon as we have lunch. Thank God it's summer vacation, or his school would be riding me again."

"And it's been like this . . . ?"

"For days."

Currier lifted a dumpling to his lips with chopsticks and chewed. Some lump of gluten and pride, insoluble in tea, stuck in his Adam's apple. "Maybe it's time to think about a very low-dose regimen of an antidepressant."

The word filled me with animal panic. He saw.

"Eight million children in the country take psychoactive drugs. They're not ideal, but they can work."

"If eight million children are taking psychoactive drugs, *something* isn't working."

The senior research professor shrugged. Concession or objection—I couldn't tell. I searched a for a way out. "Could Robbie be . . . I don't know. Starting to tolerate or habituate to the sessions? Could the effects be wearing off faster?"

"I can't imagine. In most subjects, we see durable improvement lasting for weeks after each training."

"Then why is he sliding down again?"

Currier raised his gaze to the television screen on the wall opposite our table. In the record heat, clusters of lethal bacteria were spreading up and down the Florida coast. The President was telling reporters, *Maybe it's entirely natural. Maybe it isn't. People are saying . . .*

"Maybe his reactions are entirely understandable."

"What do you mean?" I asked, although my neck hair knew.

His frown was remarkably like his smile. "Clinicians and theorists are rarely going to agree on what constitutes mental health. Is it the ability to function productively in hard conditions? Or is it more a matter of appropriate response? Constant, cheerful optimism may not be the healthiest reaction to . . ." He nodded at the TV.

I had an awful thought: Maybe the last few months of neural feedback were hurting Robbie. In the face of the world's basic brokenness, more empathy meant deeper suffering. The question wasn't why Robin was sliding down again. The question was why the rest of us were staying so insanely sanguine.

Currier flipped a hand in the air. "He's scoring much higher on self-control and resilience. He's so much better at coping with uncertainty than he was when he first came to see us. All right: So he's still angry. He's still depressed. Honestly, Theo? I'd be concerned if he *weren't* upset, these days."

We finished eating. Martin argued over the morality of my paying for our tab, but the fight wasn't vigorous. We walked back across campus. I'd made a mistake, going out without sunblock. It was only June, but I couldn't breathe. Currier struggled, too. He held a surgical mask to his face. "Sorry. I know how ridiculous this looks. But my allergies are off the charts." At least we weren't in Southern California, where weeks of Code Red air from wildfires had sealed millions inside.

The protection of DecNef seemed to be ending. For a while it had kept Robin happy and me safe from having to drug my son. Now even Currier was suggesting it. One small conflagration at school and the choice would no longer be mine.

"He keeps asking me how Aly fought a losing battle for years without getting beaten by it." Currier's expression was unreadable behind his mask. I pressed on blindly. "I wonder the same thing. She used to get angry. She got depressed. A lot." I didn't much care to tell her old birding friend about her night terrors. "But she blew right through."

His smile was audible, even behind his mask. "His mother had some prize brain-body chemistry."

We paused on University Avenue near the Discovery Center, where our paths divided. I braced myself for another suggestion that it was time for the trial-and-error of child brain cocktails. But Currier removed his mask and nursed an expression that I couldn't decode.

"We could learn her secret. Robin could tell us himself."

"What in the world are you talking about?"

"I still have Aly's run."

Angers flooded me from many directions, none of them useful. "You *what*? You saved our recordings?"

"One of them."

I knew without asking. He'd pitched my Admiration and Grief and her Vigilance. He'd kept her Ecstasy.

"You're saying you could train Robin on Aly's old brain scan?"

Currier sized up the wonder of it down on the pavement near his feet. "Your son could learn how to put himself into an emotional state his mother once generated. It might be motivating. It could answer his question."

The colors of Plutchik's wheel spun around me. Stabs of orange interest gave way to shards of green fear. The past was turning as porous and ambiguous as the future. We were making it up, the story of life in this place, as surely as I made up the bedtime stories of alien life my son hadn't yet outgrown.

I looked down both long diagonals of the sidewalk intersection: not an Asian student in sight. I'd missed something obvious, in over thirty years of reading and two thousand science fiction books: there was no place stranger than here.

THE QUESTION GOT HIM OUT OF BED. He looked at me, his face a nursery of stars. *They have Mom's* brain? *She's in the experiment?*

I answered with every adult reservation, but it didn't matter. He all but jumped me.

Holy crow. Dad! Why didn't you tell me?

He took my face in his palms and made me swear solemnly that I wasn't lying. It was like the two of us had stumbled on a video clip that no one knew existed, the record of a day that had been sealed off forever. Peace came over him, as if all would be well now, whatever the outcome. He turned his head to look out through his bedroom window at the summer rains. His eyes had a calm resolve, resigned to anything existence might throw at him. He'd never be laid low again.

I WAS PACING IN THE LAB'S FOYER when he came from the first session. He'd trained for ninety minutes. Colored dots, musical pitches, and other feedback helped him to find and match the patterns of his mother's brain. I smiled, faking a calm I didn't have. Robin must have known I was crazy for anything he could tell me.

Ginny brought him from the test room. Her arm draped over his shoulder while his hand reached up to clutch the sleeve of her lab coat. Ginny looked as casual as I was trying to be. She leaned down and asked, "You cool, Brain Boy? Want to sit in my office for a minute?"

He loved to sit at Ginny's desk and read her collection of hipster comics. Ordinarily he'd have jumped at the offer. He shook his head. *I'm cool.* Then, as his mother had reminded him a million times in life, he added, *Thank you.*

For an hour and a half, he'd been feeling his way around Aly's limbic system. Each time he'd raised and lowered pitches or steered icons toward targets on the screen he was steering himself into the bliss that had been Alyssa's once, years ago—a lark we'd taken part in on an otherwise ordinary day. In Robin's head, if nowhere else, he was talking to his mother again. I needed to know what she was saying.

He saw me from across the laboratory suite. His face lit with excitement and hesitation. I saw how badly he wanted to tell me where he'd just been. But he didn't have words for that planet.

He let go of Ginny's sleeve and slid out from under her arm. Her professional face betrayed a stab of abandonment. Robin approached me, something new in his walk. His stride was looser, more experimental. Ten feet away he shook his head. Reaching me, he grabbed my upper arm and pressed his ear against my chest.

"Good one?" The syllables came out of me, anemic.

It was her, Dad.

I flushed in the back of my legs. It occurred to me, too late, what an overactive imagination like Robin's might do with so rich an inkblot.

"It felt . . . different?"

He shook his head, not at the question but at my dissembling. We made another appointment for the next week. I chatted with Ginny and a pair of postdocs. It felt like my classic nightmare where I'm lecturing in public and only belatedly discover my skin is green. Robin patted me on the back and nudged me toward the hallway, out of the emotional incubator, into the world.

We walked to the parking lot. I peppered him with questions, everything but what I was too adult to ask. He answered with monosyllables, more stymied than impatient. Only when I put my pass in the parking garage machine and the gate lifted did he open up.

Dad? You remember that first night in the cabin, in the mountains? Looking through the telescope?

"I do. Very well."

That's what it was like.

He held his hands in front of his face and spread them. Some memory amazed him, either blackness or stars.

I turned on Campus Drive toward home, keeping my eyes on the road. Then, in a voice I barely recognized, the alien on the front seat next to me said, *Your wife loves you. You know that, right?*

I WATCHED FOR SOME DIFFERENCE. Maybe I cued myself, knowing whose feelings he was learning to emulate. But it seemed to take just two sessions for the black cloud he'd sunk into after his disastrous stint at the Capitol to break up into wisps of cirrus.

I came to wake him on a late June Saturday. He groaned at the shock of consciousness and sudden sun. But now, at least, he lifted his head off the pillow and grinned as he moaned.

Dad! Am I training today?

"Yes."

Yay! he said, in a funny little voice. *Because, you know, I could really use it.*

"Could you use a little paddle in the boat afterwards?"

Serious? On the lake?

"I was thinking just out in the backyard."

He growled deep in his throat and bared his teeth at me. *You're lucky I'm not a carnivore.*

Choosing his clothes for the day left him wistful. *Ah, this shirt. I forgot about this one. This is a good shirt! How come I never wear this shirt?* He came out to the living room half-dressed. *Remember that pair of furry socks Mom gave me, with separate toes, and little claws on each one? What happened to those?*

The question made me flinch. I'd trained on his old brain for so long. I was sure a squall was coming. "Oh, Robbie. That was a hundred sizes ago."

I know. Geez. I was just curious. I mean: Are they still somewhere? Is some other kid wearing them and thinking he's half-bear?

"What made you think of *those*?"

He shrugged, but not in evasion. *Mom.* Eerie thoughts came over me. But before I could challenge him, he asked, *What's for breakfast? I'm starving!*

He ate everything I put in front of him. He wanted to know

what was different about the oatmeal (nothing) and why the orange juice was so tangy (no reason). He sat at the table after I cleared it, humming some melody I couldn't make out. The raging curiosity I felt over the source of Aly's recorded *Ecstasy* that long-ago day flooded through me again. My son—*her* son—had glimpsed it, but he couldn't tell me.

I took Robbie in to the neuro lab for another session with his mother's brain print. He and Ginny fell into their familiar routine. I watched him for a few minutes as he moved shapes around on his screen by telekinesis. Then I walked down the hall and dropped in on Currier.

"Theo! What a pleasure!" He must have meant something different by the word than everyone else did. Every syllable the man spoke irritated me. I needed a stint or two in his empathy machine. "How's the boy doing?"

I made the case for guarded optimism. Martin listened, his face reserved.

"He's probably generating a fair amount of auto-suggestion."

Of course Robin was auto-suggesting. *I* was auto-suggesting. The changes might be entirely imagined. But brain science knew that even imagination could change our cells for real.

"Is there anything new about this round of training? Changes in the AI feedback? Was Alyssa's recording of different neural regions?"

"Different?" Currier's shoulders rose; his mouth approximated a smile. "Sure. We've boosted the scanning resolution. The AI keeps learning about Robin and getting more efficient the more Robin interacts with it. And yes, Aly's scan is of an evolutionarily older part of the brain than the target templates we worked with in the earlier session."

"So, in other words . . . nothing at all is the same." I'd asked what I came to ask. Everything except what I wanted most to know.

And I was pretty sure that Currier wouldn't be able to tell me what Aly herself had refused to say.

But then I thought: Maybe he could. The idea crept across my clammy, conductive skin. Maybe Robbie wasn't the first to visit Aly's brain print. But I was afraid the question might make me look crazy. Or I was too afraid of the answer to ask.

ROBBIE EVEN ENJOYED INFLATING THE BOAT. Usually he gave the foot pump two minutes of half-hearted kicks before giving up. That day, he didn't even ask for help. The watercraft rose from a puddle of floppy PVC without a complaint from my son.

We put in near a sign that gave the fishing limits in Spanish, Chinese, and Hmong. Robin slipped off the dock while getting into the boat. He wailed as his shoes sank into the mud and the lake soaked up to his knees. But the instant he scrambled back into the boat, he looked at his legs, puzzled. *Well. That's weird. Getting so worked up about water.*

We paddled out in the flat-bottomed dinghy, taking forever to go a hundred yards. He scoured the shore as he rowed. I should have known what he was looking for. Birds: the creatures that had kept all his mother's demons at bay. He'd always been interested in them. But interest had turned to love, deep in his spine, as he trained on the print of her brain.

A sleek, gray form shot across our bow. He waved me to stop paddling. The first notes of distress in days tinged my son's voice. *Who is he, Dad? Who is he? I couldn't see!*

A resident so common even I knew its name. "Junco, I think."

Dark-eyed or slate? He turned to me, sure I could tell him. I couldn't. His mother spoke, up close to my ear. *The robin is my favorite bird.*

We rowed some more, the slowest form of transportation known to humankind. In deeper water, he lifted his paddle. *Could you take over, Dad? I'm kind of preoccupied.*

I worked from the stern, passing my paddle from side to side to keep us from spinning. A butterfly more staggering than any stained-glass window landed on Robin's downy forearm where he rested it on the boat. Robin held his breath, letting the visitor stumble, fly, and land again on his face. It walked across his closed eyes before flying away.

Robbie lay back against the gunwales and appraised the sky. His eyes sought out all the thousands of points of light from our night in the Smokies, every one of them still up there but erased by the light of day. The two of us glided underneath invisible stars, crossing the placid lake in an inflatable boat.

I'd imagined we were alone. But the more I watched Robin, the more I joined the party. Flying things, swimming things, things skating across the lake's surface. Things that branched over the shore and fed the water with rains of living tissue. Chatter from every compass point, like some avant-garde piece for a chorus of random radios. And one enormous life in the boat's bow, a thing that was me but wasn't. When he spoke, I startled so hard I almost capsized us.

Do you remember that day?

He'd left me far behind. "What day, Robbie?"

The day you two recorded your feelings?

I remembered it with weird precision. How Aly and I craved each other afterward. How we locked ourselves in our room. How she wouldn't tell me the source of her ecstasy. How she'd called through the closed door to reassure our son that everything and everyone were *so okay.*

There was something funny about the two of you. You were both act-ing strange.

He couldn't have remembered that. He'd been so young, and nothing about that afternoon would have been remarkable enough to impress itself on him.

Like you both had a big secret.

Then my wife was whispering. *You remember the secret, don't you, Theo?*

I paddled against our spin and slowed my breathing. "Robbie. What made you think of that?"

He didn't answer. Alyssa kept teasing. *Of course he remembers. His parents were acting weird.*

"Did Dr. Currier mention something about that day? Was he asking you things?"

Robin rolled over onto his belly, rocking the boat. He squinted at the far shore, trying to see into the past. *Did Mom have a tattoo or something?*

He could not have known about that. I didn't dare ask him how he did. She'd gotten the thing before we met. She needed a psychic boost to power her through a disastrous first year of law school. To push back against the demoralizing crush of L1, she hit upon the idea of sowing the world's tamest wild oat. Four scalloped petals around a tiny center of stamens and anthers, inked into her skin.

"It was supposed to be a little flower. Her namesake plant."

Sweet alyssum.

"That's right."

But something happened to it?

"She didn't like the way it turned out. Someone told her it looked like a deformed smiley face. So she asked the tattooist to turn it into a bee."

And the bee ended up looking funny, too.

He was rattling me. "That's right. But she stuck with the bee. She didn't want to end up with a funny-looking horse tattooed all over her."

His face was turned toward the water. He didn't smile.

"Robbie? Why are you asking?"

His shoulder blades stuck out through his polo shirt like amputated wings. *Dad. What do you think she was thinking, that day? It's so weird. It's . . . like walking into a forest a million years old.*

I wanted to beg. Send me word—just one small thing that survived what happened to her. I'd lost the gist of her, the feel. And Robbie couldn't tell me. Or he wouldn't.

He rested his chin on the side of the boat and gazed into the lake. The bobbing surface of the water was the ocean of another world, one in a story I'd read when not much older than he was. He was looking for the thousands of fish that the dark green water hid from the eyes of air-breathers.

What's the ocean like, Dad?

What was the ocean like? I couldn't tell him. The sea was too big, and my bucket was so small. Also, it had a hole. I put my hand on the back of his calf. It seemed like my best available answer.

Did you know that the world's corals will be dead in six more years?

His voice was soft and his mouth was sad. The world's most spectacular partnership was coming to an end, and he'd never see it. He looked up at me, with Aly's ghost planted right into his brain. *So what are we supposed to do about that?*

THE FIRST TIME TEDIA DIED, a comet tore off a third of the planet and turned it into a moon. Nothing on Tedia survived.

After tens of millions of years, the atmosphere came back, water flowed again, and life sparked a second time. Cells learned that symbiotic trick of how to combine. Large creatures spread once more into every niche of the planet. Then a distant gamma ray burst dissolved Tedia's ozone shield and ultraviolet radiation killed most everything.

Patches of life survived in the deepest oceans, so this time it was faster coming back. Ingenious forests set out again across the continents. A hundred million years after that, just as a species of cetacean was beginning to make tools and art, a neighborhood star system supernovaed, and Tedia had to start again.

The problem was that the planet lay too near the galactic center, packed in too closely to the calamities of other stars. Extinction would never be far away. But there were periods of grace, between the devastations. Forty resets in, the calm lasted long enough for civilization to take hold. Intelligent bear-people built villages and mastered agriculture. They harnessed steam, channeled electricity, learned and built simple machines. But when their archaeologists revealed how often the world ended, and their astronomers figured out why, society broke down and destroyed itself, millennia before the next supernova would have.

This, too, happened again and again.

But let's go see, my son said. *Let's just have a look.*

By the time we arrived, the planet had died and resurrected itself a thousand and one times. Its sun was almost spent and would soon expand to engulf the entire world. But life went on assembling endless new platforms. It didn't know any better. It couldn't do otherwise.

We discovered creatures high up in Tedia's jagged young mountains. They were tubular and branchy and they held so still for so long that we mistook them for plants. But they greeted us, putting the word *Welcome* directly into our heads.

They probed my son. I could feel their thoughts go into him. *You want to know if you should warn us.*

My frightened son nodded.

You want us to be ready. But you don't want to cause us pain.

My son nodded again. He was crying.

Don't worry, the doomed tubular creatures told us. *There are two kinds of "endless." Ours is the better one.*

SUMMER FLOODS THROUGHOUT THE GULF contaminated the drinking water of thirty million people, spreading hepatitis and salmonellosis across the South. Heat stress in the Plains and the West was killing old people. San Bernardino caught fire, and later, Carson City. Something called Theory X had armed militias patrolling the streets of cities throughout the Plains states, searching for unspecified foreign invaders. Meanwhile, a novel stem rust triggered wheat crop failure throughout China's Huangtu Plateau. In late July, a True America demonstration in Dallas turned into a race riot.

The President declared another national emergency. He mobilized the National Guard of six states, sending the troops to the border to combat illegal immigration:

THE GREATEST THREAT TO THE SECURITY OF EVERY AMERICAN!!

Wild weather throughout the Southeast triggered an outbreak of *Amblyomma americanum*, the Lone Star tick. Robbie loved the story. He asked me to read him anything I saw about it. *It might not be a bad thing, Dad. It might even save us.*

He said strange things these days. I didn't always challenge him. This time I did. "Robbie! What a horrible thing to say!"

Seriously. The infection makes people allergic to meat. No more meat eaters could be an amazing thing. Our food would go ten times farther!

The words made me queasy. I wanted Aly to intervene with the boy. But that was the problem: she was intervening already.

He trained a fourth time on the template of his mother's ecstasy. And then a fifth. Each session left him a little more happily baffled. He spoke less and less, even as he looked and listened more. He drew into his notebook with the speed of a growing plant.

He came into my study after dinner, where I sat writing code. *Was I better yesterday than I am today?*

"What do you mean?"

Like, yesterday I felt like nothing could touch me. Today? Arrrggh!

He roared the roar of impatient rage his mother always did, when confronted with inane bureaucracy. But even as he sank his claws in me and shook with a frustration he couldn't name, his aura felt large and loose. He'd grown easy in his new skin.

The days brightened. He sat with his digital microscope for hours at a time. He could stare at simple things and sketch for the better part of an afternoon. The backyard birdhouses, the contents of an owl pellet, even the mold on an orange entranced him. He still fell into old fears and angers. But they leached out of him faster, and low tide left behind all kinds of treasures in the exposed and tranquil pools.

The boy who stood on the steps of the Capitol waving his handmade placard was gone. I ought to have been relieved. But I'd go to bed at night feeling something toward my once-anxious child that seemed an awful lot like mourning.

I did a terrible thing. I sneaked a look in his notebooks. Over the millennia, millions of parents have done worse, though usually for better reasons. I couldn't pretend he needed policing. I had no reason to eavesdrop on his thoughts. I simply wanted to listen in on his ongoing séance with Aly.

It happened on the first of August, when he asked if he could camp in the yard. *I love it out there at night. So much going on. Everything talking to everything else!*

You could hear the sounds from the house well enough: the choirs of tree frogs, the massed cicada choruses, and the solos of night birds that hunted them. But he wanted to be inside the sounds. It surprised me, my timid son asking to spend the night outdoors by himself. I was glad to encourage him. The world might be dissolving, but our backyard still felt safe.

I helped him pitch the tent. "Sure you don't want company?" I wasn't really offering. My mind was already planning my illicit evening reading.

I waited until his tent light went out. His notebooks were on top of his student desk, propped up between geode bookends. He trusted me. He knew I'd never spy on him. I found his current one, its cover emblazoned with the words PRIVATE OBSERVATIONS OF ROBIN BYRNE. I pored through the pages, feeling no guilt at all until I saw what they contained. Not a single word about his mother, or about me, either, for that matter. Not a line of his own private hopes or fears. The entire book was devoted to drawings, notes, descriptions, questions, speculations, and appreciation—the proof of other life.

Where do finches go when it rains?
How far does a deer walk in one year?
Can a cricket remember how to get out of a maze?
If a frog ate that cricket, would he learn the maze faster?
I warmed a butterfly back to life with my breath.

One mostly blank page declared:

I love grass. It grows from the bottom, not the top. If some-thing eats the tips, it doesn't kill the plant. Only makes it grow faster. Pure genius!!!

Underneath that manifesto he'd drawn a grass stem with all the parts labeled: *blade, sheath, node, collar, tiller, spike, awn, glume . . .* He'd copied the names from somewhere, and yet the seeing was all his. He'd circled a spot on the open blade and put a question mark next to it: *What is the fold in the middle called?*

My face flushed with two shames. I was spying on my son's notebooks. And I was getting my first good look at a blade of grass. The oddest feeling came over me: the pages had been dictated from the grave. I put the notebook back in place. When he came back into the house the next morning and went to his room, I was afraid he might smell the prints of my fingers on his pages.

WHAT ABOUT AN ADVENTURE? he asked, and he took me on a walk around the neighborhood. I'd never seen him walk slower or swivel his head more. *Ecstasy* wasn't right. Alyssa's zeal softened in Robin, to something more fluid and improvised. Half the world's species were dying. But the world, his face said, would stay green or even greener. He was all right now with every coming disaster, so long as he could just get outdoors.

He shocked me by greeting a young couple who came down the sidewalk toward us. *How far are you going today?*

The question made them laugh. Not far, they said.

We're not going far, either. Maybe just around the block. Although, who knows?

The young woman regarded me, the muscles around her eyes praising me for a job well done. I denied all responsibility.

Down the sidewalk, he grabbed my elbow. *Hear that? Two downy woodpeckers, having a chat.*

I worked to hear it. "How do you know?"

Easy. "Downy goes down." Hear how the song sinks a little, at the end?

"Well, yes. But I mean, how do you know that the downy's song goes down?"

And there's a house wren. Per-chick-oree!

I wanted to shake him by the shoulders. "Robbie. Who taught you this?"

Mom knew all the birdsongs.

He must have known that he was spooking me. Maybe he was chiding me for my ignorance. I'd birded with Aly all through courtship. But after we married, I left that task to other people.

"That's true. She did. But she studied them for years."

I don't know them all. I only know the ones I know.

"Are you studying them somewhere? Online?"

Not really studying. I just listen and like them.

Where had I been, during all that listening? On other planets.

We walked, Robbie listening and me fretting. I was running a calculation I didn't know how to complete. How different was he from who he'd been months ago? He'd always sketched, always been curious, always loved living things. But the boy at my right elbow was a different species from the boy who'd played with his birthday microscope in our rented cabin in the woods less than a year earlier. Fascination had made him invincible.

Two more steps and he froze in place. He waved me forward, pointing down at the sidewalk, pantomiming. On the concrete, the shadows of a nearby ironwood tree played against a field of sandy sunlight. They looked like layers of Japanese ink paintings on coarse paper, floating over one another in ghostly animation. His face broke out in contagious joy. But Robbie's happiness and mine were as different as a tern on a thermal and a rubber-band prop plane. I got restless long before he did. He might have stayed there all afternoon watching the spectral silhouettes if I hadn't prodded him away.

Three blocks from our house, we reached the tiny neighborhood park. He pointed to a slender fountain of a tree trunk in the corner of the playground near the swings.

That's my favorite. I call it my redhead tree.

"Your *what?* Why?"

Because it has red hair. Serious! You've never seen it?

He steered me toward the low-hanging branches. When we reached the tree, he twisted a leaf. There, on the underside, in the junction of the side veins and the midrib, were tiny patches of red hair.

Scarlet oak. Cool, right?

"I had no idea!"

He patted me on the back. *That's okay, Dad. You're not the only one.*

Shouts came from down the street. Three boys a little older than

Robbie were trying to dislodge a stop sign. Concern clouded Robin's face. *People are so strange.*

He let the leaf go, and the branch sprang back into place. I looked up at the column of tree, where every leaf was now red-haired. "Robbie. When did you learn all this stuff?"

He reared back and gawked at me, the only creature out here that baffled him. *What do you mean, "when?" All along!*

"But have you been teaching yourself?"

His whole body demurred. *Everybody out here wants me to know them.* In another moment, he'd entirely forgotten I'd ever asked him anything. He showed me an ant mound and a burrow dug under the wall of a small pavilion. *I don't know whose that is, yet.* He got down on his haunches and watched the opening for long enough to make me restless. *Whoever's in there is fantastic.*

He walked under the tunnel of maples and doomed ash trees as if he were in a submersible at the bottom of the Marianas Trench. I tagged along in the wake of his rotating gaze. But still, I wasn't looking. I couldn't clear my head of a question that had nagged at me for weeks. It came out of me even as I was thinking of some new way to suppress it. "Robbie? When you do the training? Is it like Mom's there?"

He stopped and grabbed at a section of chain-link fence. *Mom's all over.*

"Yes. But—"

Remember what Dr. Currier told us? Whenever I train myself to match the pattern, then what I'm feeling . . .

Was what she was feeling. The lemon-colored wedge, that grand prize on Plutchik's wheel of fortune. He had Ecstasy, while I was stuck on Apprehension, Envy, or worse.

He started up again, and I followed. His hand swept along the length of suburban street. *Dad? It's like that planet we went to. The one where all the separate creatures share a single memory.*

HE POINTED DOWN THE BLOCK toward the sign-vandalizing boys. *Let's see what they're doing.*

This wasn't Robbie. Real Robbie was back in the house, playing his solo farming game, watching videos of his two favorite women, and cowering from the rest of humanity. But this boy took me by the arm and pulled.

We'll just say hi, okay?

Words that Aly cajoled me with a thousand and one times in this life. I questioned the wisdom of heading into that cloud of testosterone. Then it hit me: A large part of this experiment consisted of training my son to unlearn the worst of the traits he'd gotten from me. In this lawless little boondock of Sol 3 that had me so cowed, my son had somehow grabbed the crown of confidence.

The three preteens glanced up from their destruction to sneer as we got close. Two of them wore ads for running shoes. The third wore camo pants and a shirt reading THESE COLORS DON'T RUN, THEY RELOAD. They stopped kicking at the sign, but in a way to suggest that they'd finish the task the moment we were gone. I'd seen a pre-election poll the week before. Twenty-one percent of Americans thought society needed to be burned to the ground. A stop sign probably seemed an easy place to start.

Before I could fake authority and tell them to go home, Robbie called out. *Hey! What are you guys doing?*

The one in the reload shirt snorted. "Burying our goldfish."

Robin's eyes widened. *Really?* All three boys snickered. I watched my son recoil a little, before snickering back. *We had to bury our dog once. Do you know about the owl?*

The boys just stared, trying to decide if he was mentally challenged. At last the smallest of the three, the one in the baseball cap reading I'M NOT REALLY THIS UGLY, said, "What are you talking about?"

The great horned owl. In the white pine by the Catholic church. The thing is huge! He spread his hands to half his height. *Come on! I'll show you.*

The two small guys checked with the big one, who wavered on the corner of Disgust and Interest. Robin turned and motioned for them to follow. Amazingly, they did.

Robin led us around the block to a mat of accumulated brown needles under the branches of a big white pine. He pointed, and we four looked up. *Shh. There he is.*

"Where?" one of my companion thugs bellowed.

Robin shushed again, exasperated. He whispered through clenched teeth, *Arggh! Right. Up. There!*

I searched for half a minute before realizing I was looking into the eyes of the magnificent bird. It must have been two feet tall, but the crazed camouflage of its feathers disappeared into the pine's fissured bark. Only the whitewash on the trunk beneath and the golden rings of its pitiless stare betrayed it. The whole neighborhood would have been out under the tree, if they'd known.

RELOAD boy whipped out his phone to take pictures. The tiny kid in the NOT THIS UGLY cap pulled out his phone, too, and began texting. The third kid shouted, "Shit!" and the great creature stooped, bobbed twice, and straightened into the air. Its huge, tapered wings opened as wide as I was tall. They pressed on the heavy air and the bird disappeared over the roof of the house across the street.

Robin looked ready to lay into them for scaring the creature off. But he merely sighed at giving away such a valuable secret. He caught my eye and tipped his head, down the street toward our escape route. He didn't talk again until we were out of earshot.

The great horned owl's conservation rating is "Least Concern." How stupid is that? Like: unless they're all dead, we shouldn't be concerned.

Even his anger seemed bountiful. I draped my arm across his shoulders. "How did you happen to find him?"

Easy. I just looked.

THE DAYS GREW SHORTER and summer ran its course. One night in mid-August, he asked for a planet before bed. I gave him the planet Chromat. It had nine moons and two suns, one small and red, the other large and blue. That made for three kinds of day of different lengths, four kinds of sunset and sunrise, scores of different eclipses, and countless flavors of dusk and night. Dust in the atmosphere turned the two kinds of sunlight into swirling watercolors. The languages of that world had as many as two hundred words for sadness and three hundred for joy, depending on the latitude and hemisphere.

He was thoughtful, at the story's end. He lay back on his pillow, hands clasped behind his head, looking up at the idea of Chromat on his bedroom ceiling.

Dad? I think I'm done with school.

His words collapsed me. "Robbie. We can't start this again."

What about homeschooling? He seemed to be reasoning with someone on the roof.

"I have a full-time job."

As a teacher, right?

He was calm as a skiff on a windless pond. I was capsizing. I wanted to shout, *Give me one good reason why you can't sit in a classroom like every other child your age.* But I already knew several.

Eddie Tresh is homeschooled, and his parents work. It's easy, Dad. We just fill in a form and tell Wisconsin that you're going to do it. We can get some course packets and stuff online, if we want. You wouldn't have to spend any time on me at all.

"Robbie, that's not the problem."

He turned to look at me and waited for my objections. When none came, he rolled over on one elbow and retrieved a battered paperback from his little student desk next to the bed. He handed me the volume: Aly's old field guide to the birds of the eastern U.S.

"Where did you get this?" My tone made even me flinch. I

seemed to want to criminalize my son. He got it off the bookshelf in my bedroom—where else?

I can learn by myself, Dad. Give me the name, and I'll tell you what it looks like.

I flipped through the book, now filled with tiny checkmarks next to the species he knew. One of his parents was already homeschooling him.

I want to be an ornithologist. They don't teach you that in the fourth grade.

The field guide felt as heavy as it would have on Jupiter. "School prepares you for a lot more than just your job." He looked at me, concerned for how lame and tired I sounded. I fumbled my fingers into the hashtag sign he'd taught me. "Life skills, Robbie. Like learning how to get along with other kids."

If it really taught kids that, I wouldn't mind going. He scooched over on the bed and consoled my shoulder. *Here's how I look at it, Dad. I'm almost ten. You want me to learn everything I need for being an adult. So school should teach me how to survive the world ten years from now. So . . . what do you think that'll look like?*

The noose tightened, and I couldn't slip it. He must have learned the argument from all those Inga Alder videos.

Really. I need to know.

Earth had two kinds of people: those who could do the math and follow the science, and those who were happier with their own truths. But in our hearts' daily practice, whatever schools we went to, we all lived as if tomorrow would be a clone of now.

Tell me what you think, Dad. Because that's what I should be learning.

I didn't need to say anything out loud. With his newly learned powers, Robbie had only to look in my eyes, move and enlarge his inner dot, and read my mind.

Remember how Pawpaw just kept getting sicker and sicker and wouldn't go to the doctor, and then he died?

"I remember."

That's what everybody's doing.

I didn't much want to remember my father. Nor did I want to discuss bottomless catastrophe with my nine-year-old. The house was peaceful and the night was calm. I fingered Aly's book, with its dozens of new checkmarks.

"Bachman's warbler."

Bachman's warbler, he repeated, as if in a spelling bee. *Male? Black cap, fading to gray. Green body, yellow belly, white under the tail.*

I'd gone to the wrong school. He'd learned more in one summer, on his own, than he'd learned in a year of classroom. He'd discovered, on his own, what formal education tried to deny: Life wanted something from us. And time was running out.

Critically endangered, he concluded. *Possibly extinct.*

"You win," I said, as if there had ever been a contest. "And lesson one is figuring out how this homeschooling thing works."

WE FILED OUR FORM OF INTENT with the Department of Public Instruction. I built a little curriculum: reading, math, science, social studies, and health. Mine was better than what he'd been getting. The day we withdrew him from school, he ran around the house singing "When the Saints Go Marching In." He mimed all the instruments and knew all the words.

The change took time, sweat, and many more babysitters. My hours were somewhat flexible, and he loved to come to campus with me. In a pinch, I set him up at the library. But my other students didn't get the best of me that semester. My own work for publication ground to a standstill. I had to cancel appearances at conferences in Bellevue, Montreal, and Florence.

It surprised me that we only needed 875 hours of instruction a year. Since Robbie now wanted to learn things even on weekends, that came to less than two and a half hours a day. He had no trouble keeping up with the public curriculum. He polished off his online self-exams with glee. We traveled everywhere that reading, math, science, social studies, and health let us travel. We studied at home, in the car, over meals, and on long walks through the woods. Even shooting penalty kicks against each other in the park became a lesson in physics and statistics.

I built him a Planetary Exploration Transponder—basically my aging tablet computer, gussied up with enamel paint to look futuristic and cool. I created a special sign-on for him, locked down to a grade school browser that limited him to a handful of child-geared sites and a few educational games. He didn't mind the constraints. Near-Earth orbit was still orbit.

Between trying to tutor him through his curriculum, preparing two undergrad lectures and a grad seminar in biomarkers, continuing to flail against the Asian grad student visa crisis, and writing copious emails to colleagues apologizing for missed deadlines, I felt like NASA in the wake of the *Challenger*. Stryker gave up on me and dissolved our research partnership. For the first time since coming to Wisconsin, I had to file an annual activity report with no significant publications.

Robin woke me up one Saturday, half an hour before the sun, ending the first few hours of deep sleep I'd had in days. At least he was waking me with joy and not a tantrum. *Where am I going today, Dad? Come on. Give me a new treasure hunt.*

I searched for something that would keep him busy long enough for me to clear my own backlog of work.

"Draw me the outlines of eight countries in West Africa. Then fill them each with four drawings of their native plants and animals."

Easy-peasy, he declared, charging out of the room for his trusted PET. By three p.m., the job was done. At the pace he was setting, he threatened to have the 875 hours of fourth grade finished by the end of summer.

I HAVE A GREAT IDEA, Robbie said. *Dr. Currier's lab could take a dog. A really good dog. But it could be a cat or a bear or even a bird. You know that birds are a lot smarter than anybody thinks? I mean, some birds can see magnetism. How cool is that?*

I'd taken him to my office for the afternoon while I got things ready for the new academic year. He was playing with a toy programmable scale that showed your weight on Jupiter, Saturn, the moon, or anywhere in the solar system.

"Take a dog and do what, Robbie?" His thoughts these days often grew richer than he could say.

Take him and scan him. Scan his brain while he was really excited. Then people could train on his patterns, and we'd learn what it felt like to be a dog.

I failed to rise above adult condescension. "That's a cool idea. You should tell Dr. Currier."

His scowl was gentle compared to what I deserved. *He'd never listen to me. Which is sad, you know? I mean, think about it, Dad. It could just be a regular part of school. Everyone would have to learn what it felt like to be something else. Think of the problems that would solve!*

I can't remember how I answered him. Three weeks later, I learned that a prominent ecologist at the University of Toronto used parts of my atmospheric models to map how the Earth's own ecosystems might evolve under steadily rising temperatures. Dr. Ellen Coutler and her grad students saw thousands of interconnected species failing in a series of cascading waves. Not a gradual decline: a cliff.

Robbie was right: we needed universal mandatory courses of neural feedback training, like passing the Constitution test or getting a driver's license. The template animal could be a dog or a cat or a bear or even one of my son's beloved birds. Anything that could make us feel what it was like to not be us.

HE DROPPED A GLASS BOWL on the kitchen tiles. It shattered into pieces. One sliver cut his bare heel as he jumped back. A year ago, he would have spun out in tears or rage. Now he simply grabbed his hurt foot and held it in the air. *Oh, snap! Sorry, sorry!* After we washed and bandaged him, he insisted on sweeping up his mess. A year ago, he wouldn't have known where to find the broom.

"Impressive, Robbie. Like you're coming at this whole life thing with a totally different game plan."

He burrowed a slo-mo fist into my soft underbelly and laughed. *Actually? It's kind of like that. Old Robin would be all: Waaah!* He pointed up at the ceiling. *New Robin is up there, looking down on the experiment.*

He tented his hands in front of his lips. It was the funniest gesture, like he was channeling Sherlock Holmes. Like he and I were old dudes, reflecting on the long and winding road that had deposited us in front of a fireplace in the common room of an assisted living facility. *Remember how Chester would tear up a book or pee on the carpet? You couldn't really get mad at him because, he was just a dog, right?*

I waited for him to complete the thought. But it turned out the thought was already complete.

I BROUGHT ROBBIE IN for his last training of the summer. By then the whole lab was in awe of him. Ginny gave Robbie comics and took me down the corridor, out of earshot. She stood shaking her head, not sure how to say what she needed to. "Your son. I just. Love your son."

I grinned. "Me, too."

"He's getting amazing. When he's around, I feel, I don't know . . ." She looked at me, her eyes at a loss. "Like I'm a little more here? He's contagious. A viral vector. We all feel happier when he's here. We all start looking forward to him two days before he comes in." Embarrassed but happy, Ginny backed away and returned to the training.

I watched the session from the control room. Robin had become a virtuoso. His pleasure was proportionate to the ease with which he animated his screen on nothing but thought. He and the AI improvised a duet, each harmonizing with the other. I looked on from the outside, unable to hear a note of the unfolding symphony. Robin's face ran the gamut of squints, scowls, and smirks. He seemed to be chattering with someone in a language that had only two native speakers.

I'd seen this before. Robin was almost seven. He and Alyssa were doing a jigsaw puzzle on a folding card table, under a brass elbow lamp. The pieces were large and their count was low. Aly could have done the whole thing by herself in two minutes. But she was holding back, slowing down, keeping him in the game, making an evening of it. And he repaid her in all the colors of a child's delight. The two of them played off one another, amusing themselves with silly anatomical descriptions of the pieces they were looking for, racing each other to the shrinking pool of candidates. Four months later, Aly would be gone. That evening disappeared with her, until it came back to me unbidden as I watched Robin playing with her all over again.

Currier asked me to join him in his office. I sat across his desk, separated from him by a mound of spiral-bound papers. "Theo, I need to ask a favor."

The man had given me priceless free therapy. He'd turned Robin around and staved off who knows what disasters. Technically, I probably owed him a favor.

Currier toyed with an elaborate Japanese wooden puzzle box that only opened to a long ritual of memorized steps. "We think we might have something viable. A significant treatment modality." I nodded and held still, like Chester when Aly read him poems. "And your son is our most powerful argument. He has always been a high-performing decoder. But now . . ." Currier set down the half-completed puzzle box. "We'd like to start putting the word out."

"You've been publishing all along, haven't you?"

He smiled at me the way my father used to when I swung hard and popped it up. "Sure we have."

"And conferences? Colloquia?"

"Of course. But now we're fighting to keep our funding."

"Tell me about it." After a dozen glory years, astrobiology was going begging. But it surprised me to hear that even Currier's practical science was strapped for cash. I'd never imagined that all research would have to show a profit. But then, I'd also never imagined that the Secretary of Education would cut funding from grade schools that taught evolution.

Currier's eyes asked for forgiveness in advance. "We need to think about technology transfer while we can. This is a technology very worth transferring."

"You want to license it."

"The entire process. As a highly adaptable mode of therapy for multiple psychological disorders."

My son didn't suffer from a *disorder*. "Just tell me the favor."

"We're showing the work at professional gatherings. To journalists and people in private industry. Can we include a clip of him?"

I stumbled on *private industry*. I don't know why. Everything on this planet had been commodified, long before my time. Currier wouldn't meet my eye. The Japanese puzzle box had his full attention. "We can use the videos of the trainings we've been making since the beginning."

I couldn't recall his having mentioned video to me. I must have agreed to it, on some form.

"He'd be anonymized, of course. But we'd like to mention what makes his progress so singular."

Boy learns bliss from his dead mother.

My brain was too slow for the rash of calculations. I believed in science. I wanted Robin to be part of some larger useful thing. I wanted people to see what was happening to him. He might become a virus of well-being, like Ginny said. But this plan of Martin's tripped a warning buzzer.

"That doesn't sound very safe."

"We'd be showing two minutes of pixilated and voice-altered video to researchers and health professionals."

I felt petty and superstitious. Worse: self-serving. Like I'd had the meal and now refused to pay my share of the check. "Can you give me a couple of days?"

"Certainly." He was more relieved than felt right. Perhaps to ingratiate me, he asked, "Does he glow as much at home as he does in the lab?"

"He's been beatific for weeks. I can't remember the last time he had a fit."

"You sound mystified."

"Shouldn't I be?"

"Imagine what he's inhabiting."

"I'd like to do more than imagine."

Currier frowned, not getting me.

"I'd like to train as well." I'd become more and more obsessed with the idea after each of Robin's sessions. I needed access to my dead wife's mind.

Currier's frown turned to an embarrassed grin. "Sorry, Theo. I'm afraid I wouldn't be able to justify the cost of that. Right now we're struggling to pay for the legitimate experiment."

Flustered, I veered away. "I wanted to ask . . . The more Robin trains, the more he resembles Alyssa. The way he taps on his temple and chews on the word *actually* . . . it's eerie. He's learned half the birds Aly knew."

The idea amused him. "I assure you. He can't get that from the training. He can't get anything from her brain print at all except a feel for that one emotional state of hers that he's learning to emulate."

And yet she was teaching him, one way or the other. I didn't insist. I felt like a superstitious hunter-gatherer in a magic cargo cult. Instead, I said, "To tell you the truth, I'm not sure that emotional state really was her."

"Ecstasy? *Not Aly?*"

A spark passed between Martin and me. I read it without any feedback training at all. The man's eyes shied away from mine, and I knew. My whole program of willful ignorance fell apart, revealing the truth beneath a suspicion I'd nursed forever. It wasn't just my own bottomless insecurity: I never knew my wife of a dozen years. She was a planet all her own.

THAT NIGHT, ASTRONOMERS AROUND THE WORLD COLLECTED more information about the universe than all the astronomers in the world collected in my first two years of grad school. Cameras five hundred times larger than the ones I'd trained on swept arcs across the sky. Interstellar consciousness was waking up and evolving eyes.

I sat in front of the large, curved monitor in my study, tapping into oceans of shared planetary data, while my son lay belly-down on the carpet in the other room, browsing his favorite nature sites on his Planetary Exploration Transponder. Around the country, my anxious colleagues were preparing for war. And I was being recruited.

For eight years, I'd crafted worlds and generated living atmospheres, gradually assembling something my fellow astrobiologists called the Byrne Alien Field Guide. It was basically a taxonomic catalog of all kinds of spectroscopic signatures collated to the stages and types of possible extraterrestrial life that might make them. To test my models, I'd looked upon the Earth from far away. I saw our atmosphere as pale, fuzzy pixels of light reflected off the moon. I'd fed those pixels into my simulations, and the black lines written into their spectra checked the validity of my evolving models and helped me tweak them.

But my life's work had entered a holding pattern. Like hundreds of my fellow researchers, I was waiting for data—real-world data from real worlds, *out there*. Humanity had taken its first step toward discovering whether the cosmos was breathing. But that step stalled in midair.

The Kepler scope succeeded beyond all our dreams. It filled space with new planets everywhere it looked. Thousands of its candidate worlds were waiting to be confirmed, without enough researchers to confirm them. We knew now that Earths were common. There were more of them than I'd dared hope, and closer by.

Yet Kepler never saw a single planet straight on. It cast a wide net, watching for the faintest imaginable dimming of suns many parsecs away, and it gathered that light with a precision of a couple of dozen parts per million. Infinitesimal dips in the brightness of stars betrayed invisible planets passing in front of them. It still stupefies me: like seeing a moth crawl across a streetlight from thirty thousand miles away.

But Kepler couldn't give me what I wanted: to *know*, beyond all doubt, that one other world out there was alive. I don't know why it meant so much to me, when it left so many people cold. Not even my wife really cared all that much one way or the other. Robbie did.

To know for certain whether a planet breathed, we needed direct infrared images fine enough to yield detailed spectral fingerprints of their atmospheres. We had the power to get them. For longer than Robin had been alive—longer than Aly and I were together—I'd been one of many researchers planning a space-based telescope that could populate my every model and decide forever whether the universe was barren or alive. The craft we were backing was a hundred times more powerful than Hubble. It made our best existing telescopes look like old men with dark glasses and service dogs.

It was also a wild fling of cash and effort that made no practical difference in the world. It wouldn't enrich the future or cure a single disease or protect anyone from the rising flood of our own craziness. It would simply answer the thing we humans had been asking since we came down from the trees: Was the mind of God inclined toward life, or did we Earthlings have no business being here?

That night, a powwow gathered across the continent, from Boston to San Francisco Bay. Congress was threatening to cut the funding for our Earthlike Planet Seeker. My colleagues had assembled a hasty quorum—a hive-mind, ad-hoc defense of our life work. We teleconferenced—two dozen video windows and as many audio channels, drifting in and out of sync. As each speaker had their say, my screen filled with the face of the frail craft that spoke the words. The man with food stains all over his shirt who couldn't look even a webcam in the eye. The man who peppered every sentence with "in fact." The woman who had practiced nursing for years before becoming one of this world's great planet-hunters. The man who lost his child to an IED in Afghanistan. The man who, like me, started binge-drinking at fourteen, but, unlike me, could not rein it in these days.

—*Don't forget. Congress has twice threatened to pull the plug on the NextGen.*
—*The NextGen is the damn problem! It has been bleeding the budget dry for decades.*

The NextGen Space Telescope was a sore spot with my people. The flagship instrument was now a dozen years late and four billion dollars over budget. We all wanted it, of course. But it was more about cosmology than planet-hunting. And it stole cash from all other projects.

—*There couldn't be a worse time to pursue the Seeker. Did you see the President's tweet?*

We'd all seen it, of course. But the brilliant observer who also happened to be addicted to ethanol felt the need to post it to the text window:

Why are we pouring ever more money into a BOTTOMLESS PIT that will never return a SINGLE CENT on investment??? So-called "Science" should stop inventing facts and charging them to the American People!!

—*He's playing to the xenophobes and isolationists. All the Innies.*

—The Innies have Washington's ear. The country is bored
with astronomy.
—Then we Outies need to go to Washington and make the
case again.

My heart sank as my people made a battle plan. I didn't have another hour to spare for any other cause than the one that was taking all my time. And it wasn't clear to me that a trip to Washington would do a thing. The Seeker was just another proxy battle in the endless American civil war. Our side claimed the discovery of Earths would increase humanity's collective wisdom and empathy. The President's men said that wisdom and empathy were collectivist plots to crash our standard of living.

I turned away from the screen and glanced into the living room. Aly was sitting in her beloved egg chair, swinging her legs, as if it were almost time to have a glass of wine and find a sonnet for Chester. She looked over at me and flashed that startling smile—the small white teeth, the wide, pink gum line. She shook her head, not understanding how I could be so distressed over a conversation of so little consequence. I wanted to ask her if she loved me as much as she loved her dog. I wanted to ask her if that opossum had been worth abandoning her husband and child. But the question that came into my head—does that count for asking, with a ghost?— was even worse. Aly. Is he mine?

On cue, my trained mind reader appeared in the office doorway, brandishing his Planetary Exploration Transponder.

Dad. You won't believe this. Half of Americans think we've already been visited by beings from other worlds.

The conference on my screen broke up in laughter. The man who lost his son to Big Oil called out from across the country. *How would you like to talk to some folks in Washington?*

THE NEXT-DOOR NEIGHBOR CALLED to say that Robin was out behind the house. "He's very still. He's not moving. I think there's something wrong with him."

I wanted to say: *Of course, there's something wrong with him. He's looking at things.* But I thanked her for the information. She was just doing her part in the perpetual neighborhood watch, making sure no one ever travels too far.

I went out into the crepuscular yard to find the offender. He'd gone out in the later afternoon with a box of chalks to sketch the birch, which was still trading in late-summer greens. He took a little canvas stool. I found him sitting in the chill grass and sat down next to him. My jeans were damp in seconds. I forgot that dew forms at night. We only discover it in the morning.

"Let's see." He handed over his pastel hostage. The tree was gray by now, as was his drawing. "I'm going to have to trust you on this one, buddy. I can't see a thing."

His small laugh got lost in the roar of leaves. *Weird, Dad, isn't it? Why does color disappear in the dark?*

I told him the fault was in our eyes, not in the nature of light. He nodded, like he'd reached that conclusion already. His head aimed straight in front of him at the exhaling tree. Off to each side of his face, his hands patted the air for secret compartments.

This is even weirder. The darker it gets, the better I can see out of the sides of my eyes.

I tested; he was right. I vaguely remembered the reason—more rods on the edges of the retina. "That might make a good treasure hunt." He didn't seem interested in anything but the experience itself.

"Robbie? Dr. Currier wants to know if he can show your training videos to other people."

I'd been evading the question for two days. I hated the idea of other people appraising the changes in Robin. I hated Currier for destroying my memories of Aly. Now he had my son.

I lay back on the wet grass. I owed Currier nothing but hostility. And still, I felt an obligation so large I couldn't name it. No good parent would turn his child into a commodity. But ten thousand children with Robin's new eyes might teach us how to live on Earth.

He faced the tree, still experimenting, watching me from the corner of his eye. *What other people?*

"Journalists. Health workers. People who might set up neurofeedback centers around the country."

You mean a business? Or does he want to help people?

My question, exactly.

Because, you know, Dad. He helped me. A lot. And he brought Mom back.

Some large invertebrate in the dirt sank its mandibles into the back of my calf. Robin dug his fingernails into the soil and pulled up ten thousand species of bacteria wrapped in thirty miles of fungal filament in his small hand. He shook out the fistful of dirt and came down on the grass to lie beside me. He propped his head on the pillow of my arm. For a long time, we just looked up at the stars—all the ones we could see and half the ones we couldn't.

Dad. I feel like I'm waking up. Like I'm inside everything. Look where we are! That tree. This grass!

Aly used to claim—to me, to state legislators, to her colleagues and blog followers, to anyone who would listen—that if some small but critical mass of people recovered a sense of kinship, economics would become ecology. We'd want different things. We'd find our meaning *out there.*

I pointed up to my favorite late summer constellation. Before I could name it, Robin said, *Lyra. Some harp thingie?*

It was hard to nod, with my head against the ground. Robin pointed to the far corner of the sky, and moonrise.

You said that light gets from there to here almost instantly, right? That means everybody who looks at the moon is seeing the same thing at the same time. We could use it like a giant light telephone, if we ever get separated.

He was traveling beyond me again. "It sounds like you're okay with Dr. Currier showing people video of you?"

His shrug nudged my bicep. *It's not really my video. It probably belongs to everybody.*

Aly was there, lying with her head against my other arm. I didn't shrug her off. *Smart boy,* she said.

Remember how much Mom loved this tree? For two years he'd been asking me what Aly was like. Now he was reminding me. *She called it the Boardinghouse. She said no one has ever even counted all the kinds of things that live in it.*

I looked to his mother for confirmation, but she was gone. When the first of the year's last fireflies lit up the air a few feet from us, Robin gasped. We held still and watched them flash and blink out. They floated in slow streaks across the summer dark, like the lights of interstellar landing craft from all the planets we'd ever visited, gathered in a mass invasion of our backyard.

I CALLED MARTIN CURRIER. "Use the clip. But his face had better be totally obscured."

"I can promise that."

"And if this comes back to us in any way, I'm holding you personally responsible."

"I understand. Theo. Thank you."

I hung up on him. At least I waited until the line was dead before cursing.

This late in the world's story, everything was marketing. Universities had to build their brands. Every act of charity was forced to beat the drum. Friendships were measured out now in shares and likes and links. Poets and priests, philosophers and fathers of small children: we were all on an endless, flat-out hustle. Of course science had to advertise. Call it my belated graduation from naïveté.

Currier was a dignified salesman, at least. He pitched his results to interested parties without distorting the data. He was clear about the technique's clinical limits while still suggesting the far shores of its possibility. In a world addicted to upgrades, journalists loved his careful hints of a coming golden age.

By October, spots about the Currier Lab began appearing in the popular media. Robin and I watched him on the *Tech Roundup* show. I saw the articles in *New Science*, *Weekly Breakthrough*, and *Psychology Now*. In each venue, he came across as a slightly different person, cutting the carpet to fit the corner store.

Then came the half-page feature in the *Times*. It portrayed Currier as sanguine but circumspect. A picture of him seated next to the machine that had so often scanned Robin's feelings in real time bore the caption: "The brain is a tangled network of networks. We'll never fully map it." The man in the picture rested his chin on his hand.

Throughout the piece, Currier positioned Decoded Neurofeedback as the heir to mainstream psychotherapy, "only much faster and more effective." Solid numbers supported his claims about robustness. He downplayed the emotional telepathy angle. "The best comparison might be to the effects of a powerful work of art." But his guided tour of the technique included just enough to make DecNef feel like the next big thing:

> Well-being is like a virus. One self-assured person at home in this world can infect dozens of others. Wouldn't you like to see an epidemic of infectious well-being?

Pressed by the journalist, Currier claimed, "The critical threshold for such a thing is probably lower than you think."

Alongside the standard deviations and p-values and claims of therapeutic gains, Currier generally mentioned that tantalizing data point out on the end of the curve: a nine-year-old boy who came into the trials a bundle of rage and graduated as a junior Buddha. Sometimes, in Currier's presentations, the boy had lost his mother. Sometimes he wrestled with prior emotional disorders. Sometimes he was just a boy suffering from unspecified "challenges." Then came the video: half a minute of a pixilated Robin talking with experimenters on the day of his first session, forty-five seconds of him training on a screen while inside the tube, and another minute, one year later, of him talking to his beloved Ginny. Seeing the spliced-together clips for the first time, I gasped. My son's posture and carriage, the melody of his voice: like the before-and-after of some experimental immunotherapy. He wasn't the same person. He was barely the same species.

The film was a showstopper wherever Currier presented it. He showed the video to six hundred people at the annual conference of the American Public Health Association. At the reception after the talk, he let slip to a group of therapists the even more remarkable story behind the remarkable video. And that's when Robin's future began to get away from me.

I GAVE HIM A TREASURE HUNT about the Missis-sippi. Imagine you're a drop of water as you made your way from a glacial lake in Minnesota down to Louisiana and the Gulf. What states would you float past? What fish and plants might you see? What sights and sounds would you hear along the way? It seemed innocent enough—homework I might have done myself, thirty years ago. But thirty years ago, it was a different river.

As he often did in those days, Robbie went a little over the top. The treasure hunt turned into a week-long excursion. He drew maps and diagrams, sketches of boats and barges and bridges, whole underwater scenes replete with exotic aquatics. Days in, he appeared alongside my desk in the office, holding out the enameled tablet on which he did his research. *Requesting upgrade to the transponder.*

"What's wrong with it?"

Come on, Dad. You call it Planetary, but it's just a little kiddie browser. It doesn't let me go anywhere.

"Where do you want to go?"

He told me the things he was looking for and how he would find them.

"Fine. Use the 'Theo' sign-in today. But go back to your own account when you're done."

Goodie. You are the greatest. I've always said so. What's the password?

"Your mother's favorite bird. But flying backwards."

His eyes pitied me for choosing such an obvious secret. But he went back to work, ecstatic.

He was subdued at dinner when we both knocked off for the day. I had to draw him out. "How's life on the Mississippi?"

He spooned in some tomato soup from far away. *Not so great, actually.*

"Tell me."

It's pretty bad, Dad. Are you sure you want to know?

"I can handle it."

I don't know where to start. Like, more than half our migrating birds use the river, but they can't because they're losing their habitat. Did you know that? The chemicals that farmers spray on their stuff goes in the river, and that's turning the amphibians into mutants. And all the drugs that people pee and poop down the toilet. The fish are completely doped up. You can't even swim in it anymore! And where it comes out? The mouth? Thousands of square miles of dead zone.

His face made me regret giving him my password. How did real teachers handle this? How did they manage field trips down that river without faking the data or ignoring the obvious? The world had become something no schoolchild should be allowed to discover.

He rested his chin on his arm, on the table. *I didn't actually check this, okay? But other rivers are probably just as bad.*

I came around the table and stood behind his chair. My hands reached down to take his shoulders. He didn't look up.

Do people know this?

"I think so. Mostly."

And they don't fix it because . . . ?

The standard answer—economics—was insane. I'd missed something essential in school. I was still missing something. I stroked the crown of his head. Somewhere beneath my moving fingers were those cells that the training had reshaped. "I don't know what to say, Robin. I wish I knew."

He reached up blindly to clasp my hand. *It's okay, Dad. It's not your fault.*

I was pretty sure he was wrong.

We're just an experiment, right? And you always say, an experiment with a negative result isn't a failed experiment.

"No," I agreed. "You can learn a lot from negative results."

He stood up, full of energy, ready to go finish his project. *Don't worry, Dad. We might not figure it out. But Earth will.*

I TOLD HIM ABOUT THE PLANET MIOS, how it had flourished for a billion years before we came along. The people of Mios built a ship for long-distance, long-duration discovery, filled with intelligent machines. That ship traveled hundreds of parsecs until it found a planet full of raw materials where it landed, set up shop, repaired, and copied itself and all its crew. Then two identical ships set off in different directions for hundreds more parsecs, until they found new planets, where they repeated that whole process again.

For how long? my son asked.

I shrugged. "There was nothing to stop them."

Were they scouting out places to invade or something?

"Maybe."

And they kept dividing? There must have been a million of them!

"Yes," I told him. "Then two million. Then four."

Holy crow! They'd be all over the place!

"Space is big," I said.

Did the ships report back to Mios?

"Yes, even though the messages took longer and longer to arrive. And the ships went on reporting, even after Mios stopped responding."

What happened to Mios?

"The ships never learned."

They kept going, even though Mios was gone?

"They were programmed to."

This gave my son pause. *That's pretty sad.* He sat up in bed and pushed at the air with his hand. *But it might still be okay for them, Dad. Think of what they saw.*

"They saw hydrogen planets and oxygen planets, neon and nitrogen planets, water worlds, silicate, iron, and globes of liquid helium wrapped around trillion-carat diamonds. There were always more planets. Always different ones. For a billion years."

That's a lot, my son said. *Maybe that's enough. Even if Mios was gone.*

"They split and they copied and they spread through the galaxy as if they still had a reason to. One of the great-great-great-great-great-grandchildren of the original ship touched down on a rocky planet with shallow seas, in a small, weird stellar system rotating around a G-type star."

Just say it, Dad. Earth?

"The craft landed on a level plain in the middle of wild, waving, towering structures more complex than anything the crew had seen. These elaborate, fluttering structures reflected light at various frequencies. Many of them sported astonishing forms at their very top that resonated in lower frequencies—"

Wait. Plants? Flowers. You mean the ships are tiny?

I didn't deny it. He seemed equal parts skeptical and fascinated.

Then what?

"The ship's crew studied the gigantic waving green and red and yellow flowers for a long time. But they couldn't figure out what the things were or how they worked. They saw bees fly into the flowers and the flowers track the sun. They saw the flowers wilt and turn into seed. They saw the seeds drop and sprout."

My son held his hand up to stop the story. *It would kill them, Dad, when they figured it out. They would get on the communicator and tell every other ship from Mios in the galaxy to shut down.*

His words gave me gooseflesh. It wasn't the ending that I imagined. "Why do you say that?" I asked.

Because they would see. The flowers were going somewhere, and the ships weren't.

I BROUGHT HIM TO CAMPUS WITH ME on days when I taught. He spread out his books on the desk in my office, and while I lectured or sat on committees, Robin taught himself long division and solved word problems and decoded poems and learned why the trees outside the office window turned carroty and gold. He wasn't studying anymore. He was simply toying with things and enjoying the unfolding.

The grad students loved to tutor him. Checking in after a long October morning seminar, I caught Viv Britten, who was working on the small-scale crisis inherent in the Lambda-CDM model of the universe, sitting across the desk from my son, holding her head.

"Boss. Have you ever considered what is going on inside a leaf? I mean, really thought about it? It's a total mind-fuck."

Robin sat smirking at the havoc he'd unleashed. *Hey! Curse word!*

"What?" Viv said. "I said *freak*. It's a total mind-freak, what you're telling me."

It was all that, and more. The green Earth was on a roll, assembling the atmosphere, making more shapes for itself than it could ever need. And Robin was taking notes.

We were down on the shores of the lake over lunch, fish-spotting. Robbie had discovered that polarized sunglasses let him see into a whole new alien world beneath the mirroring surface. We were looking, hypnotized, at a school of three-inch intelligences when someone called, four feet from my shoulder.

"Theodore Byrne?"

A woman my age stood clutching a brushed-silver computer to her chest. She wore a fair amount of turquoise hardware, and the folds of her gray tunic fell over skinny jeans. Her controlled contralto voice seemed baffled by her own boldness.

"I'm sorry. Have we met?"

Her smile hung between embarrassed and amused. She turned

to my son, who, in a favorite animist ritual, was patting the almond butter sandwich he was about to eat. "You must be Robin!"

A flush of premonition warmed my neck. Before I could ask her business, Robin said, *You remind me of my mom.*

The woman looked sideways at Robin and laughed. Alyssa's and my ancestors had come from Africa, too, only from somewhat further back. She turned to me again. "I'm sorry to intrude like this. Would you have a moment?"

I wanted to ask: *A moment for what, exactly?* But my son, trained up on ecstasy, said, *We got a million moments. Right now we're on fish time.*

She handed me a business card spattered with fonts and colors. "I'm Dee Ramey, a producer for *Ova Nova.*"

The channel had several hundred thousand subscribers, with individual videos topping out at a million views. I'd never watched a minute of it, but I still knew what it did.

Dee Ramey turned to Robin. "I saw you in Professor Currier's training clips. You're amazing."

"Who told you about us?" I couldn't keep the anger out of my voice.

"We did our homework."

The penny dropped. For a guy who'd grown up on science fiction, I'd been amazingly naïve about what artificial intelligence, facial recognition, cross-filtering, common sense, and a quick dip into the planet's aggregate brain could do. At last I freed myself of stupid civility. "What do you want?"

My rudeness to a stranger shocked Robin. He kept patting his sandwich, too hard and fast. Ova Nova, *Dad. They did that story about the guy who let the botfly hatch under the skin in his shoulder?*

Dee Ramey shouted, "Wow, you watch us!"

Just the ones about how cool the world is.

"Well! We think what's happening to you is one of the coolest things we've seen."

Robin looked to me for explanation. I looked back. Realization spread across his face. Influencers wanted him for the perfect three-minute episode, one that could earn a million thumbs from strangers across the globe: *Boy Lives Again, Inside His Dead Mother's Brain*. Or maybe it was the other way around.

LIFE ASSEMBLES ITSELF on accumulating mistakes. By the time Dee Ramey showed up with plans to turn my son into a show, I'd lost count of how many parenting errors I'd already made.

Robin thought it would be fun, to become an episode alongside all of Earth's other strange inhabitants. He put his case to me over ice cream, hours after I sent Dee Ramey packing. *Honestly, Dad, think about it. I was super-miserable for so long. And now I'm not. People might like to know about that. And it'll be educational. You're all about education, Dad. Besides, it's a cool show.*

Two days later, Dee Ramey called me. "You don't understand my son," I told her. "He's . . . unusual. I can't have him turned into a public spectacle."

"He won't be a spectacle. He'll be a subject of legitimate interest, respectfully treated. You can be there as we film. We'll avoid anything that makes you uncomfortable."

"I'm sorry. He's a special child. He needs protection."

"I understand. But you should know that we're going to make the film, whether or not you want to take part. We'll be free to use all the materials already available, in whatever way that makes sense to us. Or you can participate and have a say in things."

Smartphones are miracles, and they've turned us into gods. But in one simple respect, they're primitive: you can't slam down the receiver.

My son was still technically anonymous. But what the *Ova Nova* researchers had discovered, others could soon find out. I'd made a mistake, and doing nothing now would only make it worse. At least I could still try to manage the way the story went public. Two days later, when my anger subsided, I called Dee Ramey back.

"I need a say in the final edit."

"We can give you that."

"You are not allowed to use his real name or say anything that would make him easier to identify."

"That's fine."

My son was a troubled boy, hurt by seeing what the sleepwalking world could not. An offbeat therapy had made him a little happier. Maybe showing him on camera being himself could beat whatever sensationalism Ova Nova might create out of Currier's clips and sales talks.

Robin sat curled under my arm on the living room sofa and explained it to me, on a night when we decided to stay home on Earth. *Like Dr. Currier says. Maybe it could be useful.*

I DIDN'T GRASP WHAT WAS HAPPENING TO ROBIN until I saw the rough cut. In the video, his name is Jay. He comes into the frame, and the shot begins to breathe. He turns to look at the ducks and the gray squirrels and the lindens along the lake, and his gaze turns them into aliens for the camera to reappraise.

Next, he's lying in the fMRI tube in Currier's lab, moving shapes around on his screen with his mind. His face is round and open but a little devilish, pleased with his skill. Dee Ramey, in voice-over, explains how Jay is learning to match another set of frozen feelings laid down years before. But her explanation is beside the point. He's a child, in the full grip of creation.

Then he's sitting across from Dee Ramey, on a bench under a spreading willow. She asks: "But how does it feel?"

His nose and mouth twitch a little. His excited hands twist with explanation. *You know how when you sing a good song with people you like? And people are singing all different notes, but they sound good together?*

The journalist looks sad for half a moment. Maybe she's thinking how long it has been since she sang with her friends. "Does it feel like talking to your mother?"

His brows pinch; he doesn't quite like the question. *Nobody's saying anything out loud, if that's what you mean.*

"But you can feel her? You can tell it's her?"

He shrugs. Vintage Robin. *It's us.*

"You feel like she's there with you? When you train?"

Robin's head swivels on the stalk of his neck. He's looking at something way too big to tell her. He reaches one hand above his head to catch the lowest branches of the willow and let it slip back through his fingers. *She's here right now.*

The video blinks first and cuts away.

THEY WALK ALONG THE LAKESHORE. Jay lifts one hand to the small of her back, as if he's a doctor breaking news that's delicate but not disastrous. She says, "You must have been hurting so much."

I want to scream at her, every time. But he's paying attention to the world, not her question.

"When did the hurt start? When your mother passed, or before?"

He frowns at that word *passed*. But he figures it out on the fly. *My mother didn't pass. She died.*

Dee Ramey stutter-steps and stops. Maybe his words stun her into listening. Maybe they excite her, their weirdness promising a couple thousand more thumbs-up. Maybe I'm being cruel.

"But you've learned to match the patterns of her brain activity. So now that part of her is inside you, right?"

He smiles and shakes his head, but not in disagreement. He knows now that no grown-up gets it. He holds out his hands to the grass and sky and oaks and lindens lining the lake. Paws up in the crisp air, he waves them to include our distant invisible neighborhood, the university, the houses of friends, the Capitol, and states beyond our state. *Everybody's inside everyone.*

The video cuts to clips from early in his training. It's a different boy, hunched in a scooped plastic chair, evading a questioner in diffident monotones. He bites his lip and snarls at small setbacks. The world is out to punish him. Then footage of him painting, blissed out on line and color. I've watched the video more times than I can count. I'm responsible for a thousand of the clip's hits all by myself. But seeing the two boys side by side still stuns me.

Then he and Dee Ramey are by the lake again. "You seemed so hurt and angry."

A lot of people are hurt and angry.

"But you're not, anymore?"

He giggles, a wild contrast to the boy in Currier's clips. *No. Not anymore.*

On a bench under the trees, Dee Ramey holds one of his notebooks in her lap, turning pages. He's explaining the drawings. *That's an annelid. Incredible, you gotta admit. That is a brittle star. These things? They're water bears. Also known as tardigrades. They can survive in outer space. Serious. They could float to Mars.*

Cut to a medium shot, and he takes her down a footpath to show her something. The camera pulls in for a close-up: a patch of plants whose round-toothed leaves bead all over with tiny globes from that morning's rain. He points to the pods of fruit still hanging from its branches. *Go like this around one. Careful! Don't brush it!*

It's like he's telling a joke and can barely conceal the punch line. Dee squeals in amazement when the touch of her cupped hands makes the pod pop. She opens to look: weird green coils lie exploded on her palm. "Wow! What is *that*?"

Crazy, right? Jewelweed. You can eat the seeds!

He picks through the detonated, steampunk curls and extracts a pale green pill. Dee Ramey mugs for the camera—"I hope you're right"—and pops it in her mouth. She looks surprised. "Mm. Nutty!"

I don't remember ever teaching my son about that plant. I do remember the day I learned about it from the woman who became his mother. The years since then lie like shrapnel in my open hand.

In the video, my son never mentions the plant's other name: touch-me-not. All he says is, *Lots of good eats out here, if you know where to look.*

EVERYBODY'S BROKEN, he tells her. They sit on the beach on an upside-down kayak and watch the single low sun throw colors. Two boats in full sail skim alongside one another, back to the docks before the light is gone.

That's why we're breaking the whole planet.

"We're breaking it?"

And pretending we aren't, like you just did. The shame in her face shows up only in freeze-frame. *Everybody knows what's happening. But we all look away.*

She waits for him to elaborate. To say what's wrong with people and what might cure them.

He says, *I wish I had my sunglasses.*

She laughs. "Why?"

He points toward the lake. *There's fish in there! We could see them, with sunglasses. Have you ever seen a northern pike?*

"I don't know."

His face clouds over with incomprehension. *You would know. You'd know, if you saw a pike.*

A couple with two small kids walk the beach near them. Jay greets them with enthusiasm. He's forgotten the camera crew. His arms spin around the compass points in pleasure. The parents smile as he points out three kinds of ducks and imitates their calls. He tells them about daphnia and other water crustaceans. He shows them how to find sand fleas. The little boy and girl hang on his words.

Dusk falls in time-lapse. The show's theme music starts up, far away. Jay and his new best friend sit on their upturned boat. The lights of the city blink on in a ring around them. He says, *My dad's an astrobiologist. He's looking for life up there. It's either nowhere, or it's all over the place. Which do you want it to be?*

She looks up, where he's pointing, into the dark sky. Her expression wobbles, as if she's training to match the pattern of a feeling her mouth and eyes refuse to recognize. Maybe she's thinking about how she's going to violate her promise to me by keeping those last few words of his in the finished video. They're just too good to be lost to something so small as ethics.

Dee Ramey speaks over the shot of her upward stare. "Most of us think we're the only ones out here. But not Jay."

The shot reverses, and it's Robbie again, gazing at her with the same indiscriminate love he felt for everyone, in that narrow run of days. His face seems lit from the inside. She looks back down at him, a crumpled smile at dusk. Her later self goes on talking while the one on the screen stays mute.

"To spend time with Jay is to see kin everywhere, to take part in a giant experiment that doesn't end with you, and to feel loved from beyond the grave. I, for one, would love to hear that feedback."

But Robin has the last word. *Serious*, he says, smiling up at her in pure encouragement. *Which do you think would be cooler?*

CURRIER CALLED a week after *Ova Nova* posted the video. His voice skidded around the emotional color wheel. "Your boy's viral."

"What are you talking about? What happened?" I thought some brain infection had shown up on one of Robbie's scans.

"We've gotten inquiries from half a dozen companies on three different continents. That's not counting all the individuals who want to sign up for the training."

I considered and rejected all kinds of replies. At last I landed on, "I truly hate you."

There was a silence, more thoughtful than awkward. Then Currier must have decided I was just being rhetorical. He set to work as if I'd said nothing, filling me in on all that had happened in the last few days.

Ova Nova had dropped the video as part of a bundle called "The World Is Ending Again. What Now?" They launched the suite with a sweeping social media campaign. Other outfits picked up the news, if only to meet their own daily quota of announcements. Robbie's video caught the rapidly strobing attention of an influencer. This woman had her own lucrative video channel where she went around the world helping people get rid of things they never really wanted. Countless people around the globe were addicted to her tough love, and two and a half million of those people counted themselves as her friends. The influencer posted a link with an image of Robbie holding his hands together around a jewelweed pod. Her caption read:

IF YOU HAVEN'T PUT YOUR HEART THROUGH A
GOOD MANGLE YET THIS MORNING, TRY THIS.

The influencer followed up the invitation with several enigmatic emojis. All kinds of other influencers and non-influencers started to repost her post, and the resulting streaming jam caused the *Ova*

Nova servers to choke for an hour. Nothing built more interest in free content than the supply briefly running out.

According to Currier, the hip flooded in on Tuesday and Wednesday. Thursday and Friday, the mainstream arrived, and the late-to-the-party showed up over the weekend. Apparently, someone ripped the video and uploaded it to a pair of archive sites. Somebody else trimmed out a clip of Robin and ran it through a filter, making his eerie words sound even eerier. People were using it on message boards, in chats and text, at the bottom of their mail signatures . . .

I held the phone with one hand and poked a search into my tablet with the other. Three common words, in quotes, and there Robbie was, looking and sounding like a visitor from a galaxy far, far away.

"Shit."

Laughter trickled from Robbie's room. *I heard that!*

"What do you suggest I do about this? What am I supposed to tell him?"

"Theo. The thing is, we're also hearing from journalists."

Which meant they'd be on my front stoop in another few heartbeats. "No," I said, almost spitting. "No more. I'm done with this. We're not talking to anyone else."

"That's fine. I'd advise you not to, in fact."

Currier sounded almost composed. But then, he stood to profit massively from the flash fad. Robin did not.

I couldn't tell how much trouble we were in. Maybe the whole viral thing would blow over as quickly as it had blown up. Most of the people who were thumbing the clip and passing it along probably didn't even bother watching it all the way through. It was just a bit of weather, and there would be several more clips to thumb and pass along before the day was out.

But while Currier told me not to worry, mass cascades of error-correcting bits surged in waves of electromagnetic radiation around the planet's surface. They blasted in vertical geysers 35,786 kilometers upward into space and rained back down at 300 million meters per second. They coursed in bundles of parallel light through fiber conduits only to fan out in bursts of radio across the open air at the whim of tens of millions of grazing fingers coaxing electrons from hundreds of millions of spots on capacitive touch screens a few inches high. Robin's streams were the slightest blip in the race's desperate search for mass diversion. As a fraction of the feed produced and consumed that day, a few hundred billion bits of information were like a single pip on the surface of a strawberry at the end of an eight-course dinner. But these bits were my son, and, reassembled, they held the record of his face on a late afternoon by the side of a lake telling a perfect stranger, *Everybody's inside everyone*.

Currier said, "Let's stay calm and see how this plays out."

Hanging up on him got easier with practice.

COG CAME TO MADISON. They'd been through before, but not for a few years. Back then, they filmed my elevator pitch about using absorption lines in the light passing through a planet's atmosphere to detect life from a quadrillion miles away. Since then, COG had gone from being the poetry slam of academic lectures to becoming the chief way that most of the world learned about scientific research.

Every COG talk was delivered to a live audience in less than five minutes. The highest user-rated filmlets in the COG Madison site bubbled up to a site called COG Wisconsin. The tops in COG Wisconsin percolated up into COG Midwest, then COG U.S., and finally the coveted COG World Class. Only viewers who made it through a whole minute of a given clip could vote on it. The voters themselves climbed leaderboards for giving out the most evaluations. In this way, knowledge democratized and sciences went crowdsourced and bite-sized. My own talk topped out at COG Wisconsin, held back from the regional round by thousands of users furious that I could talk about the universe without ever mentioning God.

The organizers for COG MAD 2 sent me an email. I skimmed the first few lines and shot back my regrets, reminding them I'd taken part the last time. Two minutes later, I got a follow-up, clarifying the email I'd rushed through too quickly. They weren't recruiting me. They wanted Robin Byrne to make a cameo in a talk by Martin Currier on Decoded Neurofeedback.

I was furious. I ran a quarter mile across campus to Currier's lab. Luckily, the trot left me too winded to attack him when I found him in his office. I did manage to shout, "You stupid shit. We had a deal."

Currier flinched but held his ground. "I have no idea what you're talking about."

"You gave COG my son's identity."

"I did no such thing. I never even talked to them!" He pulled out his phone and punched up his email. "Ah. Here they are. They want to know if I would like to join your son onstage."

The penny dropped for both of us. COG had come straight to me. They had done nothing more than what Dee Ramey and *Ova Nova* had already done. Discovering the real Jay was now trivial, with so much to go on. My boy was outed. So many ships had sailed.

My hands were shaking. I picked up a logic toy from his desk—a wooden bird you were supposed to free from a nest made of a dozen sliding wooden pieces. The only problem was that nothing wanted to slide. "He has become public property."

"Yes," Currier said. For him, it was almost apology. He watched my face, psychologist by training. I was busy proving to my own satisfaction that the bird's nest was broken and couldn't be solved. "But he has given a lot of people hope. People are moved by this story."

"People are moved by gangster films and three-chord songs and commercials for cell phone plans." I was getting worked up again. Panic did that to me. Currier just studied me, waiting, until I opened my mouth and words came out. "I'll ask Robin. None of us gets to decide this for him."

Currier frowned but nodded. Something in me appalled him, and for good reason. I felt as if I were my own son, about to turn ten, seeing through adulthood for the first time.

ROBIN WAS THOUGHTFUL but cautious. *Do they want me, or do they really want Jay?*

"They definitely want you."

Cool. But what do I have to do?

"You don't have to do anything. You don't even have to say yes if you don't want to."

They want me to talk about the training and Mom's brain and stuff?

"Dr. Currier would describe all that, before you went on."

So what am I supposed to do?

"Just be yourself." The words turned meaningless in my mouth.

His eyes got that faraway look. My timid boy, who spent years avoiding contact with strangers, was calculating how much fun it might be to spill the secret of life to the general public from the lip of a large stage.

A week before the event, I started to decompensate. I regretted letting him agree to anything. If he bombed, it could scar him for life. If he crushed it, he'd climb up the ladder of COG regions and be loved by ten times more people than loved him now. Both possibilities made me ill.

The evening before the event, after Robin finished the day's last math packet, he came to me in my study, where I sat behind a stack of ungraded undergrad exams, vigorously doing nothing. He walked around behind my chair and put his hands on my trapezius. Then he called out the commands I used to get him to relax, back in the day. *Jelly up!*

I let my body go limp.

Jam tight!

I tensed again. We did a few rounds before he came around to sit sidesaddle on the arm of the chair. *Dad. Chill! It's all good. I mean, it's not like I have to make a speech or anything.*

The moment he went to bed, I called the local COG organizer—a Trotsky-looking guy Martin and I dealt with. "I have one more stipulation. After you film the talk, if I'm not happy, you don't post it."

"That's up to Dr. Currier."

"Well, I need veto rights."

"I don't think that's possible."

"Then I don't think my son is going onstage tomorrow."

Funny how you can always win negotiations you're not crazy about winning.

THREE HUNDRED PEOPLE filled the auditorium, with folks still drifting in as the morning's presenters finished. Fifteen minutes before showtime, the three of us went backstage. A techie wired up Currier and Robin and walked them through their marks.

"You'll see a red clock down on the front of the stage. At four minutes and forty-five seconds . . ." The tech drew his index finger across his throat and gurgled. Marty nodded. Robbie laughed. I wanted to puke on the floorboards.

I didn't realize the talk was under way until Currier was standing center stage in the audience applause. I held my arm around Robin, as if he might dash onstage if I let go. The tech stood on his other side, brandishing a handheld monitor and whispering into a headset boom.

Currier sounded fresh, given how often he'd pitched his research in public. He still talked about the work as if the results mystified him. He took fifty seconds to describe neurofeedback, another forty to explain the fMRI and AI software, and half a minute to summarize the effects. Minute three went to the clips of Robin. The audience was audibly impressed. So was my son, seeing them again, standing next to me in the wings of a dark, packed theater. *Geez. That's what happened to me?*

Minute four brought the reveal. Currier dropped it as if it were just another data point: the same mother whose death sent the boy into a downward spiral has returned to nurse his spirit into health. Robin twitched, under my arm. I looked down at the compact planet next to me, whose shoulder I was clasping too hard. But he was grinning, as if the boy saved from that downward spiral fascinated him.

In his last half minute alone onstage, Currier succumbed to interpretation. "We've barely glimpsed the potential of these techniques. Only the future will reveal their full possibilities. Meanwhile, imagine a world where one person's anger is soothed by another's calm, where your private fears are assuaged by a stranger's courage, and where pain can be trained away, as easily as taking piano lessons. We could learn to live here, on Earth, without fear. Now please say hello to a friend of mine. Mr. Robin Byrne."

The diminutive figure next to me shrugged off my arm and was gone. I held on to the back of my neck as he crossed the stage. He looked so small. I once saw a child his size play Mozart's Piano Concerto No. 8 at Merkin Hall in New York. The girl's hands barely stretched a fifth. I don't know how she did it, or why her parents let her. I felt the same confusion now. My son had become a tiny prodigy on his own instrument. The audience clapped wildly as Robin trotted to the floodlit center stage. There, he stabbed a hand across his front and bowed deeply from the waist. The clapping and laughter grew.

I've watched the film so often my memory is convinced I was out in the darkened hall. Currier must have thought that Robin would smile and wave, then the two of them would say goodbye. But they still had a long and fluid minute left.

The whole auditorium wants him to ask: *What's it like? How does it feel? Is it still her?* But Currier veers off into another place. He asks, "What's the biggest difference between when you started the training and now?"

Robin rubs his mouth and nose. He takes too long to answer. You can see Currier's confidence waver and hear the audience grow restive. *You mean in real life?*

The words slip through his teeth with a little lisp. The audience titters. Currier has no idea where Robin is going. But before he can get things back on the rails, my son declares, *Nothing!*

The audience laughs again, though not comfortably. The question irritates Robin. Something in those two syllables says: You know what's happening. Everyone knows, despite the code of silence. This endless gift of a place is going away. But his right wrist rotates oddly, down by his thigh, a gesture that none of the hundreds of thousands of viewers but me knows how to interpret.

Just that I'm not scared anymore. I'm all mixed into a really huge thing. That's the coolest part.

Currier gestures toward the audience, who break into applause. He puts a hand on Robin's head. My son's mother's lover. With ten seconds left, the talk ends.

ON NITHAR, WE WERE ALMOST BLIND. Of our ten major senses, sight was the weakest. But we didn't need to see much, aside from trickles of glowing bacteria. Our several well-spaced ears could hear in something like color, and we sensed our surroundings with extreme precision through the pressures on our skin. We tasted small changes across great distances. The different tempos of our eight different hearts made us exquisitely sensitive to time. Thermal gradients and magnetic fields told us where we needed to be. We spoke with radio waves.

Our agriculture, literature, music, sports, and visual arts rivaled those on Earth. But our great intelligence and peaceful culture never hit upon combustion or printing or metalworking or electricity or anything like advanced industry. On Nithar, there was molten magma, combusting magnesium, and other kinds of burning. But there was no fire.

Cool, my son said. *I'm going to explore.*

I told him not to go too far from the surface, especially the vents. But he was young, and the young suffered most from Nithar's biggest challenge. A planet where the word *forever* was the same as the word *never* was hard on its youth.

He came back from a too-brief adventure upward. He was crushed. *There's nothing up there but heaven,* he complained. *And heaven is as hard as rock.*

He wanted to know what was above the sky. I didn't laugh at him, but I was no help. He asked around and got mocked mercilessly by both his generation and mine. That's when he vowed to drill.

I didn't try to talk him out of it. I figured he could toy at the project for a few million macro-beats, and that would be the end of it.

He used the sharp tip of long, straight, heated nautiloid shell. The work was grindingly dull. It took many millions of heartbeats for his hole to reach the depth of one outstretched tentacle. But rubble dropped from on high, and that made for the first novelty on Nithar in almost never. The Hole became the butt of jokes, the object of suspicions, and the rite of new religious cults. Generations came and went, watching his infinitesimal progress. My son drilled on, with all the time in this world on his hands before bedtime.

Tens of thousands of lifetimes in, he struck air. And in one great rush of understanding, a revolution so great that nothing on Nithar survived it, my son discovered *ice* and *crust* and *water* and *atmosphere* and *starlight* and *trapped* and *eternity* and *elsewhere*.

ROBIN WAS BESIDE HIMSELF, about our trip to Washington. I was going there to help save the search for life in the universe. My most devoted full-time student was coming along for the ride.

I'm gonna make something for the trip, okay?

He wouldn't tell me what. But as Robin's legal teacher, I was always looking out for anything better than the grim social studies materials I found online. (*How Do I Save Money? What Is Profit? I Need a Job!*) A civics field trip to Our Nation's Capital, with homemade show-and-tell, seemed just the thing.

He made me wait in the car while he went into the art supply store with his life savings. He came out a few minutes later clasping a bag to his chest. When we got home, he squirreled away his covert treasures in his room and got to work. A sign appeared on his door. His balloon-letter writing had grown more playful, more like Aly's with each new feedback session:

WORK ZONE

NO VISITORS ALLOWED

I had no clue what he was up to, other than that it involved a roll of eighteen-inch-wide white butcher paper too bulky to hide. My questions succeeded only in eliciting stern warnings not to pry. So the two of us prepared for our joint field trip. While my son worked on his secret project, I polished the testimony I would present to the congressional Independent Review Panel.

The panel was tasked with making a simple recommendation: answer the world's oldest and deepest unanswered question or walk away. Dozens of my colleagues were testifying on behalf of NASA's proposed Earthlike Planet Seeker mission, over several days. Our job was simple: save the telescope from the ax of the Appropriations subcommittee, and make a world that would be able, in a few more years, to look into nearby space and see life.

The party in power was not inclined to hunt for other Earths. The heads of the review panel threatened to add our Planet Seeker to a growing graveyard of NASA cancellations. But scientists across three continents were giving up the pretense of detached objectivity and making the case for exploration, every way we knew how. That's how the son of a con man, a kid who went by the nickname Mad Dog and got his start in life cleaning out septic tanks, found himself on a plane to D.C., testifying for the most powerful pair of spectacles ever made. And my son was coming with, bringing his own campaign.

HE HUSTLED DOWN THE AISLE IN FRONT OF
ME, beaming and greeting all the passengers. He chided me as
I put his bag in the overhead bin. *Careful, Dad! Don't crush it!*
Robbie wanted the window. He watched the baggage loaders and
ground crew as if they were building the pyramids. He gripped my
hand during takeoff but was fine once we were airborne. During
the flight, he charmed the attendants and told the businessman on
my right about "a few good nonprofits" he might want to consider
supporting.

We had to change in Chicago. Robin sketched people in the gate
area and gave them their portraits as gifts. Three kids across the
concourse whispered to each other and pointed, as if they'd never
seen a living video meme before.

He was better with takeoff the second time. As we broke down
through the clouds in our final approach, he shouted over the
engines, *Holy crap! Washington Monument! Just like in the book!*

The rows near us laughed. I pointed over his shoulder. "There's
the White House."

He answered in hushed tones. *Wow. So beautiful!*

"Three branches of government," I quizzed.

He held out his finger, fencing with me. *Executive, legislative,
and . . . the one with the judges.*

We saw the Capitol from the cab on our way to the hotel. He was
awed. *What will you tell them?*

I showed him my prepared comments. "They'll ask questions, too."

What kind of questions?

"Oh, they might ask anything. Why the Seeker cost keeps going
up. What we hope to discover. Why we can't discover life some
cheaper way. What difference it would make if it never got built."

Robin gazed out the window of the cab, marveling at the mon-
uments. The cab slowed as we entered Georgetown and neared the

hotel. Robbie sat in a cloud of preoccupation, trying to solve my political crisis. I straightened his hair, like Aly used to do when the three of us were heading out into public. I felt us traveling on a small craft, piloting through the capital city of the reigning global superpower on the coast of the third largest continent of a smallish, rocky world near the inner rim of the habitable zone of a G-type dwarf star that lay a quarter of the way out to the edge of a dense, large, barred, spiral galaxy that drifted through a thinly spread local cluster in the dead center of the entire universe.

We pulled into the hotel's circular drive and the cabbie said, "Here we are. Comfort Inn."

I FED MY CARD INTO THE CAB'S READER and credits poured out from a server farm nestled in the melting tundra of northern Sweden into the cabbie's virtual hands. Robbie got out, retrieved his bag from the trunk, gazed at the very modest chain hotel, and gave a deep, appreciative whistle. *Holy crow. We are living like kings.* He wouldn't let the doorman take his bag. *It's got stuff in it!*

He whistled again in the very plain room on the ninth floor overlooking the Potomac. His civics lesson stretched out in radial boulevards below. He put his hand to the window and gazed at all the possibilities. *Let's go!*

We never made it past the Bone Hall on the second floor of the Museum of Natural History. The parade of skeletons hooked Robin by the brain stem and wouldn't let him go. He stood with his sketchbook in front of the case of perciform fishes, lavishing attention on the turn and taper of every rib. I couldn't stop staring at him from across the hall. In his loosened windbreaker and baggy jeans, he looked like an elder of one of those tiny, superannuated, wayfaring races that have been making records for billions of years, curating an account of a planet that had once thrived brilliantly but vanished without a trace.

We found a restaurant that served herbivores and walked back to the hotel. Up in our room, he grew earnest again. He sat on the edge of his bed with his hands folded in front of his face. *Dad? I wanted to wait until tomorrow to show you, but I should probably just show you now?*

Crossing to his luggage, he extracted the roll of butcher paper, a little crumpled from the journey. He set it on the floor at the foot of the beds, placed a pillow on one curled end, and unrolled. The banner was longer than the two of us stretched end to end. And it was covered in paints, markers, and inks of all colors. Down the length of it ran the words:

He had filled the scroll with bright, bold design. It seemed another thing he'd learned directly from Aly, who worked on a canvas too large for me to see. Creatures ringed the letters, as though drawn by a hand more mature than his. Stands of staghorn coral were bleaching white. Birds and mammals fled a burning forest. Ten-inch-long honeybees lay on their backs along the bottom of the banner, legs up and little X's in their eyes.

That's supposed to be pollinator decline. You think people will get that?

I couldn't say. I couldn't even talk. But then, he wasn't really waiting for my answer.

You can't depress people, though. That just scares them. You gotta show them the good life.

He lifted one end of the banner and told me to grab the other. We flipped the whole scroll over. If the first side was hell, this was the peaceable kingdom. This time the words filled the banner's middle, one row above the other:

MAY ALL BEINGS BE

FREE FROM SUFFERING

Creatures crowded in on either side: feathered and fur-covered, spiny, star-shaped, lobed and finned, bulky or sleek and streamlined, bilateral, branching, radial, rhizomatic creatures, known and unknown, creatures in the wildest array of colors and forms, all deployed between the deep green forest and the ocean blue. The sessions with Aly's brain print had made his painting more luminous, freed up his hand and eye.

He looked down at the work from above, picturing how it should have been. *I didn't know how to spell* sentient.

"You could have asked me."

But then you'd know.

"Robbie. This is better."

You think? Be honest, Dad. I only want honesty.

"Robbie. I'm telling you."

He looked down, squinting. He shook his head. *If people only knew, you know? We're all bajillionaires.* He held his hands out in front of him, as if they were full of germ plasm and treasure.

"What do you want to do with it?"

Oh, yeah. I thought, after you're done talking to the panel, that you and me could hold this up outside somewhere, with cool buildings in the background, and we could get somebody to take pictures. Then we could upload them using my name for the tags, and when people search for that freaking clip of me, they'd see this instead.

We rolled up the scroll and got ready for bed. In the dark, the hotel room glittered with dozens of LEDs of obscure purpose. Propped up in our twin beds, we might have been in the command center of a warp-drive exploratory vessel, tethered for a moment at a watering hole somewhere along an endless surveying mission.

My son's voice tested the dark. *So those people? Are they for real?*

"Which people, buddy?"

All those people who linked to my clip?

His voice was tinted with scientific doubt. My heart sank and my head revved. "What about them?"

How many of them were just laughing at me?

The room hummed at half a dozen different frequencies. Every reply seemed gutless. I took too long, and he had his answer. "People, Robbie. They're a questionable species."

He thought about this. He weighed what it meant to become a public commodity. His face soured.

"Robbie. I am so sorry. I made a big mistake."

But against the light from the window, I saw him shake his head. *No, Dad. It's all good. Don't worry. You remember the signal?*

He made it in the pool of light, twisting his cupped hand back and forth on the stalk of his broomstick arm. He'd taught me the code once, months ago, on another Earth—his invented hand sign for All Is Good.

You know how people sometimes worry: Is that person mad at me? Well, if anyone's ever wondering, I'm good with the whole world.

THE BREAKFAST BUFFET THRILLED HIM. He piled up more oat squares, blueberry muffins, and avocado toast than any creature his size should have been able to eat in a day. His lips oozed chocolate hazelnut butter as he talked. *Greatest field trip ever. And it hasn't even started!*

We planned to walk on the Mall that morning, before I testified. We talked a bit about what to see. He wanted to return to the Museum of Natural History. *To see the plants. Dad? Almost nobody knows this, but plants do pretty much all the work. Everybody else is just a parasite.*

"You are correct, sir!"

I mean, eating light? That's crazy stuff! Better than SF! His face darkened. *So why does science fiction think they're so scary?*

Before I could answer, a woman twice my age, short, avian, with eyeglasses like shop goggles, appeared at the end of our booth. "I'm sorry to intrude on your breakfast," she said, looking at Robin. "But are you . . . that boy? The one in that beautiful video?"

Before I could ask her what she wanted, he broke into a smile. *It's possible, actually.*

The woman stepped back. "I knew it. There's something about you. You're really something!"

Everybody's something, he said. The echo of the viral clip made them both laugh.

She turned to me. "Is he your son? He's really something."

"He is."

She backed away from my curtness, her words a mess of apology and thanks. When she was out of earshot, Robin gaped at me. *Geez, Dad. She was being nice. You didn't have to be mean to her.*

I wanted my son back. The one who knew that large bipeds were not to be trusted.

THE REVIEW PANEL MET in the Rayburn House Office Building, across the street from the Capitol. Robin dawdled, agog with patriotism. I tugged at him to get us to the appointed spot on time. The room was cavernous, wood-paneled, and draped with flags. Long, tiered ranks of leather-padded chairs faced a raised platform with a heavy wooden table measured out by nameplates and plastic water bottles. In the back were side tables full of coffee and nibbles.

We were late getting through security and arrived in a room filled with colleagues from around the country. A couple of them remembered Robin from when he gate-crashed the teleconference. More than a few teased Robin or asked if he was presenting. *I bet I could convince them,* he said.

The meeting started. I sat Robbie next to me. "Settle in, bud. Lunch is a long way off." He held up his sketchbook, his pastels, and a graphic novel about a boy who learns how to breathe underwater. He was fully provisioned.

The dais filled with politicians who looked like yesterday's America. They called on a NASA engineer to start things off with the latest plan for the Planet Seeker. It would settle in somewhere near the orbit of Jupiter before deploying its massive, self-assembling mirror. Then a second instrument, the Occulter, flying several thousand miles away, would position itself in the precise spot to blot out the light from individual stars so our Seeker could see their planets. The engineer demonstrated. "Like holding up your hand to block a flashlight, so you can see who's holding it."

Even to me, it sounded crazy. The first question came from the representative of a district in West Texas. His drawl sounded sculpted for public consumption. "So you're saying the Seeker part alone will be every bit as complex as the NextGen telescope, even before adding in the flying lampshade? And we can't even get the damn NextGen off the ground!" The engineer demurred, but the congressman rode over him. "The NextGen is decades overdue and billions over budget. How are you possibly going to make something twice as complicated work for the amount you're asking?"

The questions went downhill from there. Two more engineers tried to undo the damage and restore confidence. One of them pretty much imploded. The morning threatened to end before it began. Robbie had worked away for hours, barely fidgeting. Honestly, I forgot he was there. When we surfaced for lunch, he was holding up a painted page for my approval: another planet, as if seen through the Seeker, its disk swirling with the turbulent blue-green-white whose only possible cause was life.

The image was brilliant. I wanted to work it into my slide deck. We had an hour. First I steered us through the line for the catered box lunches. There were ones marked *Vegan* and ones marked *Altairian*. "You're supposed to laugh," I told my son.

I'm too Sirius.

"I see you've read the *Astronomer's Joke Book*."

I got a Big Bang out of it.

We holed up in a corner. While Robbie ate, I laid his lush painting on the floor, snapped it with my phone, mailed a copy through the air to my laptop computer, cropped and edited, then inserted it at the end of the virtual carousel I would project to a room full of people that afternoon. None of the science fiction I grew up on could have predicted such magic.

After lunch came several scientists whose work required something like the Seeker. I spoke third. I reached the stand just as the room was sliding into blood-sugar doldrums. I talked about how no other method could match direct optical imaging for finding life. I showed our best existing photo of an exoplanet—little more than a grayish blur. Even that was impressive, given that my graduate thesis advisor once assured me we'd never live to see one.

My next slide was a bit of theater: a best-guess digital simulation of what that planet would look like through the occulted eyes of the Seeker. The room gasped, as if Congress said Let There be Light and the universe obliged. I pointed out that a picture that good, with all its data, could reveal whether the planet was inhabited. I finished by showing Robbie's painting while quoting Sagan: *We make our world significant by the courage of our questions and the depth of our answers.*

Then I braced for less-than-courageous questions. The rep from West Texas came out shooting. "Can your atmospheric models tell the difference between a world with interesting life and a world that's nothing but germs?"

I said that a distant planet filled with bacteria would rival the most interesting thing ever discovered.

"Could you tell if a planet had intelligent life?"

I tried, in twenty seconds, to say how that might be done.

"And what are the odds of that?"

I wanted to hedge, but it wouldn't have helped. "No one thinks that is especially likely."

Disappointment everywhere. Another congressman asked, "Can you do your work with the NextGen, if it ever launches?"

I explained why even that magnificent instrument wasn't enough to peer directly at atmospheres. A superannuated congressman from Montana lumped the two telescopes together. "What if all these pricey toys tell us that the most interesting beings in the entire universe could have put their billions of dollars to better use right here, on the most interesting planet anywhere?"

I knew then why these men wanted to kill this project. The cost overruns were just an excuse. The country's ruling party would have opposed the Seeker even if it were free. Finding other Earths was a globalist plot deserving the Tower of Babel treatment. If we academic elites found that life arose all over, it wouldn't say much for humanity's Special Relationship with God.

I stepped down from the podium feeling like shit. Weaving my way back to my seat through a narrowing iris of light-headedness, I heard my son exclaim, *Dad! That was great!* I hid my face from him.

Afterward, we lingered in the hall outside the hearing room. I postmortemed the battlefield with my colleagues. Some were still sanguine. Others had abandoned hope. A terse alpha from Berkeley suggested I might have done better with more statistics and less child art. But one of this world's great planet hunters fussed over Robbie until he reddened. "You're so beautiful!" she told him. And to me: "You're lucky. I can't understand why my boys love *Star Wars* more than they love the stars."

WE WALKED DOWN INDEPENDENCE. Robbie took my hand. *I thought you did great, Dad. What do you think?*

My thoughts weren't fit for young ears. "Humans, Robbie."

Humans, he agreed. He smiled to himself, then lifted his gaze to the bronze *Statue of Freedom* at the top of the Capitol dome. *Do you think any aliens have found a better system than democracy?*

"Well, *better* probably looks different on different planets."

He nodded, forwarding the memory to us in the future. *Everything looks different on different planets. That's why we need to find them.*

"I wish I'd said that, back there."

He held his arms out to embrace the Capitol. *Look at this place. The mother ship!*

We followed one of the winding footpaths through the green. Robin nudged us toward the steps. My heart sank when I realized what he had in mind. The butcher-paper banner stuck out of his backpack like a space suit antenna.

Here's a good spot, right?

The difference between fear and excitement must be only a few neurons wide. Just then, one of the NASA engineers from the morning session came down the path. I waved to the man and said, "Let's do this, Robbie!" We'd be finished in a minute or two, and at least one of us would have a victory to take back home.

While Robbie retrieved the banner, the engineer and I exchanged a guarded postmortem of the day's hearing. "It's just theater," he said. "Of course they'll fund us. They're not cavemen."

I asked if he'd mind taking a picture or two of me and my son. Robin and I unfurled his masterpiece. A slight breeze wanted to take the banner from our hands. *Dad! Careful!* We tugged, and the banner stretched to full length. It billowed like the jib of a space probe filled with solar wind. In the full afternoon light, I saw details in his creatures that I'd failed to see in the hotel room.

The engineer was all enthusiasm and crooked teeth. "Hey! You *made* that? That's just great. If I'd been able to draw like that, I'd never have started with the ham radio."

I gave him my cell phone, and he took several shots from different angles and distances in the changing light. A boy, his father, the dying birds and beasts, the insect apocalypse along the banner's bottom, the background mosaic of sandstone, limestone, and marble dedicated to freedom and built by slaves: the engineer wanted to get it exactly right. Another pair of astronomers from the day's meeting saw us from a distance. They came over to admire the banner and instruct the engineer on how to take a photo. The engineer flipped my phone over to show Robbie the lenses. "We came up with digital cameras at NASA. I helped build the billion-dollar camera that we lost in orbit around Mars."

One of the astronomers held his head. "*We're* the ones who forced you NASA goons to put a camera on that thing in the first place!"

Ordinary civilians and civics tourists stopped, attracted by Robbie's scroll and the three old men happily shouting at each other. A woman my mother's age fussed over Robbie. "You made this? You did all this all by yourself?"

Nobody does anything by themselves. Something Aly used to tell him, back when Robin was little. I don't know how he remembered it.

We spun the banner around. The onlookers cheered the other side. They hemmed in to see the lush details. The aerospace engineer buzzed around, backing people off so he could take a fresh round of pictures. A shout came from a few yards down the pavement. "I *knew* it!" Somewhere in the billion revolving worlds of social media, a girl in her late teens must have seen posts of a weird little boy chirping his odd little birdsong. Now the teen milled about in this ad-hoc camp meeting, thumbing her phone through a trail of bread crumb bits back to the *Ova Nova* videocast. "That's Jay! That's the boy they wired up to his dead mom!"

Robin didn't hear. He was busy talking to two middle-aged women about how we could re-inhabit planet Earth. He was joking and telling stories. The girl who recognized him must have started a text chain, because minutes later other teens drifted in from the east end of the Mall. Somebody pulled a ukulele out of his back-pack. They sang "Big Yellow Taxi." They sang "What a Wonder-ful World." People were snapping and posting things with their phones. They shared snacks and improvised a picnic. Robin was in heaven. He and I stood holding the banner, occasionally hand-ing it off to four teens who wanted a turn. It was like something his mother might have tried to organize. It may have been the happiest moment of his life.

I was so caught up in the festivities that I didn't notice two offi-cers of the U.S. Capitol Police pull up on First Street Northwest and get out of their squad car. The teens began to heckle them. *We're just enjoying ourselves. Go arrest the real criminals!*

Robin and I lowered the banner to the pavement so I could talk to the officers. Two teens picked it up and began swirling it around like they were kite surfing. That didn't lower the temperature of the situation. Robin threaded the gap, trying to make peace between his supporters and the officers. His chest came up to their gun belts.

The senior officer's nameplate read SERGEANT JUFFERS. His badge number was a palindromic prime. "You don't have a permit for this," he said.

I shrugged. I probably shouldn't have. "We're not demonstrat-ing. We just wanted to take a picture of ourselves in front of the Capitol, with the banner my son made."

Sergeant Juffers looked at Robin. His eyes narrowed at the com-plication to law and order. No doubt it had been as long a day for him as it had for me. Things weren't good in Washington; I should have remembered that. Bullying was trickling down. "It's unlawful to crowd, obstruct, or incommode the entrance of any public building."

I glanced over to the entrance of the Capitol. I would have been hard-pressed to throw a baseball that far. I should have let it go. But he was being stupid about a thing that had given my son such hope. "That's not really what we're doing."

"Or to crowd, obstruct, or incommode the use of any street or sidewalk. Or to continue or resume the crowding, obstructing, or incommoding after being instructed by a law enforcement officer to cease."

I gave him my Wisconsin driver's license. He and his partner, whose plate read PFC FAGIN, retreated to their vehicle. The last time I was caught breaking the law was in high school, shoplifting wine from a convenience store. Since then, not even a speeding ticket. But here I was, encouraging a small boy to take issue with the destruction of life on Earth. It was not socially acceptable behavior.

In five minutes, the two of them had all the information about me and Robin anyone could use. All facts, instantly available, to anyone. In fact, they didn't need a single bit of additional data to know which side of the civil war Robin and I were on. The banner told them that.

It was not in my son's lesson about the separation of powers, but the Capitol Police fall under the responsibility of Congress and not the President. But all such distinctions had been disappearing over the last four years. Congress itself now took orders from the White House, and the appointed judges had fallen in line. A steady destruction of norms—favored by less than half the country—had united the branches of government under the President's vision. The laws did not say so, but these two policemen now answered to him.

The officers left their vehicle and waded back toward our cluster of people. As they approached, the two teens holding the banner began spinning rings around the officers. Juffers spun in place. "We're going to ask you to disperse now."

"This problem won't disperse," one of the banner-holders said.

But most of the gatherers had maxed out their political will and were drifting away. Juffers and Fagin came at the banner-holders, who let go of Robin's artwork and fled. The banner blew limp across the pavement. Robin and I chased it. There's still a crease and footprint where I stepped on it to keep it from blowing away. It's right over the painting of what must be a pangolin.

The officers watched as we smoothed, dusted off, and rolled the banner in the stiff wind. *You're probably sad right now*, Robin said to Juffers. *It's kind of a sad time to be alive.*

"Keep rolling," Sergeant Juffers said. "Let's go."

Robin stopped. I stopped with him. *If the insects die, we won't be able to grow food.*

Officer Fagin tried to take the banner, to finish rolling and wrap up the show. The move startled Robin. He clutched his artwork to his chest. Fagin, defied by something so small, grappled Robin's wrist. I dropped my end of the banner and screamed, "Do *not* touch my son!" Both men squared off against me, and I got myself arrested.

THEY CUFFED ME IN FRONT OF HIM. Then they tucked us into the sealed backseat of their cruiser for the four-block ride to USCP headquarters. Robin looked on as I got fingerprinted. His face glowed with a mix of horror and wonder. They charged me with violating D.C. Criminal Code Section 22-1307. My options weren't great. I could get a court date and make another trip all the way back to Washington. Or I could admit to the obstructing and incommoding, pay the three hundred and forty dollars plus all administrative costs, and be done with it. *Nolo contendere*, really. After all, I'd broken the law.

We walked back to the hotel in the dark. Robin was all over me. He couldn't stop smirking. *Dad. I can't believe you did that. You stood up for the ol' Life Force!* I showed him my blackened fingertips. He loved it. *You've got a record now. Criminal!*

"And that's funny . . . how?"

He took my wrist the way Fagin had tried to take his. He tugged me to a halt on the sidewalk alongside Constitution Avenue. *Your wife loves you. I know it for a fact.*

THE NEXT MORNING GOT US as far as Chicago. ORD was in a state of heightened security not safe enough to communicate to the public. Armed guards with Kevlar breastplates and canine sniffers worked their way up the concourse as we made our way to our gate. I had to keep Robin from petting the dogs.

The gate was a cocktail of jet fuel and stress pheromones. What we used to call freak weather was creating a cascade of delays and cancellations. Our connector to Madison was running late. We sat in front of a suite of four TVs, each tuned to a different band of the ideological spectrum. The moderate-liberal screen reported more drone-delivered poisonings in the Upper Plains states. The conservative-centrist one covered a private mercenary force deployed on the southern border. I pulled out my phone and attacked the two-day backlog of work. Robin sat people-watching, his face a study in wonder.

Every time I glanced up at the gate board, our flight slipped another fifteen minutes. Someone on the gate crew was ripping the Band-Aid off as slowly as possible.

Alerts rippled through every phone in the gate area. A text from the new National Notification Service flashed across everyone's screens. The message was from the President, emboldened these last two months by a series of unopposed executive orders.

> America, have a look at today's ECONOMIC numbers! Absolutely INCREDULOUS! Together, we will stop the LIES, SILENCE the nay-sayers, and DEFEAT defeatism!!!

I muted the phone and returned to work. Robbie sketched. I thought he was drawing people in the gate area. But when I looked again, his figures turned into radiolarians and mollusks and echinoderms, creatures that made Earth seem like a crazy 1950s issue of *Astounding Stories*.

I worked, ignoring the fidgeting in the chair to my left. A substantial woman, her head on a swivel, was berating her phone. "Is something going on out there?"

Her phone answered in the sassy voice of a young actress. "Here are today's best events in the Chicago, Illinois, area!"

The woman caught my eye. I looked away, at the bank of television monitors: a cloud of acrylonitrile vapor several kilometers long was spreading through the Ruhr. Nineteen people had died and hundreds were hospitalized. A small paw clasped my forearm. Robin regarded me, bug-eyed.

Dad? Know how the training is rewiring my brain? His wave included all the craziness of the concourse. *This is what's wiring everybody else.*

The woman to my left spoke again. "There's something they're not telling us. Not even the machines know what's going on." I didn't know if she was talking to me or her digital assistant. Everyone else around us was bowed and tapping, lost in their pocket universes.

A voice came over the PA. "Ladies and gentlemen in the boarding area. We've been informed that no flights will be leaving this airport for at least two more hours."

A shout rose from the seats around us—a thwarted creature ready to strike. The woman to my left held her phone level in front of her, as if about to eat an open-face sandwich. "They just said we're in a no-fly. Yeah. Total no-fly."

Another voice came over the PA, one so homogenous it must have been synthesized. "Passengers in need of unanticipated accommodation should apply at the service counter to enter a hotel discount voucher lottery."

Robin tapped my calf with his toe. *Are we going to get home tonight?*

My reply was lost in shouts from down the concourse. I told Robbie to sit tight, then headed toward the commotion. A frustrated passenger three gates down had jabbed a ticket agent in the hand with his phone stylus. I returned to our seats, where the substantial woman was telling her phone, "It's a cover-up, right? It's those HUE people. Am I right? It goes deeper than you think."

I wanted to warn her that it was no longer legal to say certain things in public.

Robin eyed the gate, humming to himself. I leaned in. The song was "High Hopes." High apple pie in the sky hopes. Aly used to sing it to him in his infancy, while bathing him.

WE MANAGED TO MAKE IT HOME. Robbie went in for the neurofeedback session he'd missed, and I put out a rash of fires. A few days later, he took me birding. Holding still and looking had become his favorite activity in all the world. Naturally, he assumed it would bring out the best in me, too. It didn't. I held still. I looked. All I could see were the dozens of outings my wife had asked me on, before giving up and going birding with someone else.

We went to a preserve fifteen miles out of town. We came to a confluence of lake, meadow, and trees. *Right here*, Robin declared. *They love edges. They love to fly back and forth from one world to another.*

We sat in tall grass by a boulder, making ourselves small. The day was crystalline. We shared Aly's old pair of Swiss binocs. Robbie was less interested in spotting individual birds than he was in listening to the calls fill the ocean of air. I didn't realize how many kinds of calls there were until my son pointed them out. I heard a song, wildly exotic. "Whoa. What's that?"

His mouth opened. *Serious? You don't know? That's your favorite bird.*

There were jays and cardinals, a pair of nuthatches and a tufted titmouse. He even identified a sharp-shinned hawk. Something flashed by, yellow, white, and black. I reached for Aly's binoculars, but the prize was gone before I got them up to my eyes. "Did you see what it was?"

But Robin was tuned in to other thoughts, receiving them over the air on some unassigned frequency. He gauged the horizon, immobile for a long time. At last he said, *I think I might know where everybody is.*

It took me a while to remember: The question he'd latched onto so long ago, on a starry night in the Smokies. The Fermi paradox. "Then hand them over peacefully, buddy. No questions asked."

Remember how you said there might be a big roadblock somewhere?

"The Great Filter. That's what we call it."

Like, maybe there's a Great Filter right at the beginning, when molecules turn into living things. Or it might be when you first evolve a cell, or when cells learn to come together. Or maybe the first brain.

"Lots of bottlenecks."

I was just thinking. We've been looking and listening for sixty years.

"The absence of evidence is not the evidence of absence."

I know. But maybe the Great Filter isn't behind us. Maybe it's ahead of us.

And maybe we were just now hitting it. Wild, violent, and godlike consciousness, lots and lots of consciousness, exponential and exploding consciousness, leveraged up by machines and multiplied by the billions: power too precarious to last long.

Because otherwise . . . How old did you say the universe is?

"Fourteen billion years."

Because otherwise, they'd be here. All over. Right?

His hands waved in every direction. They froze when something primordial signed the air. Robbie saw them first, still mere specks: a family of sandhill cranes, three of them, flying southward in loose formation toward winter quarters that the young one had not yet seen. They were late leaving. But the whole autumn was weeks late, as late as next spring would be early to arrive.

They drew near along a liquid thread. Their wings, gray shawls trimmed in black, arched and fell. The long dark tips of their primary feathers flexed like spectral fingers. They flew outstretched, an arrow from beak to claws. And in the middle, between the slender necks and legs, came a bulge of body that seemed too bulky to get airborne, even with all the pumping of those great wings.

The sound came again, and Robbie grabbed my arm. First one, then another, then all three birds unspooled a chilling chord. They came so close we could see the splashes of red across the bulbs of their heads.

Dinosaurs, Dad.

The birds passed over us. Robbie held still and watched them wing away to nothing. He seemed frightened and small, unsure how he got here on the edge of woods, water, and sky. At last his fingers loosened their grip on my wrist. *How would we ever know aliens? We can't even know birds.*

WE SAW SIMILIS FROM A LONG WAY AWAY. It was a ball of perfect indigo, glinting with the light of the nearby star it captured.

What's that? my son asked. *People must have made that.*

"It's a solar cell."

A solar cell that covers the whole planet? Crazy!

We made a few rotations around the globe, confirming him. Similis was a world trying to capture every photon of energy that fell on it.

That's suicide, Dad. If they hog all the energy, how do they grow their food?

"Maybe food is something else, on Similis."

We went for a look, down to the planet's surface. It was as dark as Nithar, but much colder, and silent aside from a steady background hum, which we followed. There were lakes and oceans, all frozen under thick ice. We passed underneath scattered, blasted snags that must have been thick forests once. There were fields of nothing, and grassless pastures of slag and rock. The roads were abandoned, the towns and cities empty. But no sign of destruction or violence. Everything had fallen into decay slowly, on its own. The world looked as if all the residents had walked out and been taken into the sky. But the sky was covered in solar panels, pumping out electrons at full tilt.

We followed the hum down into a valley. There we found the only buildings still intact, a vast industrial barracks guarded and repaired by ever-vigilant robots. Great conduits of cabling channeled all the energy captured by the solar shell into the sprawling complex.

Who built this?

"The inhabitants of Similis."

What is it?

"It's a computer server farm."

What happened to everyone, Dad? Where did the people go?

"They're all inside."

My son frowned and tried to picture: a building of circuitry, infinitely bigger on the inside than on the outside. Rich, unlimited, endless, and inventive civilizations—millennia of hope and fear and adventure and desire—dying and resurrecting, saving and reloading, going on forever, until the power failed.

FOR HIS TENTH BIRTHDAY, the boy who once could not be roused in the morning without wailing like a howler monkey brought me breakfast in bed: fruit compote, toast, and pecan cheese, all artfully arranged on a platter accompanied by a painted bouquet of mums.

Get up, dude. I'm training today. And I have so much homework to do before we go. Thanks to you!

He wanted to walk to Currier's lab. The lab was four miles from our house, a two-hour walk in each direction. I wasn't crazy about spending half a day on the adventure, but that was all the birthday present he wanted.

Maples blazed orange against the sky's deep blue. Robbie took his smallest sketchbook. He held it in the crook of his arm, scribbling into it as we walked. He slowed down for the most banal things. An ant mound. A gray squirrel. An oak leaf on the sidewalk with veins as red as licorice. He and his mother had left me far behind, Earthbound. I needed a moment alone with Aly myself, to visit that ecstasy whose source she never revealed to me. Currier had turned me down for the training once before. But this morning felt like ultimatum time.

Despite my constant prodding, we got to the lab ten minutes late. I came in the door apologizing. Ginny and a pair of lab assistants were huddled in conversation. They broke off, startled to see us. Ginny shook her head, distressed. "I'm so sorry, guys. We need to cancel for today. I should have called."

I couldn't tell what was up. But before I could press her, Currier appeared from the back hallway. "Theo. Can we talk?"

We headed to his office. Ginny snagged Robin by the shoulder. "Want to check out the sea slugs?" Robin lit up, and she led him away.

I'd never seen Martin Currier move so slowly. He waved for me to sit. He remained standing, hovering near the window. "We've been put on hold. The Office for Human Research Protections sent an interdiction letter last night."

My first thought was for my son's safety. "Is there a problem with the technique?"

Currier swung to face me. "Aside from how promising it is?" He waved an apology and composed himself. "We've been told to halt all further experiments funded in whole or part by Health and Human Services, pending a review for possible violations of human subject protection."

"Wait. HHS? That doesn't happen."

His mouth soured again at my quaint objection. He crossed to his desk and sat. He pecked at his keyboard. A moment later, he read from the screen. " 'There is concern that your procedures may be violating the integrity, autonomy, and sanctity of your research subjects.' "

"*Sanctity?*"

He shrugged. It made no sense. DecNef was a simple, self-modulating therapy showing good results. Labs across the country were conducting far dodgier trials. More drastic experiments were being run inside the bodies of hundreds of thousands of kids every day. But someone in Washington was keen to enforce the new human protection guidelines.

"The government doesn't arbitrarily shut down reasonable science. Did you do something to alienate someone in power?"

Currier inhaled, and it dawned on me. *He* hadn't done anything. My meme of a son had. The elections were coming, and the parties were neck-and-neck. In a single gesture, designed to make the news, agents of the chaos-seeking administration had played to the Human Sanctity Crusade, slapped down the environmental movement, pissed on science, saved taxpayer money, thrown red meat to the base, and shut down a novel threat to commodity culture.

Marty held my gaze—a neural feedback all its own. He was

having as much trouble with the idea as I was. The law of parsimony demanded a simpler explanation. But neither of us had one. He pushed his rolling chair away from the computer and massaged his face with both hands. "Needless to say, this kills any chance of licensing the technique. If I were a paranoid person . . ." He was paranoid enough to leave the thought unfinished.

"What will you do?"

"Comply with the investigators and make my case to the appeals board. What else *can* I do? Maybe it'll turn out to be a short-lived nuisance."

"And in the meantime . . . ?"

He looked at me askance. "You want to know what will happen to him, without any more treatments."

It shamed me, but he was right. The trap evolution shaped for us: the entire species might have been on the line, and I'd still worry first about my son.

"The honest answer is: We don't know. We have fifty-six subjects pursuing some form of feedback. They're all going to be yanked violently out of their training. We're in uncharted waters. There's no data for what happens next." He looked around his office, the inspirational posters and 3-D brain teasers. "With luck, he has achieved permanent orbit. Maybe he'll keep making gains on his own. But DecNef could be like any other kind of exercise. When you stop working out, the health gains degrade and you regress back toward your body's set point. Life is a machine for homeostasis."

"What do I do if there are changes?"

He seemed to want to ask a favor, scientist to scientist. "I'd ask you to keep bringing him in for evaluation if I could. But I can't, until this investigation is over."

"Clear," I said. Although nothing was.

ROBIN WAS PHILOSOPHICAL, WALKING HOME. *It's still the experiment, right? Whatever happens, we'll learn something interesting.*

I wasn't sure if he was consoling me or educating me in the scientific method. I couldn't concentrate. I was thinking of all the legitimate scientific research that might be shut down between now and Election Day, on no better grounds than political caprice. We were, as Marty said, in uncharted waters.

"It's temporary. They're just on hold for a while."

Do they think the training is dangerous or something?

The maples were too orange. My mail notification sounded. I could smell winter on the air, two thousand miles and three days away. Robbie tugged at my sleeve.

This isn't because of Washington, is it?

"Oh, no, Robbie. Of course not."

He twitched at the tone in my voice. My mail bell dinged again. Robbie stopped in place on the sidewalk and said the strangest thing. *Dad? If you went to sea or to war . . . if something happened to you? If you had to die? I would just hold still and think of how your hands move when you walk, and then you'd still be here.*

After dinner, he asked me to quiz him with flash cards of state flowers. Before bed, he entertained me with tales from a planet where a day lasted only an hour, but an hour lasted longer than a year. And years had different lengths. Time sped up and slowed down, depending on your latitude. Some old people were younger than young people. Things that happened long ago were sometimes closer than yesterday. Everything was so confusing that people gave up on keeping time and made do with Now. It was a good world. I'm glad he made that one.

He shocked me by kissing me good night, on the mouth, the way he always insisted on when he was six. *Trust me, Dad. I'm a hundred percent good. We can keep the training going by ourselves. You and me.*

THAT FIRST TUESDAY IN NOVEMBER, online conspiracy theories, compromised ballots, and bands of armed poll protesters undermined the integrity of the vote in six different battleground states. The country slid into three days of chaos. On Saturday, the President declared the entire election invalid. He ordered a repeat, claiming it would require at least three more months to secure and implement. Half the electorate revolted against the plan. The other half was gung-ho for a retry. Where suspicion was total and facts were settled with the like button, there was no other way forward but to do over.

I wondered how I might explain the crisis to an anthropologist from Promixa Centauri. In this place, with such a species, trapped in such technologies, even a simple head count grew impossible. Only pure bewilderment kept us from civil war.

I FOUND HIM IN THE BACKYARD on a too-warm, late autumn day, drawing into a notebook as if his colored pencil were a scalpel. He jerked when my shadow fell across the grass in front of him, and he rushed the notebook shut. His stealth surprised me. He switched to his math problems worksheets—two-digit multiplication—and slipped the incriminating notebook under his folded legs as if it might disappear back into the grass and soil.

The last thing I wanted was to ransack his private thoughts again. But given the situation, it felt wise to have a look. I waited three days, until Robbie took an afternoon bike ride down to the railroad tracks to look for migrating monarchs on the last milk-weeds. Then I combed through his bookcase and his bedroom's prime hiding spots until I found the book. In between his field notes was a two-page splash of lines and colors. The painting looked like a child's Kandinsky. It had that rush of modernist excitement shared by a generation of artists about to go up in flames. Underneath, he'd written, in a small, shaky hand: *Remember what she feels like! You can remember!!!*

ON MONDAY MORNING I had to go into his bedroom to rouse him for breakfast. I'd made his favorite tofu scramble, but when I tried to tickle him awake, he shouted at me. His own volume startled him. *Dad! I'm sorry. I'm really tired. I didn't sleep so good.*

"Was it too warm in here?"

He closed his eyes, watching some remnant animation on the inside of his lids. *There weren't any more birds. That's what happened. In my dream.*

He rallied and got up. We had breakfast and enjoyed a reasonable day, although his homework, as always now, took longer than before. We played bocce in the park and he won. Coming home, we saw an eagle take a mourning dove, and though Robbie flinched at the sight of the tearing beak, he still drew it from memory when we got back to the house.

I'd fallen so behind in my teaching that I was in danger of having my tenure revoked. But after dinner I took him by the shoulders and said, "How do you want to spend the evening? Name your galaxy."

He knew his answer. With one admonitory finger, he commanded me to sit on the couch. He poured me a glass of pomegranate juice—the closest thing to wine available—and went to the bookshelf to retrieve a beaten-up anthology. He put it in my hands.

Read me Chester's favorite poem. I laughed. He kicked my shins. *Serious.*

"I'm not sure which one was his favorite. Should I read you your mom's?"

He didn't even bother to shrug—just a flick of his small hands. I read him Yeats's "A Prayer for My Daughter." Maybe it wasn't Aly's favorite. Maybe it was just the one I remember her reading to me. It's a long poem. It was long for me back then, in my thirties. For Robin, it must have felt geological. But he sat still for it. He still had some concentration left. I was tempted to skip to the end, but I didn't want him to discover, twenty years later, that I'd cheated him.

I was fine until stanza nine. That one had some long pauses in it, as I read.

> Considering that, all hatred driven hence,
> The soul recovers radical innocence
> And learns at last that it is self-delighting,
> Self-appeasing, self-affrighting,
> And that its own sweet will is Heaven's will;
> She can, though every face should scowl
> And every windy quarter howl
> Or every bellows burst, be happy still.

Robin sat still for the whole long trip. He didn't even twitch until I finished. Even then, he stayed curled against my flank. In that clear soprano voice, he said, *I didn't get it, Dad. Chester probably got more of it than I did.*

I had promised him months ago that we'd talk about getting another dog. Nothing had kept me from following through but selfish cowardice. I nudged him with my flank. "We still need to get you a birthday present, Robbie. Should we look for a new Chester?"

I thought the words would galvanize him. He didn't even lift his head. *Maybe, Dad. It might help.*

THE FIRST MELTDOWN CAME as we were driving back from the shoe store at the mall. We were six blocks from home, on the edge of our quiet neighborhood, when I hit a squirrel. The thing about squirrels is that they think the car is a predator. Natural selection has shaped them to evade pursuers by cutting back and running right into you, as you carry straight on down the street.

The thing threw itself under my wheels with a fur-muffled thump. Robin swung around to stare at the sentient being in the road behind us. I saw it, too, in the rearview mirror, a lump on the asphalt. My son screamed. In the closed car, the sound turned wild, long and bloodcurdling, and it converged on the word *Dad*.

He undid his seat belt and opened the passenger door. I screamed, too, and grabbed his left arm to keep him from stepping out of the moving car. I rolled to a stop on the side of the residential street. He was still howling, tearing against my grip and trying to jump out. I held him until he stopped struggling. But the end of the struggle was not the end of his howls. He calmed down enough to light into me again.

You killed it! You freaking killed it!

I told him it was an accident, that everything had happened too fast for me to make any choice at all. I apologized. Nothing made any difference.

You didn't even slow down! You didn't even . . . Mom died instead of killing an opossum, and you didn't even take your foot off the gas!

I tried to stroke his hair, but he shoved me away. He turned to look out the back window. "Robbie," I said. But he wouldn't look away from the lump in the street. I asked him to say something, to tell me what he was feeling. But he held his face into his hands. There was nothing to do but start the car and head home.

There, he headed straight to his room. At dinner, I knocked. He opened the door a crack and asked if he could skip the meal. I said he could eat in his room if he wanted. I loaded up a bowl with fried apples, which he loved. But when I went in at seven-thirty, the bowl was untouched. He was lying in bed in his plaid pajamas, with the lights out and his hands behind his head.

"Would you like a planet?"

No, thanks. I have one.

I sat in my study and pretended to work. A reasonable hour for sleep took forever to arrive. I woke from a nightmare with a tiny hand clamped around my wrist. Robin was standing by my bed. In the dark, I couldn't read him. *Dad. I'm going backwards. I can feel it.*

I lay there, dumb with sleep. He had to spell it out.

Like the mouse, Dad. Like Algernon.

IN THE SHORTENING DAYS, I worked to keep Robin at his lessons. He liked me to sit and do them with him. But the moment I turned to my own work, he lapsed into a trance.

He and I made it through the equinox, and harder still, the holidays. I lied to Aly's family, telling them that we were celebrating somewhere else. By mutual agreement, the two of us spent the week alone. We snowshoed through the blanketed cornfields just outside of town. Robbie made ornaments for the tree from sketches cut out of his field notes. On New Year's, all he wanted was to play endless games of Concentration with the Songbirds of the Eastern U.S. playing cards that he'd gotten me for a Christmas present. He was asleep by eight.

Throughout January, he slipped in small steps from color back to black-and-white. In early February, I gave him a one-week break from classes, apropos of nothing. He needed it. He began playing his farm game again on the computer, after months away. He was touchy when I told him to give it a break. Before the week was over, he wanted to get back to his school assignments. He didn't have the focus to sit more than half an hour at a shot, but he was desperate to learn something. I knew I would have to bring him to a doctor if this went on much longer.

Give me a treasure hunt, Dad. Anything.

"How much of that butcher paper roll do you have left from Washington?"

He made a face. *Don't remind me about Washington. I got you in trouble.*

"Robin! Stop."

I got Dr. Currier's whole experiment shut down. And now you see what's happening!

"That's not true. I talked to Dr. Currier two days ago. There's a chance the lab will be up and running soon."

How soon?

"I don't know. Maybe by summer." In that moment, it didn't feel like a lie. And it made him sit up like an alerted prairie dog. *I'd tell it again.*

The thought of a reprieve seemed to give him strength. Just imagining doing the training again was almost as good as doing it. Somewhere in the universe, there are creatures for whom that's always so. He picked at his shoelaces, stilled by contrition. He told his shoes, *There's a bunch of that roll left.*

In fact, he had about ten feet. We trimmed a foot off one end. "Nine feet. Perfect. Roll it out in the living room."

For real? He took some persuading. He rolled out a paper path through the middle of the room.

"All right. Nine feet, for four and a half billion years. That's half a billion years per foot. Let's make a timeline."

He rallied a little and held up a finger. He went to his room and returned with a basket of pens and brushes. Then we both got down on the floor and went to work. I penciled in the major waypoints: the end of the Hadean, one foot into our scroll. Immediately after that, the start of life. Robbie penned in those first microbes, hundreds of colored specks you almost needed a magnifying glass to see. He filled the next four feet with a rainbow of cells.

Five feet in, I marked the moment when competition gave way to networking and complex cells swarmed the Earth. Robbie's cells swelled a bit and gained a little texture. For two more feet, his forms unfolded into worms and jellyfish, seaweed and sponges. When I finally stopped him that night, he was himself again.

That's a good day, he declared, as I tucked him in.

"Agreed."

And we haven't even gotten to the big stuff yet.

He was out in the living room when I woke the next morning,

adding, refining, touching up, and waiting for me to mark the start of the main event. I penciled it in—the Cambrian explosion, just over a foot from the end of the scroll.

Dad, there's no room left. And everything's just starting. We need wider paper.

His arms flung outward, then dropped to his side. Enthusiasm and distress had become the same thing. I left him to it and took up my own delinquent modeling. All morning long he stayed at it. A parade of giant creatures fanned out across the width of the paper. He ate lunch on the floor, perched over his growing masterpiece. He stood and stepped back, mouth wide with pride and ire. A moment of study from above, and he dropped back down into the thick of things.

All that afternoon, we worked alongside each other. I checked in once or twice, but his immense journey was flowing along at full tilt, and the last thing Robbie wanted was help from anyone. At five, cross-eyed from too much coding, I quit to make dinner. The day had been so fine that I wanted to reward him, and that meant mushroom burgers and fries.

I put in my earbuds to listen to the news while prepping the meal. The stem rust that had killed a quarter of the wheat harvest in China and Ukraine had been found in Nebraska. Fresh water from a dissolving Arctic was flooding into the Atlantic, swirling the protective currents like a hand passed through a smoke plume. And a hideous infection was hitting cattle feedlots in Texas.

I forgot myself, forgot that my son was crawling on the floor in the other room. I shouted something vile, and louder than I realized. Because of the earbuds, I didn't hear Robin until he was tugging on my shirt. He startled me, and I jumped. He got flustered and defensive. *Well, don't just ignore me! What's the matter?*

"It's nothing." I took out my buds and stopped the app. "Just the news."

Something bad? It's something bad. You swore pretty hard.

I made a mistake. "It's nothing, Robbie. Don't worry."

He sulked over dinner and slammed through the meal. But way too quickly, he seemed to forgive me. By the time I broke out the cocoa almonds, he was smiling again. I was stupid not to guess.

After we finished, he went back to his spot on the living room floor while I returned to my computer. I was tweaking one of my algorithms for volcanic eruptions on water worlds when a thumping came from across the house. I cursed again. It sounded like a small mammal had gotten into the walls of Robin's bedroom and was making a nest between the studs. I'd never be able to get it out and save my house without sending my son into another spiral.

There was another thump, several more, too metronomic to be anything but human. It sounded like a plumber making serious mistakes. I went for a look.

The sound came from Robin's bedroom. I opened the door and saw him curled up in the corner holding his Planetary Exploration Transponder and banging his head against the wall. It was a slow-motion, soft, exploratory head-slamming, like an experiment in final penance.

I rushed him, shouting. Before I could pull him away from the wall, he barreled to his feet, through my arms, and out of the room. I stopped only long enough to check the tablet. On the screen, a group of demented cows stumbled into each other. They'd lost control of their bodies. One of them slipped to the ground, lowing in confusion. The close-up cut to an aerial shot of a staggering animal mass hundreds of creatures wide.

The story was all over the net: brain contagion, tearing through Texas's four and a half million head of cattle, spreading from feedlot to feedlot with industrial-scale efficiency. Robin had logged in to my account and found it, using my password that I never changed: his mother's favorite bird, flying backward.

Screaming started up from outside, looping over the agonizing video. *Stop! Enough! Stop!* I ran from the room and outside. He was alone in the dark backyard. No threat anywhere, no one at all but my wailing child. He dropped like a deadweight the moment I reached him. His screams grew worse when I tried to embrace him. *That's enough. Stop. Stop!*

I dropped to my knees and took his face. My own shouted whispers were half comfort, half muzzle. "Robbie. Hush. Don't. It'll be okay."

That word *okay* drew a shriek that shattered me, so out of control, up close to my ear. I recoiled, and he broke free. He was across the yard and around the corner of the house before I could get to my feet. I chased him back inside. He was coiled again in the corner of his room, battering the wall with his brain. I broke through the doorway and threw myself between the wall and his skull. But he finished the moment I reached him. He slumped in my arms. A sound came out of him as awful as his screams. A long, low gurgle of defeat.

I cradled him and stroked his hair. He didn't fight. Aly had stopped whispering in my ears, the moment I most needed her. My brain searched for something to say that wouldn't make him lash out again. Every possibility felt inane. We lived in a place where feedlots were subsidized, but feedback was prohibited. I should never have brought him to visit this planet.

"Robbie. There are other places."

He lifted his head to glare at me. His eyes were small and hard. *Where?*

His body went limp. The rage had cleaned him out. I let him lie a while longer. Then I got him up and into the kitchen, where I iced his forehead. In the bathroom, he washed and brushed his teeth in a stupor. The lump came on, plump and dark, a thousand-year egg set above the brow of his right eye.

He didn't want to read or be read to. He violently rejected a trip through space. He lay in bed, staring at the ceiling. *Why did you hide it from me, Dad?*

Because I was afraid of exactly what had happened. That was the honest answer, and still I hid. "I shouldn't have."

What's going to happen?

"They'll be put down. They probably already have been."

Killed.

"Yes."

Won't it spread? With animals packed in like that? And getting moved around all over the place?

I told him I didn't know. I do now.

Lying in his narrow bed, he looked impossibly pale. His hand reached out from under the sheets to cover his eyes. *Did you see them? How they were moving?* In the stillness, his whole body jerked, like that galvanic jolt just before sleep. He grabbed my hand for balance. His upper arm felt wilted and useless.

Last month, he said, then lost his way. *Last week? I could have handled this.*

"Robbie. Buddy. Everyone goes up and down. You'll—"

Dad? He sounded petrified. *I don't want to go back to being me.*

"Robbie. I know it feels like the end of the world. But it isn't."

He pulled the sheet up over his face. *Go away. You don't know what's happening. I don't want to talk to you.*

I held still. Anything I said might drive him screaming back out into the dark yard. Minutes passed. He seemed to soften. Perhaps he started to fall asleep. He slid the sheet from off his face and lifted his head from the pillow.

Why are you still here?

"Aren't you forgetting something? May all sentient beings—"

He held up a flaccid hand. *I want to change the words. May all life. Get free. From us.*

THE VISITORS SHOWED UP the next Monday. It wasn't yet ten. I was reading an email thread from folks at NASA, with the latest on the Seeker. It wasn't good. Robbie was spread over the dining room table, learning the provinces of Canada. They rang the front bell, a woman and a man in puffy coats, he cradling a briefcase on his chest. I opened the door a little. They offered their hands and IDs: Charis Siler and Mark Floyd, caseworkers with the Children, Youth and Families Division of the Department of Human Services. It would have been within my rights not to let them in. But that didn't seem wise.

I took their coats and led them into the living room. Robin called out from the far side of the wall. *Is somebody here?* For a moment he sounded like the boy in the film. Like Jay. He tumbled into the living room, confused at the sight of daytime strangers in the house.

"Robin?" Charis Siler asked. Robin studied her, curious.

I said, "I've got visitors, Robbie. How about you take a bike ride?"

"Sit for a minute," Mark Floyd commanded.

Robin looked at me. I nodded. He climbed into Aly's favorite swivel egg chair and swung his legs against the ottoman.

Floyd asked Robin, "What are you working on?"

I'm not working. Just doing a geography game.

"What kind of game?"

Something he made. Robin aimed his thumb at me. *He knows a lot, but he gets things wrong sometimes.*

Floyd grilled him about his studies, and Robin answered. If the state meant to check on his curriculum, they had a satisfactory answer. Charis Siler watched the volley of questions and answers. After a bit, she leaned in and asked, "Did you hurt your head?" And everything clicked at last. She stood and crossed the room to examine the bruise, which protruded from his right brow like a blue carbuncle. "How did that happen?"

Robbie demurred, reluctant to tell a stranger what his animal self had done. He shot me a look. My head barely inclined. Siler and Floyd saw it, I'm sure.

I hit it. His words were tentative, almost a question.

Siler held his hair back with two fingers. I wanted to tell her to get her hands off my son. "How did that happen?"

The fact spilled out of Robin. *I hit it against the wall*. Honesty was his downfall.

"How, honey?" Siler sounded like the school nurse.

Robbie snuck me another sheepish look. Our visitors intercepted it. My son touched his bruise and looked downward. *Do I have to say?*

All three turned to me. "It's okay, Robbie. You can tell them."

He lifted his head, defiant for five seconds. Then he let it drop again. *I was angry.*

"About what?" Charis Siler asked.

About the cows. Aren't you angry?

She stopped in mid-prosecution. I thought for an instant that she felt ashamed. But the tiniest muscles in her face said bafflement. She didn't know which cows he meant.

The situation was heading south. I caught Robin's eye and tipped my head toward the front door. "You want to go check on the owl?" He shrugged, defeated by adult stupidity. But he murmured goodbye to the guests and slipped from the house. The door closed behind him, and I turned on my prosecutors. Their masks of professional neutrality enraged me.

"I have never laid a finger on my child in anger. What do you think you're doing?"

"We received a tip," Floyd said. "It takes a lot for someone to phone in an alert."

"He was frightened. Really, really upset over this bovine viral encephalopathy. He's sensitive to living things." I didn't add what I should have—that we all should have been terrified. It still seemed a child's fear.

Mark Floyd reached into his briefcase and retrieved a folder. He opened it on the coffee table between us. It was filled with two years of papers and notes, everything from Robbie's initial suspension from third grade to my arrest in Washington for a public incident in which I'd employed my son.

"What is this? You've been keeping files on us? Do you keep files on all the troubled kids in the county?"

Charis Siler frowned at me. "Yes. We do. That's our job."

"Well, my job is to take care of my son the best way I know how. And I'm doing exactly that."

I don't remember what transpired after that. The chemicals flooding my brain prevented my hearing much of what the caseworkers said. But the gist was clear: Robin was an active case in the system, and the system was watching me. The next suggestion of abuse or improper care and the state would intervene.

I managed to stay contrite enough to get them to the door without more drama. Out on the stoop, watching their car pull away, I saw Robbie at the end of the block, astride his stopped bike, waiting for the moment when he could come safely home. I waved him in. He got up in the saddle and pedaled full-out. He did a flying dismount and left his bike lying in the lawn. He trotted to me and clasped me around the waist. I had to peel him off before he'd talk. The first words out of his mouth were, *Dad. I'm ruining your life.*

THE RIVER OF FORMS IS LONG. And among the billions of solutions it has so far unfolded, humans and cows are close cousins. It wasn't surprising that something on the fringe of life—a strand of RNA that codes for only twelve proteins—was happy, after one small tweak, to give another host a try.

Los Angeles, San Diego, San Francisco, Denver: none of them matched the density of an industrial-scale feedlot. But human mobility and relentless commerce made up for that. And still, back in February, no one was all that worried. The virus tearing through the beef industry was being upstaged by the President. Week after week, he kept pushing back the rescheduled elections, claiming that digital security in several states was not yet adequate and that various enemies were still poised to interfere.

When the third Tuesday in March came along, it surprised the entire fatigued country when the polls did open at last. But it shocked only half of us when another wave of irregularities were declared insignificant and the President was named the winner.

THE SIGNAL CAME FROM XENIA, a small planet in a modest star system near the tip of one spiral arm of the Pinwheel Galaxy. There, at the start of a night that lasted for several Earth years, something like a child held up something not quite a flashlight to something quite unlike the Earth's night sky.

Near the child stood the closest living thing to what might be called its parent. On Xenia, the entire species of intelligent beings contributed a little germ plasm to birth each new child. But each Xenian was given one child to raise. On Xenia, everyone was everyone else's parent and everyone else's child, everyone's older sister and younger brother all at once. When one person died, so did everyone and no one. On Xenia, fear and desire and hunger and fatigue and sadness and all other transitory feelings were lost in a shared grace, the way that separate stars are lost in the daytime sun.

"There," the something-like-a-father said to its something-like-a-child, in something almost like speech. "A little higher. Right up there."

The little one lay back, floating on its living kinship raft above the intelligent soil. It felt its not-quite arm nudged by a process of assistance no one from Earth would have a name for.

"There?" the younger one asked. "Right there? Why didn't they ever answer?"

The older one replied not in sound or light but in changes in the surrounding air. "We bathed them in signals for thousands of their generations. We tried everything we could think of. We never managed to get their attention."

The sequence of chemicals that the young one emitted was not quite a laugh. It was a whole verdict, really, an entire astrobiological theory. "They must have been very busy."

THE DAYS LENGTHENED. Sunlight made a comeback. My son did not. He was certain that he'd failed me, that he'd failed all the creatures he was forced to outlive. He sat curled up in Aly's egg chair or hunched at the dining room table staring at his school-work. An hour would pass while he held himself crumpled and still. Once I glimpsed him holding his palms out in front of his face, mystified by all the life that still passed through them.

It was in my power to help him. The time for fear and principle was past. All I had to do was accept a few future risks, and I could ease his present pain. He needed medication.

One night, after a bath, he lingered in the bathroom for so long that I had to check on him. He was standing with a towel wrapped around his boy's slight body, staring at the mirror. *It's gone, Dad. I can't even remember what I can't remember.*

This is what I miss most about him. Even when his light went out, he was still looking.

My spring break was days away. I'd been preparing in secret. I sprang the idea on him. "How about a gigantic treasure hunt?" His shoulders fell. He was done with discovery. "No, Robbie. A real one."

He eyed me, suspicious. *What do you mean?*

"Put your pajamas on and meet me in my office."

He obeyed, too curious to refuse. When he appeared at the side of my desk, I handed him a sheet of paper filled with names, two dozen in all. Spring beauties. Sharp-lobed hepatica. Trailing arbutus. Bishop's cap. Fire pink. Six kinds of trilliums.

"Know what these are?" If he didn't when he started to nod, he'd figured it out by the time the nod was done. "How many can you find and draw?"

His limbs began to jitter. He snarled in distress. *Dad!* I held his arm to calm him.

"I mean for real. From life."

Puzzlement kept him from melting down. His hand paddled the air, begging me to be reasonable. *How? Where?* As if flowers would never happen again, for someone so fallen.

"How about the Smokies?"

He shook his head, refusing to believe. *Serious? Serious?*

"Totally, Robbie."

When?

"How about next week?"

He searched my face to see if I was lying. For the first time in weeks, hope trickled out of him. *Can we stay in the same cabin again? Can we sleep outdoors? Can we go to that river with the rapids where you and Mom went?* Then the full awfulness of life washed over him again. He raised the list of wildflower names up to eye level and groaned. *How am I supposed to learn all of these in one week?*

I vowed that when we came back from the woods, I'd make an appointment with his physician and start him on a new treatment.

THE RIDE DOWN MADE HIM RESTLESS. His smallest thoughts now required endless reassurance. He couldn't stop asking about the past. Through most of Illinois and all through Indiana and Kentucky, he talked about Aly. He wanted to know where she grew up and what she studied in school. He asked how we met and how long it took us to get married and about all the places we visited before he came along. He wanted to know everything we'd done together on our honeymoon in the Smokies, and what Alyssa had liked best about those mountains.

When he wasn't grilling me, he was studying an Appalachian wildflowers book I'd gotten him, indexed by color and organized by the time of blooming. *What's a "spring ephemeral"?*

I corrected his pronunciation and told him.

Why do they go so fast?

"Because they're down in the shade on the forest floor. They have to germinate and bud and bloom and fruit and set their seed before the trees leaf out and it's game over."

What was Mom's favorite spring wildflower?

I must have known once. "I can't remember."

What was her favorite tree? You can't remember her favorite tree?

I willed him to stop asking, before I forgot the little I'd ever known.

"I can tell you her favorite bird."

He started shouting at me. It was a long trip.

I MANAGED TO RENT the same cabin we stayed in so long ago, the one with its wraparound deck open to the woods and stars. We crunched down the steep gravel drive, chasing the shadows of trees. Robin bolted from the car and took the front steps two at a time. I followed, with the bags. Inside, all the light switches still bore their labels—*Hallway, Porch, Kitchen, Overhead*—and the cabinets were still covered in the same color-coded instructions.

Robbie tore into the living room and flung himself onto that couch emblazoned with its procession of bears, elk, and canoes. Three minutes later he fell asleep. His breathing was so peaceful I left him there to sleep through the night. He woke only when dawn poured in.

That morning we hit the trails. I found a climb not far inside the boundary of the park that faced the southern sun while backing onto a damp ledge. Every twenty yards we came across another wet outcrop packed with more species than a manic terrarium. You could have cut out a chunk, loaded it into the cargo bay of an interstellar spacecraft, and used it to terraform a distant Super Earth.

Robin clutched his list. He was finding new flowers left and right. But he'd lost his ability to name things. *Are these rue anemones, Dad?*

He'd found a clump identical to the picture in his field guide. "I don't know. What do you think?"

Well, the petals don't quite match up. And the little thingies in the middle are a lot longer.

I looked at the picture and then at him. He'd lost his confidence. Four months ago, he would have been correcting the book. "Trust yourself, Robbie."

He fretted and waved his hands in the air. *Dad. Just tell me.*

I confirmed his guess. He drew a clumsy little clump of rue anemone. He went on to find, then worry over, both true and false Solomon's seal. Then he drew those, too.

Only drawing gave him a little peace. With a sharp pencil in his hand and a log to sit on, he was still okay. But it took him forever to re-create the ghostly purple streaks lining the inside of a spring beauty. He raged against the shakiness of his trout lilies. And, honestly, his draftsmanship had shriveled a little, from the airy, open boldness of a month before.

The checklist filled in. He found ten, then a dozen species of ephemerals in full flower, faster than any stranger to this place would have imagined. Each new find filled him with dogged satisfaction. Before we were half a mile up the ridge, he found every kind of plant that I'd put on my challenge. He looked back down along the wall of sun-covered, wet rock so packed with cooperating experiments. *Spring will keep coming back, whatever happens. Right, Dad?*

There were strong arguments either way. The Earth had been everything from hell to snowball. Mars had lost its atmosphere and fizzled away to a frigid desert, while Venus descended into hammering winds and a surface hotter than a smelter. Life could crash and spin out, pretty much overnight. My models said as much, and so did the rocks of this planet. Here we were, in a place fast becoming something new. Predictions were shaky from a sample size of one.

"Yes," I told him. "You can count on spring."

He nodded to himself and headed up the ridge. We came around a switchback onto a level stretch. The forest cleared from one step to the next. Lush laurel undergrowth surrendered to open stands of oak and pine. My phone pinged. It shocked me to be in coverage, even up here. But it was the job of coverage to cover every uncovered spot on Earth.

I checked. I couldn't help it. I flicked past the lock screen—Aly and Robbie on his seventh birthday, their faces painted like tigers. Seventeen messages in six different text chains waited for me. I looked up to see Robbie heading down the trail, his gait almost easy again. I sneaked a look at the texts, fearing the worst. But I failed to imagine what that might be.

The NextGen Telescope was dead. Thirty years of planning and ingenuity, twelve billion dollars, the work of thousands of brilliant people from twenty-two countries, the hope of all astronomy, and our first good chance to see the contours of other planets. The newly reelected President had killed it with glee:

> ## THE BIGGEST FRAUD PERPETRATED ON BELIEVERS SINCE THE ATTEMPTED COUP!!!

My colleagues were scrambling in the ruins, pouring out their fury, grief, and disbelief. I typed in something, five words of uncomprehending solidarity. The message queued but wouldn't send.

Down the trail, Robbie knelt at the foot of a hemlock, fixed on something. I put my phone away and headed toward him. He stood as I approached. *Did Mom ever hike this trail?*

Fierce as death is love. "What were you looking at?"

He kept his eyes on a spot in the rhododendrons, back down the ravine. *Did she?*

"I don't think so. Why?"

Then could we just go to the river? The one she liked?

"It's early yet, bud. I thought we'd head down after lunch. We're going to camp there tonight."

Could we just go now? Please?

We headed back over the ridge, along the rock seeps and their packed bouquets. He bore down the mountainside. I tried to slow him to look. "Check out the fire pinks. They were barely open when we came up. Can you believe what they've done in one hour?"

He looked and declared his amazement. But he was elsewhere.

We came out at the bottom of the mountain and got back in the car. I drove to the other trailhead, the one we'd hiked a year and a half ago. The one my wife and I had hiked on our honeymoon a decade before that. I'd seduced her, as we walked, with stories of the thousands of exoplanets popping up all over, where there had been none for all of human history.

How long before you find the little green men?

"Very little," I told her. "Probably not men. Maybe not even green. But we'll both live to see them." Neither of us would.

Robin sensed something, as we got the frame packs from the car and slung them on. He waited until we were on the first switchback, a quarter mile down the trail. He stopped under a stand of freshly flowering serviceberry and looked at me sideways. *Something's bugging you.*

Some primal part of my brain imagined that if I never spoke the fact out loud, it might yet turn out otherwise. "It's nothing. I'm just a little thoughtful."

It's me, isn't it?

"Robbie. Don't be ridiculous!"

My screaming got us in trouble with the Child Protectors. They're going to take me away from you, aren't they?

It's hard to hug someone half your height when you're both wearing frame backpacks. My attempt only confirmed his suspicions. He pushed away and started down the trail. Then he stopped, turned, and warned me with a drawn finger.

You shouldn't try to protect me from the truth.

"I'm not." My hand went up and traced a squiggle in the air, a flick three inches high and two across. It meant, *Forgive me, I'm making a lot of mistakes.* His head dropped a millimeter. That meant, *Me, too.*

"Robbie, I'm sorry. It's bad news. We heard from Washington."

They're killing the Seeker?

"Worse. They're killing the NextGen."

He cupped his ears and gave a soft cry, like something half in flight. *That's crazy. All those years. All that work and money. Didn't they hear your talk?*

I swallowed a bitter laugh.

What about the Seeker?

"Not a prayer now."

Never?

"Not while I'm alive."

He couldn't stop shaking his head. *Wait. That's not right.* He frowned, doing the math in his head. The years it had taken to conceive, design, and build the NextGen. The wasted years of planning that had gone into the Seeker. The years that would have to pass before anyone dared propose a space-based telescope again. And the years left to me. Math wasn't Robin's strongest subject. But it didn't have to be.

What are they going to do with it?

A question sure to wreck the sleep of astronomers and ten-year-olds everywhere. A twelve-billion-dollar device meant to travel fifty thousand times farther from Earth than the Hubble, align its eighteen hexagonal mirrors into an array with a precision less than one ten-thousandth of a millimeter, and peer to the universe's edge would, presumably, be scavenged and carted away in pieces—history's most expensive shipwreck.

Dad. Everything's going backward.

He was right. And I had no idea why.

The trail narrowed to a single track and passed through a long tunnel of rhododendrons. I watched him from behind, struggling under the weight of his pack and the force of realization. We crested and began the mile-long dive back down to the water. He stopped short and I almost knocked him over.

All those civilizations out there. They're gonna wonder why they never heard from us.

WE REACHED THE SITE, tucked into a crook in the steep river. Robin shed his bulky pack and metamorphosed back into a boy.

Can we sit by the water first, before we pitch the tent?

The day was fresh and clear, with hours of light left and no chance of rain. "We can sit by the river for as long as it takes."

As long as what takes?

"To figure out the human race."

He tugged me the dozen yards down to the river's edge. The stream smelled newborn and green. We each found a rock to sit on, right up on the shore. He dipped his hand into the racing current and winced at the cold. *Can we put our feet in?*

The NextGen was dead. The Seeker, too. My models would never be tested. My judgment was shot. The force and freedom of the white cascades filled the air. "We can try."

I stripped off my boots and heavy hiking socks and plunged my bruised feet into the water's swirl. The freezing water probed the edge between relief and pain. Only when I pulled my legs out of the icy flow did I realize they were numb. Robbie was shaking, pumping his feet in the shallows to warm them.

"That's enough for now, okay?"

He lifted his stiffened limbs out of the current. From mid-calf downward, he was brick-red. *Red-footed booby bird!* He grabbed his toes in agony and tried to thaw them. His laugh was a sob of pain. He scoured the water for something. I was afraid to ask him what. A different boy, in a different age, on a different world, once told me that his mother had become a salamander. I stared downstream with him, hoping for a sighting to redeem the day.

Robin made it out first. *Heron!*

I didn't think he had such stillness left in him. The bird, a foot deep in the water, fixed on nothing. So did Robin, for a long, hypnotic time. They stared each other down, my son's forward-facing eyes and the bird's sideways one. DecNef had ebbed from Robin, but not the knowledge of how to lock in to shimmering feedback. Someday we'll learn again how to train on this living place, and holding still will be like flying.

Tall bird stalking. Every five minutes, half a step. The bird was a piece of standing driftwood. Even the fish forgot. When the heron at last jabbed out, Robin shrieked. The strike crossed two meters with barely a lean-in from the bird. It came back upright, a meal the size of astonishment dangling from its mouth. The fish seemed too big to slip down the bird's throat. But that baggy gullet opened, and in another moment, not even a bulge betrayed what had happened.

Robin whooped, and the sound startled the heron into flight. It bent, kicked, flapped its massive wings. It looked even more pterodactyl as it lifted, and the croaking it made as it took off was older than emotion. The clumsy launch turned graceful. Robin hung on the bird as it threaded the undergrowth and was gone. He went on staring at the spot where the great thing had disappeared. He turned to me and said, *Mom's here*.

We put our shoes back on, turned upstream, and worked our way for a hundred yards along the stony banks to the spot where my whole family had once swum, if not all at the same time. As we came up to the pools beneath the rapids, I swore out loud. Robin blanched at the word. *What, Dad? What?*

He didn't see until I pointed. The whole stretch of stream was covered in cairns. Stacked-up rocks rose everywhere, from both banks and from the boulder tops in the middle of the stream. They looked like Neolithic standing stones or tapering Towers of Hanoi.

Robin quizzed me with a look, still not understanding.

What's wrong with them, Dad?

"Those were your mother's worst nightmare. They destroy the homes of everything in the river. Imagine creatures from another world materializing in our airspace and tearing up our neighbor-hoods, again and again."

His eyes darted, searching out the chub and shiners and trout and salamanders and algae and crayfish and waterborne larvae and the endangered madtoms and hellbenders, all sacrificed to this turf-marking art. *We have to take them down.*

I felt so weary. I wanted to set life down and leave it by the side of the water. Instead, we went to work. We demolished the tow-ers within our reach. I knocked mine down. Robin dismantled his one at a time, peering through the clear water for the best place to replace each stone. When we finished with the stacks on the near bank, he looked across to the stacks in the middle of the stream. *Let's get the rest of them.*

Two thousand five hundred miles of rock-strewn rivers ran through these mountains. Human industry would reach them all. We could dismantle cairns every day, all summer and fall long, and the towers would rise again next spring.

"They're too far. The current's too strong. You felt how cold it is."

A look comes into the eyes of every ten-year-old, the first hint of the long war to come. Robin wavered on the threshold of daring me to stop him. Then he sat down on a rock covered with lichen a thousand years old.

Mom would do it.

His mother, the salamander.

"We can't today, Robbie. That water is pure snowmelt. Let's come back in July. The cairns will still be all over the place. I guarantee."

He gazed at the green-lined channel that plunged through the forest and down the mountain. The song of a veery seemed to appease him. His breathing deepened and slowed. A hatch of gnats

swarmed above the rapids and a flurry of early bluish-white sul-
phurs puddled around a pool near his feet. In this place, it would
have been hard for anyone, even my son, to remember his anger for
long. He turned to me, too quickly my friend again. *What are we
making for dinner? Can I work the cookstove?*

IN CAMP, NO ONE could touch us. We pitched the tent close to the riverbank and spread our sleeping rolls on the ground. We set up kitchen in a blackened fire ring, and Robbie cooked lentils with tomato, cauliflower, and onions. The meal left him ready to forgive me everything.

We hung our packs in the same old sycamores, by the water. The sky through our gap in the tulip poplars and hickories was so clear that we tempted fate again and took off the tent fly. Soon it was dark. We lay side by side, on our backs, under the transparent mesh, looking up into the blue-black wash, where stars remade the rules in all quarters of the night.

He nudged me with his shoulder. *So there are billions of stars in the Milky Way?*

This boy made the world good for me. "Hundreds of billions."

And how many galaxies in the universe?

My shoulder nudged his back. "Funny you should ask. A British team just published a paper saying there might be two trillion. Ten times more than we thought!"

He nodded in the dark, confirmed. His hand waved a question across the sky. *Stars everywhere. More than we can count? So why isn't the night sky full of light?*

His slow, sad words stiffened the hairs up and down my body. My son had rediscovered Olbers' paradox. Aly, who had been away for so long, leaned her mouth up to my other ear. *He's quite something. You know that, don't you?*

I laid it out for him, as clearly as I could. If the universe were steady and eternal, if it had been around forever, the light from countless suns in every direction would turn night as bright as day. But ours was a mere fourteen billion years old, and all the stars were rushing away from us at an increasing rate. This place was too young and was expanding too fast for stars to erase the night.

Lying so close, I felt his thoughts racing outward into the darkness. His eyes skipped around the sky from star to star. He was drawing pictures, making his own constellations. When he spoke, he sounded small but wise. *You shouldn't be sad. I mean, because of the telescope.*

He spooked me. "Why not?"

Which do you think is bigger? Outer space . . . ? He touched his fingers to my skull. *Or inner?*

Words from Stapledon's *Star Maker*, the bible of my youth, lit up in a backwater of my brain. I hadn't thought about the book in decades. *The whole cosmos was infinitely less than the whole of being . . . the whole infinity of being underlay every moment of the cosmos.*

"Inner," I said. "Definitely inner."

Okay. So, maybe the millions of planets that never launch the telescope are just as lucky as the millions of planets that do.

"Maybe," I said, and turned my head away from him.

That one, there. He pointed. *What's happening on that one?*

I told him. "On that one, people can split in half and grow back as two separate people, with all their memories intact. But only once in life."

His arm swung to the far side of the sky. *And that one? How about over there?*

"On that one, chromatophores all over a person's skin always give away exactly what they're feeling."

Cool. I'd like to live there.

We flew around the universe for a long time. We traveled so far that the waxing moon, two days from full, rose over the mountains' rim and blotted out the stars. He pointed to one of the last bright lights remaining. Jupiter.

On that one? All your memories never get weaker, and they never go away.

"Ouch. A broken bone? A fight you have with somebody?"

The way Mom's skin smelled. Seeing that heron.

I looked where his finger pointed. The light was dimming in the full wash of the moon. "Do you want to go there?"

His shoulders lifted off his sleeping pad. *I don't know.*

Something called in the woods. It wasn't a bird and it wasn't any mammal I'd ever heard. The cry pierced the dark and hung above the roar of the river. It might have been pain or joy, grief or celebration. Robbie jerked and grabbed my arm. He hushed me, although I made no sound. The shout came again, farther away. Another call provoked another response, overlapping in the wildest chords.

Then it stopped, and the night filled up with other music. Robin turned and grabbed me harder, his face lit by moonlight. Every creature alive would feel all things they were built to feel.

Listen to that, my son told me. And then the words that would never weaken and never go away: *Can you believe where we are?*

IN THE DARK OF OUR SNUG TENT, ten inches from my face, Alyssa whispered, *Why does it matter so much?*

We'd hiked for eight hours until my feet bled. We'd swum together in the wild cascades. My exhaustion was so complete that I had struggled to light the camping stove and cook our dinner. I can't remember what we ate. I only remember how she asked for more.

I wanted to collapse facedown on my inflatable pillow and die for a week. She wanted to keep me up all night and talk philosophy. *Does it make any difference at all if it happened anywhere else? It happened here. That's everything, right?*

I was brain-dead. I could barely get my subjects to agree with my verbs. "Once is an accident. Twice is inevitable."

She pressed my chest and said, *I like this marriage business.* She sounded surprised, as if that discovery settled all matters.

"Find any trace of it anywhere, and we'll know that the universe wants life."

She laughed so hard. *Oh, the universe wants life, mister.* She rolled over on top of me, compact but planetary. *And it wants it* now.

For a minute, we were everything. Then we weren't. I must have fallen asleep afterward, because I woke again to an otherworldly sound. In the dark, someone was singing. I thought at first it was her. Three fluid, looping notes: the briefest melody trying out endless new keys. I looked at Aly. Her eyes in the darkness were wide, as if the wistful, three-note tune were Beethoven. She grabbed my arm in mock-panic.

Honey! They've landed. They're here!

She knew the name of the singer. But I failed to ask her, and now I'll never know. She listened, until the bird went silent. The wake filled at once with the hum of other creatures, a mesh spreading in all directions through the six different kinds of forest surrounding us. She held still in simple ecstasy, the one our son would for a moment learn.

This is the life, she said. *If I could keep this with me forever . . .*

Such a small difference, between *forever* and *once*.

I DRIFTED OFF, WITHOUT KNOWING. The zipper of the tent opening woke me. I couldn't figure out how he'd gotten dressed and halfway out of the tent before I knew it. "Robbie?"

Shhh! he said. I couldn't figure out why.

"Are you okay?"

I'm good, Dad. Super-good.

"Where are you going?"

Number one, Dad. Be right back. In the moonlight, his hand twisted like a spinning globe, his old signal to me that all was well. I lay my head down on my inflatable pillow, pulled the lip of my winter-weight bag around my neck, and fell back asleep.

The silence woke me. Right away I knew two things. First, I'd been asleep for longer than I thought. And second, Robin wasn't there.

I dressed and left the tent. The grass we'd pitched in was damp with dew. His shoes and socks lay by the opening. The flashlight, too: no need for it. The moon in the clear sky turned the Earth into a blue-gray aquatint. Navigating the roots and rocks was as easy as walking by streetlight.

I called but heard nothing back, over the sound of the rapids. Rounding the site, I shouted louder. "Robin? Robbie! Buddy?" A muffled moan came from the stream, a few feet away.

I reached the bank in seconds. In the silver light, the rapids were a jumble of shards. He'd told me something once: *The darker it gets, the better I can see out of the sides of my eyes.* My head swiveled from downstream to up. He was curled over a boulder in the middle of the flow, embracing it.

Five feet into the current, I hit slickness. A stone turned under my foot and I tumbled. I struck with my right knee and left elbow, scraping both open. The freezing surge washed me ten yards downstream before I caught hold of another large rock. I crawled back upstream, working from stone to stone on my hands and knees. Every foot seemed to take minutes. Nearing the boulder, I saw everything. He'd been dismantling cairns. Turning the river back into a safe home.

He was soaked up to the top of his rib cage. His whole body was quaking. He tried to reach out, but his arm swung limply in the air. Slurred sounds came from his mouth, nothing like words. His whole body shook under my hand like the flank of a frightened beast. He felt so cold.

Time came apart. I couldn't decide what I was supposed to do. His pulse felt so weak I was afraid to lift him. If I tried to crawl back with him through the cascades, it would have meant submerging him in freezing water for longer than he might survive. I gathered him up to carry him to the bank. On my second step, I lost my footing and dunked him in the water. Terrible noises came out of him. No one could have crossed those wet rocks upright, with a weight in their arms.

I lifted him onto the tiny island he'd been hugging and held him in place while I climbed up next to him. I stripped off his pants and shirt, taking forever to get the wet clothes off his skin. His T-shirt clung in a heap on the narrow boulder; his tiny jeans slipped off and washed downstream. His shivering got worse. I tried to dry him, but only succeeded in speeding the chill of evaporation.

I fought to stay calm and concentrate. I needed to wrap him in something warm, but my own clothes were wet from my fall. His breath came out in shallow, labored sighs. I tucked his knees to his chest, removed my soaked shirt, and huddled my torso around him. But my skin was as cold and wet as his.

I lifted my head. The world was silvered and still. Even the river tumbled too slowly to be real. We were miles from the trailhead. Mountains blocked all cell coverage. The nearest person was across the ridge. And still I yelled. My screaming distressed Robin, and his moaning got worse. Even if someone by some miracle heard me, they'd never find us in time.

I rubbed and patted him, calling his name. The patting turned to slaps. He stopped moaning, stopped responding in any way. Purpose leaked from his body. Even with all my friction, his skin slipped from red toward blue. I leaned in again to wrap him in my wet arms, but it was no good. I needed some other way to get him warm. A few minutes more, in the cold spring air without any clothes, and he'd be gone.

I looked up. The tent with my dry thermal sleeping bag was just above the bank, no more than twenty feet away. I curled around him on the rock and tried to seal a layer of air around his torso. The shivering went on, but I couldn't hear a heartbeat.

A voice said, *Try*. I left him curled on the rock and stumbled through the rapids to shore. I scrambled up the rocky, tree-lined bank. The tent zipper tore as I fought with it. I grabbed the sleeping bag and ran back to the river. On the bank, I wrapped the bag around my neck and somehow thrashed my way back to the boulder without falling. I wrestled the bag around him and sealed it. Then I covered him with my body. I sheltered him as best I could, searching for the sound of his breath above the rushing water.

A long time passed before I could accept that he no longer needed me.

THERE WAS A PLANET that couldn't figure out where everyone was. It died of loneliness. That happened billions of times in our galaxy alone.

THE UNIVERSITY GAVE ME COMPASSIONATE LEAVE. After the funeral, after long days with Robbie's relatives and everyone who counted us as friends, I felt no need to speak to anyone ever again. It was enough to stay inside, to read his notebooks and look through his drawings, and to write down everything I could remember about our time together.

People brought food. The less I ate, the more they brought. I couldn't bring myself to pay a bill or cut the grass or wash a dish or watch the news. Two million people in Shanghai lost their homes. Phoenix ran out of water. Bovine viral encephalopathy jumped from cattle to people. Weeks passed before anyone realized. I slept in the day and stayed up at night, reading poems to a room full of sentient beings who were everywhere but here.

I didn't answer my phone. Now and then I skimmed voice mails and glanced at texts. Nothing needed answering. I wouldn't have had answers, anyway.

Then one day, a message from Currier. *If you'd like to be with Robbie, you can be.*

"OKAY," SAYS THE MAN I NO LONGER HATE. "Relax and hold still. Watch the dot in the middle of the screen. Now let the dot move to the right."

I don't know how. He says it's the easiest thing in the world. Wait until it starts to move itself. Then stay in that state of mind.

He's risking a lot for me, breaking the law. We'll all be breaking it, soon enough. But Martin is more than merely criminal. He's spending a budget that he doesn't have, powering these machines with energy that will soon be hard to come by at any price. He runs the scanner himself, having laid off all his staff. Like so many others, his lab is folding.

I lie in the tube and tune myself to a print of Robbie. One that they recorded last August, when he was at his best. Just being in this space helps me breathe. I learn to move the dot, to grow it and shrink it and change its color. Two hours fly by. Currier says, "Would you like to come again tomorrow?"

I'm not sure why he's helping me. It's more than pity. Like lots of scientists, he's a sucker for redemption. And for some reason, he's deeply invested in my progress. It would take much more advanced brain science than his to explain that one. It's a question for astrobiology, in fact. Goldilocks planets can turn rain and lava and a little energy into agency and will. Natural selection can prune selfishness into its opposite.

I come the next day, and the day after that. I learn to raise and lower the pitch of the clarinet, to slow it down and speed it up and turn it into a violin, simply by letting my feelings match his. The feedback guides me, and all the while, my brain learns how to resemble what it loves.

AND THEN ONE DAY, MY SON IS THERE, inside my head as sure as life. My wife, too, still inside him. What they felt, then, I now feel. Which is bigger, outer space or inner?

He doesn't say a thing. He doesn't have to. I know what he wants from me. He only wants to see what's out there. Light travels at three hundred thousand kilometers a second. It takes ninety-three billion years to cross from one end of space to the other, past black holes and pulsars and quasars, neutron and preon and quark stars, metallics and blue stragglers, binaries and triple-star systems, globular and hypercompact clusters, coronal, tidal, and halo galaxies, reflection and plerion nebulae, stellar, interstellar, and intergalactic disks, dark matter and energy, cosmic dust and filaments and voids, all spun from the laws folded up into vibrations far smaller than the smallest units we have names for. The universe is a living thing, and my son wants to take me for a quick look around while there's still time.

We rise together into orbit high above the place we've been visiting. The thought occurs to him, and I have it. *Can you believe where we just were?*

Oh, this planet was a good one. And we, too, were good, as good as the burn of the sun and the rain's sting and the smell of living soil, the all-over song of endless solutions signing the air of a changing world that by every calculation ought never to have been.